family
line

family line
Written by John H. Matthews
Copyright © 2018 John H. Matthews

ISBN: 978-0-9975670-9-0

Library of Congress Control Number:
2018907440

Published by
Bluebullseye Press
www.bluebullseyepress.com
A division of Bluebullseye LLC

Edited by Ginger Moran

Cover and book design
Copyright ©2018 John H. Matthews

Cover photo by Annie Spratt

family
line

john h. matthews

bluebullseye press

To my grandfather,
who gave me my first big-boy bicycle,
told me my first dirty jokes,
and left behind the stories
that inspired this book.

And to my son, Brennan,
whose imagination inspires me
every day by creating something
new out of whatever is in
front of him.

Also by John H. Matthews

The South Coast

Ballyvaughan

Designated Survivor

Red Grace: A Grace Short Story

Chapter 1

THE CEMENT WALL was cold and rough against my head while the flicker of a fluorescent light insisted I not sleep. I thought of everything other than what I should be thinking about, the body on my living room floor and that I'd probably just gotten away with murder. It had occupied my conscious thoughts for too long and once the act had been committed it was a memory to be discarded like a playground brawl or a song heard in an elevator.

A blood red blanket covered the ground outside the backdoor this morning, a layer of leaves that had fallen from the Japanese maple overnight. I'd stopped and thought about walking around them, avoiding stepping on the random and temporary beauty that would mark the beginning of a day so different than the one that would end. But I'd accepted their fate along with my own and walked across them, the prints of my work boots pressed into the surfaces of the leaves.

If I am wrong, I'll accept my punishment. Perhaps I was too careless and some artifact of the crime absolves me of my innocence. But I am confident that at any time the sheriff will walk in and release me from the confines of the small county jail. There was always the smallest chance, a chance I had known well before pulling the trigger, that my story wouldn't be believed and the rest of my life would be spent in the state prison down south in McAlester.

My memories aren't a concern. I've spent my life hiding secrets from everyone near me that a couple more, no matter how violent or tragic, were another pinpoint. The story I'd told the sheriff's deputy was one of quick reaction, a flurry of moments strung together that were over before I knew they'd begun. It was a cliché not worthy of crime shows on television because it was a story so mundane that it would be hard not to believe, no claims so wild as to require further investigation.

This night had been planned for months. The yellow pages from a legal pad were now ash at the bottom of the wood burning stove in my living room. Those pages would be proof of my guilt, of the planning and forethought, everything that made a prosecutor's job easy for a quick conviction. But I hadn't acted suddenly, a trail of clues in my wake. I'd taken my time, watched and waited. No fingerprints had to be wiped down to hide tracks. There were no witnesses to provide a conflicting version of events.

This is not a story of redemption or revenge. It is not a last will and testament or a confession scribbled out on a deathbed. It is a statement of facts, a reenactment of history told as accurately as it can before the memories are gone, the blood flow to that part of my brain cut off by the foreign object that I can sense growing, working its way into my shortened future while removing my past. Like all stories it deserves to be heard from the beginning, from the first time I had the dreams that would become such a part of my life, and the window into so many deaths.

The red leaves would be gone by now, destroyed by the footsteps of deputies and paramedics going in and out of the house while I sit here. The blood on the living room floor would still be there for me to clean up once released.

Chapter 2

THE COCA-COLA STRUCK my dry lips and for a moment felt like it was burning. It was at least a year since I'd had one. I sat on the curb with my bag of schoolbooks on the sidewalk beside me, legs stretched out onto the main road through town, the Mother Road some called it. I savored every sip of that pop, making it last so long that the final drops were warm in my mouth. My father never bought it, or much of anything else. Once a week I'd ask for money to stop at the store in town on my way home from school so we'd have food in the house.

I wanted to keep the bottle, to help me remember how it tasted and felt. If my father found it I'd have to explain how I afforded the ten-cent drink. I took one last pull at the green glass bottle, pointing it straight up in the air and waiting for any last drops that clung to the inside to fall down to my tongue. After nothing came out, I stood up to return it to the rack of empty bottles inside the store then thought again and dropped it into my canvas bag along with my schoolbooks and the notebook I wrote my stories in then started the two-mile walk home. The boots I wore were hand-me-downs from my older brother. The leather soles worn thin, the rocks of the road pushed their way through into my feet with each step.

The paved road of town turned to gravel just past the post office. I tried to walk on the narrow strip of green grass that somehow survived between the dusty rocks of the road and the tall brown grass that grew up through the barbed-wire fence that kept cattle on the other side. Every few feet there were large clumps of bright orange Indian Paintbrush growing around the fence posts. I'd brought some home to my mother once and she put them in a vase on the kitchen table like I'd brought home a dozen red roses. When dad came in and sat down he just stared at them for a minute then asked why the hell there was a bunch of weeds on the table.

I never minded the long walk. It was time between the violence that surrounded twelve-year-old schoolboys and the silence that surrounded my father at home. Though not a violent man, Joseph Hudson had struck me a few times. A wide berth was given, an unspoken agreement to keep out of each other's way. I thought Larry leaving would bring me and Dad closer, instead it put more distance.

The cows and horses along the way were all familiar to me. I gave them names and made up stories of their conversations to each other, often writing them down late at night when I was supposed to be sleeping. Deep into the middle of one of these stories I came to the end of the long and rutted dirt driveway into my own yard, having daydreamed through more than half of my walk.

My stomach tightened when I saw the blue and white Chevy pickup sitting at an angle in front of the house. My father never got home before me. I tried to think of how long I'd sat to drink the soda or if I'd taken too much time walking home, even though I left school early. Then the black and white Ford Fairlane the county sheriff drove came into view just past my father's truck.

I considered turning around, heading back into town or, even better, to my hiding spot a mile away in the neighbor's pasture. I was still far enough down the drive that my father likely hadn't seen me yet. The sight of the sheriff's car was unusual. When dad would be picked up from a barroom fight in the middle of the afternoon the sheriff would take him to the station to sober up, not give him a ride home. They had known each other for years, since high school at least, so certain allowances were given. Not once had my father been charged for the offenses he committed while drunk.

The front door of the house opened. The screen door swung freely and clapped into the house, the spring that would pull it back into the threshold broken long ago. Sheriff Cole walked out onto the porch then spoke into the darkness of the doorway, the words not audible from a distance. His hand reached into the void then went to his hip, resting on top of the rarely used revolver. The sheriff nodded then went to his car. It started with a rumble then slowly rolled down the driveway toward me.

Please don't stop, I thought as hard as I could, trying to will the vehicle to keep moving. I kept walking up the edge of the driveway, avoiding looking up at the oncoming car.

The Fairlane came to a stop beside me.

"You get in there now, Wes," the sheriff said. "Your father needs you."

A deep red bruise was forming around the left edge of the officer's mouth and traces of dried blood stretched across his cheek where he'd tried to wipe it off with the back of his hand.

The car moved again and turned left onto the gravel road, a cloud of brown dust swelled up and gave chase as the vehicle gained speed. I turned to the house and saw my father standing on the porch, the screen door held open with his right hand, a cigarette in his left. He'd quit smoking at least a dozen times in the last three years. I learned to stay away from him the first couple of weeks, if he made it that long. It had only been six days since he'd again smoked his final cigarette, tossing the rolling papers into the trash.

"Come on, Wes."

Just fast enough to not be accused of taking my time, I walked to the house, up the five steps to the porch then through the door he held open for me.

Thick smoke hung inside from the cigarettes my father and the sheriff had smoked in the small front room, an ashtray overflowing on the table between the two chairs facing the window. The acrid scent of my father's cheap tobacco he bought and rolled himself always hurt my nose. A softer smell rested on top of it, almost sweet, of the brand the sheriff smoked.

"Let's sit down," he said. "We need to talk."

My father rarely uttered more than three words in a row to me. The thought of sitting down to talk with him was foreign. The mere fact of being his child was not enough in common for him to have a close relationship or create any need for conversation. I chose the furthest chair, the wooden straight back in the front window. It was my favorite piece of furniture in the house, where my mother would sit to sew when she had been healthy. Even when she was sick she would sometimes insist on being placed in the chair, her sewing supplies in the basket beside her feet, in an effort to feel normal. My father foiled my plan and picked up a stool from beside the fireplace and carried it over to me. I watched his familiar movements, his left leg not bending far enough and causing the slightest irregularity in his step. He was a tall man, over six feet, with sandy brown hair and a slight and sinewy body that was deceivingly strong.

He settled down on the stool, elbows on his pointy knees, and looked at me. It was only then that I saw the redness around the man's eyes. My father was an oilman that maintained the giant pump jacks that spotted the Oklahoma landscape. He could take apart an engine the size of a car and put it back together without breaking a sweat. Once he had a huge wrench take the skin off the back of his hand. He wrapped it with his handkerchief and finished putting the motor back together before tending to the wound. He was not a man that cried.

"Wes," he said. "Lawrence is gone."

I tried to figure out what he was saying. Of course Lawrence was gone. He left months ago for Fort Bliss.

"Yeah. I know."

"No, you don't, Wes." I couldn't remember the last time I'd heard him use my name, much less so often. "Your brother was sent to Vietnam last month."

We didn't have a television but I knew about the war and had heard of other kid's brothers and fathers who had gone to Vietnam. Billy Lansing got to leave school two weeks before Christmas and didn't come back until February because his father had gone to Vietnam.

"Okay." I thought more about Billy Lansing. He'd been different since coming back to school, quiet and withdrawn.

"Wes, your brother is dead. He was killed in the war. He was killed in Vietnam."

I turned my attention back to my father and thoughts of Billy Lansing faded as quickly as they had entered my mind.

Dead.

The word hung in my ears. I wasn't naïve, I knew what death was and had experienced it several times. When I was nine I watched my mother fade from a beautiful woman to debilitated and bed bound until she finally died in her sleep, her breath struggling through the disease that had eaten her lungs. Then there had been the dogs, mostly killed by coyotes that ran rampant in the fields at night. The cows all died the same winter two years ago, my father no longer able to afford the feed to keep them healthy and too proud to ask for help.

But Lawrence was just a kid. He'd gone off to the Army when a letter came in the mail telling him he had to go. We shared a bedroom our whole lives until the day the bus pulled out of Stroud with him in a window seat, halfway back, waving at me with a sad smile. We'd sat together on the edge of his twin bed hours earlier.

"Do you have to go?" I asked.

"Yeah, I do," he said. "I got drafted, so they're making me go. But I was gonna sign up anyway, just like Dad and Grandpa did."

"Why do you wanna go?"

"It's a way out of here, out of Stroud, out of Oklahoma," Lawrence said. "I don't want to work the farm, fix oil pumps, just grow old out here. I wanna get out."

"You don't have to work the farm or the oil fields," I said. "You know Grandpa wants you to work with him."

"Fixing tractors? Nah. We both know he'd rather have you there anyways."

"But I don't want you to go."

"I know," Lawrence said. "But I have to. I'll be back to visit when I get leave. Maybe I'll take you with me when I come back."

"You understand what I'm telling you?" My father's voice shook me from the memory.

"Yes. Larry's dead." I stared at the floor. "Can I go now?"

He ran his hands across his face. His knuckles were red and fresh blood stained his shirt cuff. A scar ran down the back of his left hand, the rough pink line of skin disappeared under his shirtsleeve.

"Go."

Chapter 3

THE SCREEN DOOR slammed against the wall with a crack as I pushed through. Then I ran.

The late afternoon sun was just above the trees and everything before me glowed with the golds and reds of autumn. My side began to hurt but I didn't slow down, going faster than I usually ran, faster than I'd ever run before. I didn't stop until I reached the abandoned church in the neighbor's pasture a mile away. At the outside wall of the stone building I bent over and vomited out what little was left in my stomach.

I watched as the dry red clay soaked up the remainder of the Coca-Cola. After wiping my shirtsleeve across my mouth I walked around to the opening in the side of the church that had been made years earlier to allow cows to go in and out for shelter. I sat down in the far corner, away from the long rays of light that were still hanging on outside.

The church still had the engraved keystone with Theodore Roosevelt's face on it above the door, a product of the Works Progress Administration in the late 1930's. Once, when I rode past it in my father's truck, he told me he'd gone to church here when he was younger. I acted uninterested, not wanting to let him know where I spent my time when I wasn't at home or school.

The town and surrounding area had experienced a small boom from the work the government was bringing in and from the development of more oil production. But it didn't take long for most of the new residents to tire of the hot summers, hard winters, and lack of any amenities. The larger towns and cities offered more and people moved. The building ended its time as a church after only twenty years and it didn't take long to be welcomed back as a part of the earth. Grass and plants began to grow out of the spaces between the large red and orange stones that formed the walls. The wooden floor was gone, used for some other building or firewood years ago, leaving only the rough dirt underneath.

I sat hidden in the dark corner, knees to my chest. My mind raced too fast to think of any one thing for very long, like the needle on a compass constantly being spun around. When I would begin to focus on my brother I shook my head, sending the needle waving back and forth again in search of true north.

The glow from the hole in the wall grew softer and longer as the sun moved down in the sky until a beam of light, filtered by half bare branches outside, struck a young tree trying to grow inside the church. A random seed that landed had somehow taken root and now a life no taller than three feet and smaller around than my thumb struggled to live in the confined space. It received vital sunshine for only an hour or two every evening as the sun moved toward the horizon, but was protected from the harsh winds that moved across the flatness of Lincoln County. Perhaps the seed that had fallen was more fortunate than others, sheltered from the elements that killed so much more life than it fostered.

My mind slowed as the final light faded, the wavering needle settling into a direction. I thought about the dime and the bottle of pop. It had been during afternoon recess. My classroom was made up of three grades, sixth, seventh and eighth. I tried to keep away from the older kids on the playground and avoided anyone my own age as well. Today I had filled the fifteen-minute break by sitting on top of the large rock out behind the school building, at the far corner of the field that was used as a playground.

I had been the first to the rock, a popular spot at recess, and once I'd taken my place atop the stone nobody else cared to be near it. I'd sat there and watched the older kids play kickball and the younger ones do whatever they could find to do, which usually involved wrestling or fashioning rifles out of dead branches and playing war. The sun was reflecting off the brown stone and I was warm even in the cool fall air, but I wasn't about to give up the prime spot.

I'd closed my eyes and pointed my face to the sky. The

warmth surrounded me. Everything else on the playground faded away. For a moment I had seen my brother, standing in front of me. His uniform hung on his slight body and the heavy rifle slung over his shoulder, then he fell to the ground. Another boy in a uniform ran over to him, his helmet falling behind him to show thick black hair, then it all disappeared into an array of brilliant colors that swirled then faded until there was only blackness again.

I'd opened my eyes and saw three teacher's faces and a dozen more of kids from my classroom all gathered around me. I was lying on the ground at the base of the big stone.

"What happened?" I said.

"You fell off the rock," one of the teachers replied.

"I don't remember falling."

"I think you passed out," the teacher said.

As the teachers helped me up the other kids walked away, some laughing at me, others going on about their previous conversations as if it had been a common occurrence. I was taken inside and looked over by the teachers.

"Did you have any lunch?" I was asked.

"Yes, ma'am," I lied.

The teachers spoke amongst themselves, too quietly for me to hear. Ms. Albertson, my teacher, came back over to me. She had long brown hair and a smile that made you feel warm if you were fortunate enough to be the recipient. I spent most of my time in class watching her movements, listening to her quiet voice that somehow projected across the room with no problem. I would try to remember how my mother moved and talked and smiled but when I did, those memories fading with time, it would end up being Ms. Albertson I'd see.

"Here you go, Wesley." She handed me the dime. "Why don't you get going home and buy yourself something to drink on the way."

There was still two hours of school left but I didn't argue. I thanked her and walked out of the office, that coin clutched so tightly in my hand it left indentations of the ridges on my palm.

I now sat in the old church and thought about the vision of my brother and I closed my eyes, hoping to see him again, hoping to prove what my father said wasn't true. When we were younger we'd play army out in the yard. He always wanted to pretend to be our grandpa, fighting in World War I. I always ended up being the Germans and learned to defend myself in our mock fights that would go far beyond gentle playing.

The night rolled in and the temperature dropped fifteen degrees in as many minutes. The darkness in the country is a force, something tangible to the senses. If the moon isn't out it is impossible to see five feet. The blackness surrounds you as the night is palpable on your skin.

"Wesley."

I looked up and Larry was standing there, his uniform had changed from baggy fatigues of the battlefield to the formal dress blues, fitted and shaped to his body. His left chest was covered with too many round and square medals of different colors, too large for the uniform. Light reflected off of them into my eyes.

"I've come back for you, Wesley," Larry said. "Just like I said I would."

I tried but found myself unable to speak inside the dream.

"Come on, Wesley." The vision of Lawrence moved toward me, reaching his hand out. "Let's go."

I reached out, my hand seeming a million miles from his even though he stood right in front of me. Stretching further, he only grew further away as his body turned to dots of light that spread out from each other then faded like embers flying off of a fire.

I woke up, blinking my eyes in the darkness, my body cold. It took me a moment to remember where I was.

The wind had picked up ahead of a storm that was moving in. The wood and tile roof of the old church had been replaced with corrugated tin and the wind came in and out between the sheets of thin metal and created music like I had never heard before. It was dark and dissonant and seemed to come from every direction and for the first time in my favorite place I was scared. I could feel the vibrations of the sounds on my skin, reverberating through my body. I knew the coyotes came out at night looking for the weaker calves and dogs that wandered too far from their homes. A twelve-year-old boy would be no match for the wild animals.

I felt for my bag of schoolbooks then remembered being home and leaving it beside the chair in the front room where my father had spoken with me, the empty Coca-Cola bottle hidden inside. The thought of my brother's death hit me again like I'd just heard it and for the first time I cried. I wrapped my arms around myself in the darkness and leaned my head against the rough stone wall of the church and cried until I knew I had to go out into the darkness.

I stood and felt my way around the building until I was outside. The quarter moon was low on the other side of the building but provided just enough light to help me to the road.

Every noise made me jump as I took each step with caution, trying not to make noise to attract a coyote or to trip over one of the larger rocks on the gravel road. I had no idea what time it was, only that it was late. My flannel shirt provided no protection from the cold night air and I tried to pick up my pace to warm up and get home.

During the day I would cut across fields and jump fences, shortening the trip, but it was too dark for that. Taking the road distorted my sense of progress, unsure of any landmarks in the darkness. To my left was the open cow field and to my right were dense woods, my only way of knowing I was at least headed in the right direction. Every few steps I was certain I heard rustling just behind the façade of overgrown weeds that hid the dark maze of trees. Great animals, fierce and hungry, flashed through my thoughts and I quickened my steps.

Lights flashed behind me and I stepped to the side of the road as they grew bigger and brighter until the blue and white Chevy pickup skidded to a stop beside me and for the first time in years I was relieved to see my father.

Chapter 4

THE LOW AUTUMN sun found its way through the gaps in the curtains in my bedroom window. A spotted pattern of light crawled across the wallpaper. I stared up through the dust floating gently in the beams of light, smoothly spinning and never touching as though each had its own gravitational pull that allowed them to dance to an endless and silent piece of music. Once the sun rose far enough the glow would fade and the dance would become invisible again until the next morning's performance.

This was the only bedroom I'd ever had, except for the spare room I'd slept in at Grandpa's up in Jay every so often. I shared this one with my brother even when I was in a crib. The wallpaper had never been changed from the people who'd lived in the house before us, a faded pattern of green holly leaves that looked way too much like Christmas to be in a bedroom. Mom had talked all the time about changing it but never did, wanting something more appropriate for a boy's room, she'd say.

Rolling to my side to face away from the window, I saw the empty twin bed a few feet away. Fragments clicked together as the memories from the day before leaked into my mind and I pushed them away and broke the fragments apart again, not ready to think about that, not now, not yet. It was back there, waiting to be reckoned with, but I wasn't ready. I wanted another day, at least another moment, to pretend he was still alive, still walking on the earth. I turned to the sound of my wind-up alarm clock ticking out the seconds on the bedside table.

9:38. Late for school.

I jumped up and pulled on the clothes from the day before that my father had done his best to fold and place on the chair across from my bed after carrying me in, asleep from the ten-minute ride home. The smell of the field was still on the clothes and on me and my breath had the stink of vomit. I brushed my teeth quickly and tried to get a comb through my thick hair but gave up, leaving it looking worse than it had before I started.

My father sat at the kitchen table, a stack of papers in front of him. Some of them were bills, I knew that much. Sometimes I heard him on the telephone, still arguing with the insurance company and hospital about Mom. He never spoke of her, willingly at least. I'd ask questions sometimes. There were memories that I couldn't tell were real or made up and I just wanted to know, but was usually met with a grunt, then an order to do my chores or go to bed.

"I'm late for school," I said.

He didn't look up, a pen in his right hand following the lines of words in a thick document. "It's Friday. I thought you could stay home," he said. "I have a pump to go check near Prague. You can go with me."

I thought again of Billy Lansing and his disappearance from school last year, remembering that his father hadn't come back from the war. Once he was back in school it wasn't for long and he was gone, the seat in the second to last row just empty again. I'd overheard the teachers saying that his mother packed him and his baby sister up and moved them north to Kansas to be near her sister and how hard it must be for her to be a widow.

"Sure." I looked to the stove after the scent of fresh fried eggs and bacon hit my nose. "You made breakfast?"

Looking at the eggs I realized I'd never gotten to my chores last night and my father must have gone out and collected them. This was usually grounds for his few words, louder than usual and sometimes a few strikes from a switch pulled from a bush outside or his open hand if nothing else was nearby.

"Eat up, and make a sandwich for later. We won't be stopping for lunch."

I grabbed a plate and scooped up the rest of the eggs then sat and ate them as if they would disappear if I didn't.

Work was rare for my father. Since Mom died, he spent more time at the bar or locked up than he did in the oil fields. His reputation as one of the best mechanics in the state had deteriorated and only a few oil lease owners would call him anymore, and usually only as a last resort. He'd been fortunate for years, always in demand. Each morning he'd make a call to an office in Cushing then be off on the road, sometimes putting in fourteen hour days and covering hundreds of miles.

The pickup loaded with tools, my father pointed us out of town toward the large oil fields southwest of Stroud. My forehead rested on the passenger window as I watched the land go by. The flatness of central Oklahoma was only in contrast to hillier places. There might not be mountains and valleys, but the earth moves here. The fields rise and fall gently, rolling along with the car in shades of green and brown, broken by splashes of color in the flowers and weeds. I'd never seen anywhere else but had a hard time picturing it being any better than this. Larry wanted out of here and I couldn't understand why. I guess he didn't see the beauty I saw.

My dad broke the quiet. "Your teacher called this morning."

I didn't move. It seemed to require more force to hold still than it would to respond to my father so I finally gave in.

"Yeah?"

"She said you had an accident on the playground yesterday."

I pulled myself upright, a bright red splotch stretched across my forehead from the cold glass.

"I fell off the big rock."

"That thing's still there?" he said. "We played on it when I was a kid."

I had never even considered the fact that my father was once a school child, much less that he went to the same small building where I attended class now.

"I had my first kiss on that rock. Marilu Albertson surprised me while I was sitting up there one day. Do the popular kids still stake claim to it every recess?"

I didn't know how to react to the information. What little I knew about my father was from first hand experience of being his child and living in the same house.

"Yeah. But I got to it first yesterday and had it to myself."

"How'd you fall off?"

I didn't know what to say. I wasn't even sure how it had happened. "I guess I fell asleep."

The crisp October air poured in as he rolled the window down. He pulled a cigarette from his pocket that he'd assembled at home and lit it with the silver lighter that was never far from him. After taking a long pull followed by a slow exhale, the cabin filled with smoke in defiance of the open window.

"Did you have a dream?"

I resisted turning to stare at my father.

"I don't know," I said. "I mean, I don't remember."

We rode in silence as more of the cigarette was taken in. I could hear the catch in my father's breath as he inhaled, the same I'd heard from my mother. He then threw the butt to the highway and rolled the window up, trapping his final exhale of smoke inside the enclosed cabin.

"It's just you and me now, Wes."

"I know."

"We might as well learn how to talk to each other." My father recited the words as if he'd practiced them. "I know I'm not good at it, but I wanna try."

I could see him fidgeting on the vinyl seat, a sign of weakness in an otherwise confident man. He didn't know how to talk to his own son but spent hours at the bar in town with men he barely knew.

"Your dream, did it seem real?" He looked away out the side window as he said it.

I thought of my brother, standing before me in his loose fitting fatigues, rifle hanging off his shoulder like an afterthought. Certainly my father couldn't know.

"I saw Larry," I said. "I guess I was daydreaming about him and fell off the rock."

Time stood still between his words as he thought of what to say, in the space where ordinary conversations would end then begin anew on another topic. "Can you tell me about it?" His hesitation in asking questions was equaled only by mine to answer them. It was less a conversation than a show of resistance to communicate.

"Not much. I just saw him. He was standing there, looking at me. Then he fell down."

I saw my father's fingers tighten on the steering wheel then relax. The stale cigarette smoke hung in the cab.

"Did it look real or like a dream."

I wanted to be at the oil field, sitting in the bed of the truck scribbling in my notebook while he got his hands dirty fixing the machines that were now sitting dormant waiting on his arrival.

"It was... it was very real. But it was just a daydream."

"Ever had others like it? Ones that felt real?"

"A couple times, maybe. But not about Larry."

"I want to hear about them." A break in his voice contradicted his words.

I held my breath. These dreams were mine and nobody else's. I didn't know how to share them and I didn't know how to talk to my father about my mother. They'd been inside me, inside my brain for so long that sometimes I thought I was just making them seem real. The nights they had come to me were gone and forgotten, lost sleep at the mercy of an overactive brain.

"The first time I really remember, I guess, it was when mom was sick." I stopped talking. From the corner of my eye I saw my father straighten in the seat beside me.

"Go ahead, Wes," he said. "It's okay."

"It was brighter than a normal dream. I saw her in the kitchen making a cup of tea. It was when she was really weak and could hardly get out of bed. Don't think she'd been downstairs in a couple of weeks at that time. She took a red box from under the sink then poured something from it into her cup. She could barely even stand up but she was making a cup of tea. That was the night she—"

My words were left in the air as I flew forward on the seat, my hands stopping me from slamming into the metal dashboard as my father hit the brakes and pulled off of the road. Two cars behind us honked as they swerved to keep from hitting the pickup then flew past. The truck came to a stop, dust flying around us from the shoulder of the road. I prepared for the yelling or the hitting or both.

My dad just sat there, looking through the windshield without saying a word. We sat silently for a long time before he moved again. He put the truck in gear and pulled back up onto the road. Our conversation about dreams was over for that day. My father didn't act mad as the day went on, but I caught him looking my way a couple times, staring at me.

Chapter 5

IT WAS A month before we had the funeral. Lawrence's body had to be flown from Vietnam, through Frankfurt, Germany then to the Air Force base outside Washington, D.C., before it was brought to Tinker Air Force Base in Oklahoma City.

I stood beside my father outside a huge hanger as the Army C-130 cargo plane rolled past, its four huge propellers moving the winter air around us as it turned then came to a stop. A dozen other families were there, each small group keeping its distance from the others, clusters of mourning and distraught parents and siblings all dressed in black, contrasted by my father in his blue jeans. A line of hearses, one for each of the boys being brought home that day, were ready to take possession of the plain military caskets and drive them to their hometowns all over Oklahoma. I even saw one with an Arkansas license plate.

I scanned the caskets, identical in every way, and thought about the young men inside them, not much older than me. I already knew I wouldn't see my brother. Dad had explained that they weren't able to have an open casket due to the condition of his body. I thought of him being lowered into the dirt, soil filled in on top. There was only a little time to see this box, the last place my brother would be, before it was hidden from sight forever. I wanted to remember everything I could about it, every detail from the grain of the black stained wood to the metal hinges and lock.

Twelve soldiers were lined up in their dress uniforms and stood at attention on the far side of the row of black boxes. An Army pastor said a few words that nobody could hear over the airplanes taking off behind him. Soldiers spread flags on top of each casket that were then loaded into the hearses. A young woman not far from us let out a moaning, long cry as her family tried to calm her. I looked up at my father, whose eyes were locked onto the hearse that he knew was from Stroud then followed the casket that held his eldest son as it came to a stop behind the black car. It was gently rolled into the back and the door closed.

My father's hand came around to my shoulder and pulled me tight against his side. He was very still and we stood there, more together than we'd ever been. I felt the weight, the loss he had experienced in such a short time. A small and rare act of contact brought us closer, the only survivors of our little family. I watched the black cars, hoping they took their time before leaving.

The smell of jet fuel stuck to the air with the constant flow of aircraft taking off and landing. I looked at how many people were here running around in their uniforms and wondered why they weren't over in the war. Why did they live and Larry didn't? What was so special about them?

We followed the hearse east down Route 66 to Stroud. The driver from the funeral home wanted to take the turnpike that had been built fifteen years earlier, but dad had requested to drive on the slower road, not being one for highways or cities. The funeral was scheduled for this afternoon and the slower road was going to run us late, but he didn't care. I didn't either. These were the last moments I'd spend with Larry and I watched that big black car the entire drive. I wanted to be in that car, sitting beside the box so my hands could rest on it, feel the wood under my fingers.

We arrived at the church after three hours with no words spoken inside the cab of the pickup, but it was a silence different from the everyday quiet in our house. We both were thinking of the same thing and nothing needed to be said. I saw the flatbed truck that belonged to my grandfather and I was out and running into the church before the pickup's engine was even turned off.

I found my grandpa standing in the back of the church talking to the sheriff. I wrapped my arms around the old man's waist. He paused in the middle of a sentence and looked down at me, his face went pale.

"I'm sorry, sheriff," he said. "I lost my thought."

"We'll catch up another day," the sheriff said. "Today is for family."

"Thank you for coming, sheriff," grandpa said.

"There's no way I wouldn't be here, Jack." The two men shook hands and the lawman walked off.

"How're you holdin' up, little man?" My grandfather leaned over and wrapped his arms around me.

Jack Hudson was the counter point to everything about his own son. Where dad was reserved and soft spoken until mad or drunk, my grandfather was talkative and friendly, and above all, loving.

"I'm doin' okay," I said. "I miss him."

"I know, Wesley. I know."

The service was long and slow and my thoughts wandered, spending most of the hour resting against my grandpa's arm. After it was over I asked my father if I could ride to the cemetery with my grandfather and received only a slight nod. Dad had turned down the funeral home's offer of a limousine. He instead drove his pickup behind the hearse, my grandfather's flatbed behind him, and the handful of other cars of families and friends that had attended trailing with their headlights on. Sheriff Cole led the procession with the blue light on his roof flashing, though there were no stoplights or signs to keep the motorcade from passing.

The cemetery was at the edge of town, a faded brown field dotted with grey stones. The preacher insisted the headstones get cleaned twice a year, relying on volunteers from the church to come out with buckets of soapy water that he blessed before the scrubbing began. It was a ritual that had become part of the town. Families brought picnic lunches and the smaller children ran between the rows of stones, laughing and chasing each other. I'd come once with my mother and Larry. He chased me and she cleaned. I thought all cemeteries were like this because that was my only knowledge of them. Fun places to celebrate people and laugh and run.

While walking along the straight rows I looked at the names and years, pausing for a moment at a marker barely a foot tall. The stone was darker than the others and it was faded from too many decades in the wind and sun. Even the regular cleaning could to nothing to bring it back to its original condition. The words inscribed were worn almost smooth. 'Baby Lily' was the only name listed, not even a last name for future generations to find her grave. Below that the dates, February 16, 1896 – February 28, 1896.

Twelve days.

My 12 years on the earth seemed immortal in that moment. I knelt and placed a hand on the stone. "I'm sorry, Baby Lily."

The sky flew into blackness, voices of a dozen people faded away and left an emptiness around me. I felt scared and cold. Trembling hands held my bare skin. From inside the dark I could look up to see the young woman holding me that I didn't recognize, her hair in tangles and tears running down her face as she yelled. She was holding me in her arms against her naked chest and trying to force me to suckle but I resisted in my weakness. I was being rocked back and forth too fast, too rough.

I cried out for help but all that came was a whimpering cry, no words could form. The rocking became harder and I grew more afraid, the mother's face more frantic by the moment. There was nobody else around, just me and the woman, and her grasp on me became tighter, too tight. I tried to yell out again but the sound was transformed, stolen, into crying.

A hand pulled from under my arm, raising me out of her hands, off of the ground. "Wesley." The voice was firm yet somehow comforting. The sky opened to the overcast fall day once more. I glanced up to see my grandfather, a look of concern on his face, as I was walked further down the row. I looked back once at the worn headstone, the cries now gone.

People in dark suits and dresses, most of them nameless to me, were gathered beside a gravesite at the end as we approached. Once released from my grandfather's grip, I moved through the small crowd to the front. I saw a group of teenagers that I knew had been in high school with Larry. They were packed tightly together. The boys looked scared, as if seeing their possible future play out before them, each close to being old enough to be drafted and sent to the battlefields.

In front of me was the wide headstone with my mother's name engraved on the left side, and below it 1926-1965. I'd only seen the stone once before, a few months after her funeral. The other half had my father's name, 'Joseph Avery Hudson' already there with nothing below for the years. I thought of Baby Lily and at first hesitated to reach out. Then with one finger traced the shallow grooves in the stone, 'Loving Mother.'

I often tried to see her face or remember the feel of her hands on me when I was hurt or sad. The embrace of her arms even as they grew weaker. She had been the warmth of our home, the centerpiece of the family. Where the boys and man had distant or uncertain relationships, she was loved by all. Once when I told her I was sick and couldn't go to school, she felt my head then sent me to bed. As soon as Larry was gone she was in there with me, feeding me soup and talking with me all day. I'm sure she knew I wasn't sick and just liked having someone with her for a day.

Behind the headstone I saw the hole. It was long, narrow and deep and was waiting for my brother. Dark brown soil was piled up beside the rectangular hole, streaks of the red clay common in all the dirt in this part of the state running through it. The handles of a pair of shovels were visible on the other side of the mound. I stared at the dirt. Movement caught my eye and I knelt down to see a long earthworm working its way through the moist soil that had been disturbed and brought to the surface.

The hearse backed in and six men including my father, grandfather and the sheriff, pulled the box out and set it on the ground beside the hole, a pair of ropes underneath for lowering it into the ground after the short graveside service.

I stood between my father and grandfather beside the casket. Grandpa's hand was on my shoulder. We listened to the preacher say some more words but none of us heard them. We all stared at the box in front of us and had our own thoughts of the young man inside. Finally the last words were spoken, the final amen was pronounced and the black box was lowered down by four men in dirty work clothes and thick leather gloves to handle the ropes.

My dad leaned down and picked up a handful of the soil, rolled it in his hands for a moment, then tossed it down on top of his son's casket. I wanted to see the men shovel dirt in and cover the box, finish the ritual. Returned to the earth, as the preacher said. But they didn't. They stood where they were just out of the circle of mourners, two of them smoking cigarettes and none of them concerned about the dead boy in the casket they were there to bury.

"Can you stay with us tonight, Grandpa?"

He gave me a hug. "I wish I could," he said. "I have to be up early in the morning to deliver an engine to Joplin."

My shoulders dropped.

"How about we talk to your father and see if you can come stay with me for a few days over Christmas break?"

"Okay." The thought of spending time at my grandfather's house brought a smile to my face even though it was still over a month away. I loved walking around and climbing all over the tractors the old man fixed for a living. And when I tired of that, there were the seventy-five acres of wooded hills that rose up behind the farmhouse that begged for exploration.

The group of teenagers walked off, still huddled for safety. Arms were around shoulders and hands held hands that didn't look like they had ever touched each other.

Neighbors and friends brought more food than needed to the house. It was a ritual I knew my father couldn't understand, the party that followed the funeral. I'd watched him stand to the side, teeth grinding through it after my mother died three years ago.

Chapter 6

I STARED BLANKLY at the math problems in the open schoolbooks spread out in front of me on the kitchen table. Some of them were filled in and sloppily erased from kids breaking the rules and writing in the books years before me. There was plenty of homework to do but I had no interest in doing it. With summer break only a few weeks away I could only think about sleeping late, freedom to run around the pastures all I wanted, and spending more time at the old church writing my stories.

I startled at a hard tapping from the front door and went to investigate. I opened the door to see a soldier standing there but I never saw the man's face, my eyes glued to the dull curved metal coming from the end of his right sleeve.

Dad walked up behind me, his hand going to my shoulder. "Can I help you?"

"Sir, my name is Bill Johnson. I served with your son, Lawrence." His words were awkward and rehearsed.

Dad was frozen in the door then finally stepped back. "Please come in."

In the months since the funeral my brother's name hadn't been uttered once inside our house. A few kids at school had asked me about him but I'd just shrug and walk away rather than discuss it with anyone. His bed still sat to the right of mine, the sheets smooth and flat with an afghan our mother had made folded at the foot. I wanted it gone, out of the room, the constant reminder that my brother was never coming back. But I couldn't ask my father to take it apart.

We sat in the front room, me beside my father and the young soldier across from us in the straight back chair in the window. His shape was silhouetted against the brightness behind him, details coming in as he'd move and momentarily block the light. He sat straight, partly forward on the hard chair, shoulders square. I couldn't help but think how uncomfortable he looked and if everyone in the Army sat this way even when they weren't working. On the floor to his side was a wood box he'd carried under his arm. It had sounded heavy when he set it on the bare floor. My eyes went slowly from the box to the missing hand, up to the medals pinned to the boy's chest then to his face. Short cropped jet black hair covered his head and came down a little too far on his forehead. I felt my head swim as every hair stood up on my neck. It was the same boy I'd seen run to Larry's side in my dream.

"I'm sorry I don't have anything to offer you," Dad said. "We don't make it to the store too often."

"I appreciate it, sir. I really don't want to take up too much of your time," Bill said. "Lawrence and I were together in Vietnam. When it got bad, we made a promise to each other to go to the other's family, if it came to that."

"Thank you, son. It's an honor to meet someone who knew him, that was there with him."

"We wanted our families to know what happened, how it happened." He glanced at me and back at Dad as if to question my presence.

"It's okay," Dad said. "Wes has grown up a lot in the last few years. He deserves to hear about his brother directly."

Bill nodded and looked down at the metal where his hand had been as he collected his thoughts.

"We were on patrol along the edge of an old rice paddy that our sergeant guessed had been deserted when the war moved into that part of the country. It was knee deep in most places, deeper in others. We stopped so two of the guys could pull leeches off their legs and the rest of us could check for them, when we began to hear movement through the overgrowth," he said. "We did as we were trained and became still, and waited to see what direction the sound was going. Then bullets began to hit the ground and water around us."

I imagined the soldier staring in a mirror practicing the story, working on getting through it without breaking down. As he spoke he didn't look directly at either of us, his eyes landing somewhere between us, focusing out the back kitchen window, across the field, perhaps all the way back to Vietnam.

"Sarge ordered us to turn and head back, to retreat. I was maybe ten feet to Lawrence's left and we were running. We both heard the click and he turned to me, but he was moving too fast. His foot came off the trigger before he could stop."

Bill pulled a handkerchief out of his pants pocket and wiped his eyes. "I'm sorry, sir."

Dad nodded.

"The mine threw me maybe fifteen feet," Bill said. "I sat up, my ears ringing, trying to find Lawrence but couldn't at first. The tall grass blocked my view and there was water everywhere. Two other guys from our platoon grabbed me under the arms and kept running. Then I saw him. I told them to stop, that we needed to help Lawrence. But they said we had to get clear, that they had to get me to the medics. I didn't understand why. I felt fine except for the ringing in my ears. I pulled away from them and ran, falling to my knees in the water, but I couldn't pull him up. I was lifted back up and carried away. Even then I didn't realize until they were throwing me in the back of the truck—"

He pulled the sleeve on his right arm up six inches. The metal grapples at the end of his arm opened and closed.

"I didn't even know I'd been hit. A chunk of shrapnel bigger than a half-dollar was stuck in my elbow. They cut the arm off before I was even on the helicopter to the hospital. After finally getting stateside I spent a month at

Walter Reed in D.C. getting patched up and fitted with this thing."

"It can't be easy," Dad said.

"It isn't that bad. For the first time ever I'm glad I'm a leftie. It's the staring I have the most problem with," Bill said.

I turned my head away and tried to appear like I'd been looking out the window the whole time.

"Not the kids," Bill said. "That's to be expected. They're curious, I don't mind that. I even like talking to them about the arm, showing them how it works. It's the adults. It took me a while to realize that most of them were probably parents of other boys still over there. I do my best. When I see them looking I smile, I nod. I try to make them think that I'm okay, that this is okay." He raised the arm and looked at it. "They usually just look away."

The metal hand made a clicking sound every time it opened and closed, not just from the artificial fingers coming together, but from up inside, mechanisms working together to drive the grip. It was soft and muffled by the uniform sleeve, but still present.

"What are you going to do now?" Dad said.

"I'll go back home to Indianapolis, sir. My father sells insurance and I'll probably just work with him. Before the war I'd planned to become a police officer, but that isn't going to happen now."

"I'm sure you'll do well at whatever you choose," Dad said.

I was amazed at the words coming from my father, the encouragement and caring.

The soldier stared past us again, his eyes not seeming to be locked onto anything or even seeing anything. His calmness and resolve showed strain, a crack in the armor he was using to look like everything was fine.

"I wasn't even in the Army a year, you know," Bill said. "And we'd only been in country for a month. It seemed like forever at the time, long nights without sleeping, waiting for the sound of the bullet that would end you. Sitting up at every noise that didn't fit. We lived entire lives in those weeks, entire lives as different people. Kids carrying guns and killing other men and sometimes women. Death became a constant. But through everything we saw and did and felt, everything new and different, nothing prepared us for what it was like to come back home."

My father was turning to the side in his chair, his legs moving in their slow dance of discomfort, not at the position but the conversation. "Hows that? Wasn't coming home a relief?"

Bill shook his head slowly, almost imperceptible movement, his eyes still somewhere past Oklahoma. "Coming home was the hardest part, sir. Walking down the sidewalk in my hometown I saw people carrying their groceries and walking their dogs. Children riding bikes. It's all so... normal. Like nothing is happening thousands of miles away. Like boys aren't dying and killing. Everyone just going on about their lives. That was the hardest part of coming home. Like we were already forgotten about."

Silence was thick as the young soldier trailed off in his

thoughts, his gaze moving down to the floor then like someone had reminded him where he was, he looked at us.

"I'm so sorry, Mr. Hudson. I didn't mean to go on like that." He looked lost, unsure what to do or say next and my father unable to help him through anything like this.

Dad just nodded some more, looking over to the fireplace as if it needed inspecting right then.

"I brought something for you," Bill said. "It was something else Lawrence and I had promised."

The man picked up the wooden box then stood and stepped over to my father and handed it to him. Dad took it and sat it on his lap and looked at the grain of the mahogany, perfectly stained. The gold hinges and lock shone against the wood. I thought of the box I'd last seen with my brother inside.

"I made the box myself," Bill said. "Part of my rehab with the arm. I wanted something nice to bring it to you in."

"It's fine work." My father turned the box over in his hands, inspecting the finish, looking relieved to have something to do.

"It's not locked, if you'd like to open it," Bill said.

"I know what's inside. Thank you."

Chapter 7

I WALKED AMONG the thirsty cattle on a Tuesday afternoon, my notebook in hand. There hadn't been rain in several weeks. The fields were brown, dried up grass and weeds sticking out of the cracked soil. There was no urgency to my walking and going any faster would have made it that much hotter. Dad was at work and I spent most of each summer day at the old church.

A lone cloud passed in front of the sun offering just the sense of a drop in temperature, a moment of imaginary relief. Then it was bright again and felt worse than before. My hand was sweating where it pressed against the notebook, a moist impression of my palm left behind.

The church came into sight, the heat causing the air between me and the building to distort, to wave back and forth. In that distortion I thought I saw a movement, the smallest of changes in the scenery. I wiped the sweat from my face and eyes and looked again. Nothing was different than usual, the stone church sitting there as it always did.

I grew eager to get out of the sun, my steps getting quicker, my eyes watching the ground to keep from tripping over a dried up weed or cow pile, and almost ran into the final barbed wire fence before the church. Bending over I moved through the wires and walked up the small rise to the building, always coming to the flat facing side first and running my hand across the ancient stones as I went around the corner then through the opening. As I crossed the threshold into the shaded protection of the building I raised my eyes and saw something move, a shadow going from right to left then it turned to look at me, eyes meeting mine, then it came out of the shadows and rushed toward me.

The shape pushed past me, striking my shoulder and I fell backwards to the ground, my notebook flying open and loose pages floating down around it in the lack of any breeze. I heard the steps stop, a scuff as the person turned then slowly walked back to me. My heart was pounding and I felt paralyzed on the ground.

Silence. No steps, no sounds of breathing. I couldn't raise my head to look.

Then a quiet voice.

"Are you okay?"

I couldn't respond. Then movement and sounds as the person came around to my side and looked down at me. I saw his face for the first time. It was a boy, no older than me.

"I said, are you okay?"

I nodded then started to sit up. The boy reached his hand out and I took it. He pulled with no effort, then I was standing face to face with him.

"Yeah," I said. "I think so. You just...you scared me."

"I am sorry."

He was an inch taller, maybe two, and wore faded jeans and a jean jacket even in the heat. His face was narrow and pointed, light brown skin blending into the surroundings. Long black hair was pulled back into a ponytail. I knew who he was, or at least what he was. I'd seen the Indians around town or rolling past in old pickups, several of them lined up in the bed. They would watch you watching them, showing no emotion about it. Dad had only said to stay away from them but I didn't know why. I heard kids at school talk about how evil they were.

"Is this yours?" The boy motioned to the church.

It had been a part of me for so many years but it wasn't mine. I had only met the man who owned the land once with my father when we were at the feed store. He was tall and seemed kind.

"No. I just come here."

He nodded and looked at the building as if in approval.

"I can see why." His eyes finally came back to me and I felt him take me in all at once, size me up, then his hand came out to me. "My name is Jake."

I stared at his hand and hesitated too long, my father's words coming to me, and he pulled his hand back.

"I understand." Jake turned and started walking away and my stomach tightened up like I'd been punched.

"Wait." He turned around, hands shoved in his jeans pockets. "I'm Wesley." I saw the change in his stance, minimal motion but losing his defensive posture and a slight smile came to his face.

We moved around the church and I told him what I knew about it. He touched the stones as I do, with a reverence, a respect. He looked at the sapling and stroked the green leaves. In the dark corner of the church he became quiet then sat down on the ground in a smooth motion.

"Do you pray here?"

"No. I don't really pray."

"What do you do here then?"

I sat down facing him, aware of my posture as he sat with his back straight, shoulders back. "I sit and think. I write stories. Sometimes I draw pictures."

He nodded, always looking around at the rough ground and stone walls. "Then you pray here."

His story came out slowly, in small pieces throughout the afternoon. His family lived on the Sac and Fox Nation reservation a few miles south of town and he was in the same grade as me. He was supposed to be working today but had run off to be alone and gone too far.

"What's it like living on the reservation?"

"I guess not too different than living where you live, just everyone looks like me instead of you." He scooted over to lean against the wall, more in a way to feel the stone rather than to relax. "Most of the grown ups work off of the reservation, some in town, others on farms further out. My uncle cleans the school in Stroud."

I thought to the early mornings I would get to the school before the doors were even unlocked, sitting on the front steps until the man in green coveralls came out carrying his buckets and mops and I'd run right past him into the building, never even looking at his face.

"Yeah. I've seen him."

I didn't know what my father meant, why I should stay away from them.

"But then there are people like my great grandfather. I do not think he has been off our land since before I was born."

"What does he do?"

Jake shrugged. "He sits in his house and stares out the window. He was once the storyteller, reciting the ancient tales of the *Thakiwaki*."

"The what?"

"*Thakiwaki*. That is the real name of our tribe. You know us by what the white people call us," he said. "He has passed the history on to a younger man. All he talks about now are his visions."

I tried not to seem too interested but my pulse grew faster. "What kinds of visions?"

"Usually boring stuff like saying a visitor is coming to the tribal lands. Sometimes he knows if someone is going to die. That always sends people panicking. Everyone starts making food and visiting the house of the person he has named. Sometimes they do. I mean, you are eventually going to be right, just might be a few years."

"Do you believe him?"

"It is just the way it is, nothing to believe or not believe. If a man on the television tells you it is going to rain, do you believe him? Maybe it rains, maybe it does not. Either way it does not matter."

I didn't know this boy but felt comfortable in his presence, in my special place. His voice was calming.

"I have dreams sometimes." It came out as a whisper inside the old church.

Jake nodded matter of factly. "They come to some people, not to others."

He asked about the dreams and I told him. He didn't interrupt or ask questions, just listened. I didn't expect any answers or revelations from him and he didn't offer any. Just the act of listening, accepting was enough.

It was after more than an hour of talking that he grew quiet, his eyes going to the opening in the wall. I sat in silence with him until he quickly stood up, startling me.

"I must go."

"You gonna walk all the way back?"

"I'll go over to the main road and someone will pick me up."

I didn't want to question how he knew that would happen but he seemed sure of it. I walked to the intersection of gravel roads with him, one direction would take him down to Highway 99, the other would lead me home. He glanced back at the church like he wouldn't see it again.

"How did you find this place?" I said.

He shrugged. "I was not looking for it."

"Come visit again sometime. I live about a mile that way." I pointed up the dirt road and he nodded.

"Maybe I will. Goodbye, Wesley."

"Bye, Jake."

He moved up the road with precise movements, no waste of energy, then I turned back to the church. I felt lonely in his absence and grabbed my notebook and headed home.

Chapter 8

GRANDPA WOULD ALWAYS say that you could smell the dirt of Texas on the wind if you tried real hard. I'd sniff at the air and never knew if he was kidding me. All I ever smelled was the cow manure from the next pasture.

He was born in west Texas and lived there until heading off to the Army because it was the only thing to do in Plainview other than work a factory or the fields. With the 16th Infantry he was part of the Mexican Expedition under none other than Pershing himself, chasing Pancho Villa and his banditos around for nine months. They never caught him.

Then the United States decided to enter World War I and Pershing was ordered to take the first troops over, Grandpa right along with him. His regiment was in France and even paraded right down through the center of Paris before they found themselves in the trenches with German bullets flying over their heads.

When I was young he never spoke much about the war. A few times Larry and I had snuck into his bedroom and looked at the medals kept in a small sewing box on the bedside table. Larry would talk about going off to the Army just like him and getting his own medals. I never thought he really would. Didn't think he'd actually leave me here alone.

I sat on the front step of the old church where the sun warmed the stones, the heat coming up over me. My notebook was open on my lap as I worked through a story that had been in my head all day at school. I'd rushed home to do my chores then over to the church to write. The conversations between cows and sheep I usually wrote about had changed, turning to images I'd seen in my sleep. They were darker, sad. I was the only student ever excited about writing assignments in school. After turning in my first assignment the teacher asked me to talk after class, saying she was concerned about the subject of the story. I told her it was just a story, not that I'd dreamt it. It was what I'd been telling myself for some time.

The sound of tires on gravel came from the road and I grabbed my bag and hid behind the church, watching around the corner as dad's pickup went past on his way home from work. Once the truck was gone I packed my notebook and started the walk home. I easily could have let him see me and gotten a ride, but I still wanted to keep this place to myself. As I went through the barbed wire fence I glanced over at the road to Highway 99. I hadn't seen Jake since that first time and kept hoping he'd show up again.

My father had the most regular work he'd seen in more than two years, hauling parts back and forth between the oil fields and the large facility in Tahlequah that cleaned and prepared them to go back into service pumping oil out of the ground. It didn't pay great, but was more than we were used to. It was long hours, and he was usually gone before I even woke up and not home again until dark. But we'd found ourselves spending more time together in the last few months, even talking.

Dad had been in the Army, too, but didn't stay very long. He'd signed up as soon as he was old enough so he could go overseas along with his friends from school. They were training to fight the Germans in France, just like Grandpa had years earlier. Once when he was drunk he said he would have been at Normandy on D-Day if he hadn't broken his leg, and that it was my Grandpa's fault about the leg and I never understood that. The three boys he signed up with were all killed on Omaha Beach and I think he'd rather have been there with them.

I smelled the food before I got to the house and went around back to find dad standing over the old smoker he'd made out of an oil barrel. The smoke was thick and sweet as it came past me and made me hungrier than I already was. Not long ago if there was fresh meat being cooked, I'd look around the yard to see what animal was missing. We'd lost half our egg laying chickens in the last year. The one goat we'd ever had was the first victim of our hunger and fed us for a couple of weeks. But now he'd stop at the butcher in Cushing or Shawnee and we'd feast without the guilt of killing the closest things we had to family pets.

He saw me come around the corner of the house. "Wes." His eyes were back on the meat. "How was school?"

"Good. We're learning about the Civil War."

He nodded and reached for his beer bottle on the tree stump beside the grill. "Hungry?"

I was sure he could hear my stomach growl. "Yessir."

"Go on in and wash up and work up some sides."

In the kitchen I pulled two cans of corn and a bag of rice from the pantry. The corn was dumped into a pan to heat up while I brought water to a boil for the rice.

We sat outside to eat. The sun faded and it cooled off more but I wouldn't say anything, wrapping my arms around myself a little tighter. Dad and I sat beside each other on tree stumps left for that purpose, working the meat off down to the bone, not leaving a scrap.

It became a regular occurrence, at least once a week. He'd bring home something to cook and we'd sit outside until the stars were lit up in the sky. We were silent most of the time, but every once in a while we'd get to talking, usually about something he saw while driving all day or what Stroud was like when he was a boy. I heard him talk more that summer than I ever had, and even heard him laugh a few times.

There wasn't a warmth between us, but perhaps a thawing. We went from father and son to more like roommates, I guess. I don't think he ever thought he was a very good father, or at least didn't think he knew how to be one, so being friends was more natural to him. Occasionally he'd try to say something to seem in control, telling me to do my homework or asking if I'd done my chores. He'd usually end in a mutter, knowing what needed done was probably done.

One Saturday afternoon during the summer when it was hot outside but still cooler than being in the house, I'd been sitting outside on the grass writing in my notebook. The sun was soaking into my arms and felt good, turning my skin a soft shade of pink. Dad came out, the ever present beer bottle in his hand, and stood beside me looking out at the empty field.

"What are you writing?"

He'd never asked anything about my writing, even if it was homework. "Just a story."

"Mmm hmm." More staring at the pasture. "Want to read some of it to me?"

For a moment I tried to pretend I hadn't heard him, my hand still moving as if I were crafting new words, but just off of the paper while I thought. "If you like."

"Don't have to." He sipped from the beer and adjusted his weight to the other foot, trying to keep from looking as awkward as he did right then.

"Sure."

He glanced down at me, looked around, then sat on the grass. His lanky legs stretched out in front of him in oil stained blue jeans with his scuffed and worn boots coming out the end. A long sleeve blue denim shirt covered his arms. I always wondered how he could handle the heavy material when it was so hot.

I flipped back a few pages while I tried to pick what to read. I knew I didn't want any of my older, silly writing. But some of the new stuff was pretty obviously about Larry, though thinly disguised, and I wasn't sure how that would go over. I glanced at him still looking out at the field and picked something from a few weeks earlier.

"*Blue into green*
One becomes the other
As far as can be seen
On the horizon

Green into blue
Colors blend as
I think of you
Beyond the clouds

I see all the colors
In one place
Bending and calling
And I see your face.

But you don't answer
When I call to you
Blue into green
Green into blue."

Without looking over at him I watched from the corner of my eye. He moved his legs, kicking some mud off of one boot with the other, seeming oblivious that I'd just spoken, much less read something I had created, words I'd put together in a certain order that meant something to me. A sip from the almost empty beer. Then he mumbled with no notice. "That's good."

It was a highest praise from a man who gives no praise. It was the first time I'd shared anything I'd written other than school assignments to my teachers and I could feel myself shaking a little. Even in school we don't read out loud, the teacher fearful for what might be said in her classroom. In my head I felt I had rushed through it, read the words so quickly that he couldn't hear them right.

"Thanks."

He nodded ever so slightly then stood. He paused then his hand was on my head as he stroked my hair to the side, then he walked away.

That was as close as we'd ever been. I don't know if he'd ever held me when I was a baby, but I'm fairly certain he never changed a diaper. I know he loved my mom, but he didn't show it like some do. Occasionally it was a soft peck on top of the head while she was sitting in her sewing chair. Only once had I seen him actually hug her, the day they came home from the doctors appointment that had spelled out her fate and she'd practically fallen into his arms. She was the only person that could tell him what to do, and when she did, he did it with no questions. To me that was love, what a man does for a woman. I knew nothing of romance or intamacy, gentle touches or holding hands. It wasn't anything I'd seen. The first time I saw a high school couple making out behind the grocery store, one of the few places they could go without easily being seen by parents or neighbors driving through town, I had no idea what was happening, what they were doing. I was probably eight or nine years old. I stood there, half hidden behind a row of dented metal trash cans, as faces pressed against faces and hands moved madly across clothed bodies as if searching for something. The boy glanced around then put his hands up her shirt and it looked like he was molding clay under the thin fabric. I didn't understand it, but something inside my body did. I felt the tightness in my pants for the first time that day then ran home as fast as I could.

Chapter 9

I TRIED TO hide my smile, especially considering where we were going. It just seemed inappropriate but was hard not to. It was almost a year since Larry's funeral. We'd never been to the cemetery and I tried for three days to find a way to ask if we could go. It wasn't far from school and I could have easily walked before coming home one day or gone by myself on a Saturday morning, but I wanted to go with him. There were only three Hudsons left in Oklahoma, for all I knew, at least from our family.

I'd finally blurted it out at dinner Friday night over corn on the cob and overcooked hamburgers. Rain had been coming down so hard and fast that it was sure to flood in the lower areas and Dad stared out the back door at the grill for an hour before finally relenting and cooking inside on the stovetop. He hated burgers that weren't right off the fire. I tried to be matter-of-fact about it, not knowing how he'd react. But it came out like an accident right after asking for the butter and was interrupted by the noise of him opening another beer, causing me to have to repeat myself.

He was motionless while staring at the metal bottle cap in his hand and I thought I was going to have to say it again. Then he handed me the butter with a nod and quiet words. "Tomorrow morning." We didn't talk much more during dinner that night.

We were up early and left without even eating breakfast. You'd have thought we were headed out on a vacation as excited as I was. I asked him to stop along the dirt road and he did with no question. I jumped out of the truck and pulled a large clump of Indian Paintbrush from beside a fencepost and got back in. He looked at the orange weeds and I swear I saw the faintest hint of a smile. I tied them together with a small piece of string I'd brought and tried to imagine the looks on people's faces when they'd walk past my mom's grave over the next few days and saw them sitting there.

The brown grass was almost gone between the rows of headstones, leaving rows of muddy paths. He walked well behind me. I don't know if it was to let me have my time alone or his ambivalence to visiting the cemetery, but he eventually caught up as I placed the Indian Paintbrush. Dust caked in the dark grooves on the flat headstone had become soaked with rain, giving more depth to the words, an embellishment of the square lettering.

A year since Larry died, four years since Mom. A quarter of my life had been without her, some of the memories long gone while others were stronger and more vivid than ever. But I couldn't remember how it felt when she hugged me, as much as I tried. I know I'd loved it and whenever I would lean into her, she would wrap her arms around me and squeeze tightly, but I couldn't feel it anymore.

I stepped over to Larry's grave and saw his stone for the first time then went down on my knees as I read the words.

LAWRENCE AVERY HUDSON
JANUARY 14, 1950 – OCTOBER 8, 1968
BELOVED SON AND GRANDSON
DEAR BROTHER
SOLDIER
KILLED IN ACTION IN VIETNAM

Even as I read it I knew it was Grandpa who'd chosen the words, but it didn't matter. There was a finality in seeing it, reading it, even after a year without him, longer including when he'd left for the Army. His bed still sat next to mine, his clothes occupied the top two drawers of the dresser. I couldn't go a day without thinking about him even if I wanted because of those reminders. I wanted to think about him everyday, but knew it was time to choose when and how rather than have it thrust into the front of my brain each morning and night.

When school had started after summer break, textbooks were stacked on the front row of desks and handed back to each student. Math, English, and science books worked their way from student to student, worn covers from years of use and abuse. Ms. Albertson had walked over to me and knelt down with a different copy of the science textbook. "I thought you'd like to have this one instead." She'd flipped the front open and I looked at the list of students who had used the book and there, five rows up from where I'd write my name, was the scribbled handwriting 'Larry Hudson'. Her hand fell gently to my shoulder and lingered for a moment, then she stood and walked away.

We'd probably had the typical brothers relationship. Much of the time was spent fighting over nothing, which usually ended with him sitting on top of me until Mom made him stop. Dad didn't intervene much, always saying the roughhousing was good for boys. But Larry was very protective of me, too. He always walked to and from school with me, even in the few months after he graduated before he left for the Army.

As we pulled out of the cemetery Dad headed through town rather than taking the back streets like he always did. I didn't think anything of it until we stopped at the Rock Cafe on the far end of Main Street. We'd eaten there once when mom was still alive but I was only about five then and really didn't remember it. Not that it was anything to be excited about, but that was probably the last time we had eaten in a restaurant.

We sat at a table in the front window and ordered breakfast from the waitress who came by with her white apron and notepad. Dad spoke kindly to her which made me feel proud for some reason. While we waited for the food there wasn't much talking, though I don't know what kind of talking you do after visiting a cemetery. Then almost as abruptly as I'd blurted out my request to go visit Larry the night before, Dad began to talk.

"Would you like me to move the other bed from your room?" He was examining the Heinz ketchup bottle as he spoke, but it was as if he'd read my mind at the gravesite.

I didn't have to think about it, I already had but didn't want to sound eager. I glanced out the window at cars going by on Route 66. "Yes, sir."

He nodded and the waitress came with our food.

And that was how the decision was made to remove my brother's bed and clothes from my room. It wasn't a big discussion or fight, nobody was sad about it. Instead we ate pancakes and I poured so much syrup on mine I thought he would tell me to stop, but he didn't. By the end of breakfast we were even talking a bit, him telling me a story of when Larry was learning to walk and fell down the front steps of the house, leaving a two inch gash in his scalp.

The cafe was about half full and the one waitress moved easily around the tables taking orders and keeping water and coffee filled. I felt like someone was looking at me and glanced over at the low opening to the kitchen, plates lined up ready to be brought out to hungry diners. Just as I saw him, he turned away, not in a hurry like he'd been caught. The sharp lines of his face were familiar as well as the smooth light brown tone of his skin. After he'd turned

I could see the ball of black hair wrapped up in a hairnet on the back of his head. I wanted to go talk to him, to ask if he knew Jake, but knew my father wouldn't allow it.

We went to the cash register by the door and he paid the bill. A white piece of paper tacked to the wall caught my eye and I ran through the words printed on it. They advertised a Pow Wow on the reservation over the holiday weekend. There were drawings of feathers along the sides and one of a man dancing, wearing an ornate outfit and headdress.

Dad walked back and left a dollar on the table and had to explain why when we got out to the truck. My thoughts were on that piece of paper. It was only two weeks until Independence Day weekend.

My dad didn't put things off. If it was something within his control, when he made a decision or set his mind to something, it got done. By that evening my twin bed was centered on the wall and my clothes were divided up among all four drawers instead of stuffed into the bottom two. I thought it would feel weird, but it didn't. I was ready for the morning light to come through the window and show the dance of the dust in the air and let me think of my brother on my own terms.

We were both stuffed from breakfast and by dinnertime still didn't have any appetite. He fell asleep listening to the radio while I wrote a story about a three legged goat trying to outrun his hungry owner. It was a lot funnier than it sounds, and the first time I'd written about animals in a while.

Chapter 10

I SAW ANOTHER flyer for the Pow Wow at the store in town when I went for groceries and looked at it closer, memorizing the days and times. At home I checked the calendar from the insurance company, a photograph of Mt. Rushmore with fireworks splashed across the dark sky on the top half, the grid of dates below. The first day of the Pow Wow was Friday when Dad always came home late after stopping at the bar after work, sometimes not getting in until after I'm in bed. For the next six days I kept thinking about it until thinking turned into planning, and that Friday morning I knew what I was going to do.

The heat continued with no rain in sight. My dad watched the news every night in hopes to hear a better forecast, something to break the spell and wet the land again, to cool things off. He spent all day in his truck, sweating as he drove hundreds of miles.

Dad left for work as normal. I filled a thermos with water and made a couple of egg sandwiches to put in my backpack. I didn't have any idea how long the walk would be, but wanted to be prepared. From the box in my dresser drawer, hidden beneath socks and underwear, I pulled six dollars, all I had saved up. Enough, I hoped, to pay my way in as no price was listed on the flyer. I waited until mid afternoon to leave, sitting on the chair in the front room watching the clock on the mantle the whole time. The flyer had said events began at 7pm on Friday so I began walking at 5:30.

The fastest way to Highway 99 was back into town then turn right, but that would take me right past the bar. So I walked to the church then traced Jake's steps over to the highway. My shirt was soaked before I made that turn and I'd drank half of my water by then. The trucks flew past as I walked beside the two lane road, dust and debris flying up and hitting me. Every time I heard one coming I started to turn my head away and close my eyes. Several times I considered sticking my thumb out, trying to get a ride as the heat was wearing me down. My blue jeans were matted to my skin with sweat and I felt the burning on my thighs as they began to rough my skin.

More vehicles came past with Indians and I figured I was getting close. It was another twenty minutes of walking when I saw the line of pickups and cars waiting their turns to pay and go in. A woman in a white apron was stopping each vehicle and taking money, making change from the large pockets. She looked at me a few times then waved me over.

"You want to go to the Pow Wow?"

I nodded. "How much does it cost?" I pulled the six dollars from my pocket.

"Are you alone?"

"Yes ma'am." I was nervous. More cars pulled up to pay as she spoke to me.

"Does your mother know you are here?"

"I don't have-" I paused. "No ma'am."

She looked at the six dollars then waved her hand at me. "Put your money away, young man. Go on in."

I thanked her and walked under the green metal arch. The thumping of the drums got to me before I saw the fire and people standing around it in a large clearing past the tree line. I hid behind a large tree and watched. There were men dancing, erratic movements to a thundering beat as they spun and kicked knees up. People clapped and stomped their feet in unison, some calling out in foreign words. Before realizing I had even moved I was standing at the edge of the circle, feeling the drums in my chest, watching the dancers up close. Their eyes were closed most of the time and they sang, long exotic sounding lyrics that pulled me in.

The dance ended and the crowd dispersed. I hoped it wasn't over, that there was more to come, and followed people to see where they went next. A few people looked at me, some staring and others smiling. I watched for Jake, hoping to spot him in the crowd, to see a face I knew.

Sunset cast a warm glow through the trees then faded to darkness. Small fires throughout the park shone like beacons, drawing people from one to the other. Women squatted beside the flames and mixed foods in large pots, serving onto plates anyone who came up. The smell tingled my nose and I realized I was hungry, the sandwiches still in my backpack and likely spoiled from the heat. One cook looked up at me, her head tilting to the side in a sign of confusion at this pale face in the darkness, then she grabbed a bowl from beside her and scooped from the pot. The bowl was handed to me, then a spoon, and I sipped the broth, feeling the warmth enter my body, defying the heat of the night and cooling me. I ate more, spooning the meats and vegetables into my mouth. I heard the woman laugh along with others seated around her.

"He likes!" she called out and I just smiled.

Finishing the stew I handed my bowl back and thanked her. She waved as I walked off, still laughing. The drums were starting up again and echoed through the night air. I saw a boy go around a corner behind a small building and I ran to catch up, a black ponytail falling across a denim jacket. As I caught up the boy turned at the sound of my running. He looked at me and stepped back.

"I'm sorry. I thought you were someone else," I said. "Do you know Jake?"

His eyes dropped and he turned and walked away.

I walked back toward the large fire and the drums, trying to watch my step in the darkness while also looking for Jake.

"*Kwiyathêha.*" The voice came from my left and I stopped to look.

The old man sat on top of a picnic table that didn't seem like it could support even his slight body. Two younger men sat in front of him on the bench, passing a long white pipe back and forth between puffs.

"*Kwiyathêha,*" he said. "*Pemâkwapino.*"

I saw his aged face, wrinkles upon wrinkles with wide, bright eyes shining out, yellowed teeth when he smiled. He spoke directly to me, but I could not understand him. The words moved smoothly out of him, calm and monotone with a peak every few syllables.

"Sir?"

"*Pyâno!*" He spoke again in his own language then jabbed one of the younger men in the shoulder with a cane that had been resting across his lap.

"He wants you to come sit with him. I believe he is curious why you are here."

I glanced down the hill to the large fire and dancers then looked back at the man.

"I wanted to see," I said. "A friend of mine lives here."

The old man nodded and spoke, once again translated. "What friend?"

"A boy like me. My age. His name is Jake," I hesitated to attempt their language. "*Pyothopi.*" Jake had told me his tribal name that day, and how each family, or clan, was named for different animals. His was the deer clan.

The man straightened up, his eyes locked on me. Then he spoke in his language again to the men in front of him, and they replied. I could only listen to the sounds, not understanding any words. The old man spoke to me again but in slow, broken English.

"What do you know of *Pyothopi*?"

"I only met him once at the old church."

The wide eyes took me in, the silence lasting longer than was comfortable. Then a few more words I didn't understand with the other men. One of them stood and pointed for me to take his place on the bench. The old man put his hand on my head and turned it to see my eyes then looked off toward the big fire.

"You are the boy with the dreams," he said.

I didn't know how to respond, startled at him knowing who I was. My conversation with Jake ran past me and I looked up at the man. "You're his grandfather, aren't you? The storyteller."

He smiled then took the pipe from the other man, pulling in a long, slow breath and blowing the smoke upward into the trees, some drifting down over me.

"He told me of you. Have you any more dreams?"

"No, sir." I shook my head. "Do you know what they are? Why I have them?"

"Everyone has dreams," he said. "Some see more than others. You are like me, we see more."

"Does it mean I'm part Indian?"

The old man threw his head back laughing, slapping his knee. He spoke again to the younger men in words I couldn't understand, all of them laughing. I turned a deep shade of red and hoped they would think it was only a reflection of the fire down the hill.

"No, you are not Indian because you have the dreams. You have the dreams because your mind understands more. You sense the universe around you. Everyone is connected, you see." His hands raised up, floating over his head. "You and me, people you know, people you do not know, you are connected. You are able to see this, go into the lives of other people. It is your gift to see their fates, as I do. Others may see only happiness. We see the darkness, too, the sadness."

Drums vibrated the air and punctuated his words and my thoughts. Silhouettes of people moved past the fire down the hill. The scents of different foods drifted along with the smoke from the pipe being passed around me, a sharp scent that reeked of earth and flora and made me dizzy. The night air was heavy on my skin and I believed I could feel the people, sense them as well as see them. In one moment I loved everyone I saw, wanted to know them and talk to them. Then I thought of Jake and he came into view, clear and vivid, colors saturated and un-natural. My heart raced and my stomach tightened. In just seconds I felt the arc of a dream come and go, entering my mind and my conscious thoughts then disappear again, leaving me empty of everything but the remnants of the dream.

I stood up, uneasy on my feet as if I hadn't walked in weeks, and turned to the old man. He straightened and met my eyes and I knew he understood what had just happened. He gave a small nod, an approval to speak.

"Jake is dead," I said.

He reached his hand out and I gave him mine and he held it flat between his two palms. He stayed silent as I processed what I had seen.

"He knew." My eyes clouded over as tears rolled down my cheeks. "He knew that day at the church that he was going to die."

"He did," the old man said.

"But why? Couldn't he stop it?"

The man made no motions and said nothing, knowing I already knew that the dreams would come true. That you cannot change what is to come. Easier than I thought he could, the man stepped down from the table and put his arms around me and we walked down the hill. My stomach churned and I thought I would throw up but I took deep breaths and held it back. We stopped at the edge of the clearing where the men danced to the drums as the fire burned and sent red cinders floating up into the sky.

A man came dancing past us, more furiously than the others, eyes closed and singing in his native tongue. The old man's arm tightened on me and he leaned down and whispered in my ear.

"That is my son. That is Jake's father," he said. "He dances for *Pyothopi*."

I watched the man dance and felt the sadness and the anger coming from him. It was beautiful and frightening. He continued his dance with endless energy as if to send a message to his son and somehow I understood it. He showed his love and how he missed him, but also to let him know they would be together again someday.

When the large fire began to burn down, many people went back to their cars and pickups to leave. Others pulled out small tents and sleeping bags and set up camp beside their fires. I told the old man I had to leave, to walk home. He motioned past me and one of the younger men from the picnic table came over as if commanded.

"You were a friend of *Pyothopi*," the young man said. "I will take you home."

It took some time to get out of the park in the line of cars but eventually we were headed back north on Highway 99. He didn't slow down or point anything out, but I knew when we passed it, the ground where Jake had died.

It wasn't long after he had left me that day when the car stopped in front of him on the side of the road. He hadn't tried to run or even fight. He knew he was outnumbered and would only make it worse. The drunk boys came at him and he stood there, punches landing on his face and body, breaking his ribs. An eardrum shattered and he fell to the ground only to be kicked in the head and back. When he was finally left alone, the tires of the car shooting gravel at his limp body as it sped away, he had only minutes left to live. He died on the side of the road, alone. I had been the last person to see him alive besides his killers, the drunk teens who saw him only as an animal, something lesser because of the color of his skin.

The rain began to fall. There was no build up, just a sudden downpour that bounced off the windshield and the pavement. The temperature dropped and the Indian man rolled his window down and stuck his arm out, singing a song I couldn't understand. As we drove past, I saw my dad's truck at the bar and smiled, knowing my adventure would remain a secret.

I thanked the man as I got out in front of my house and took my time walking to the porch. The rain felt good on my skin after the hot day and a part of me believed it was a message from Jake telling me he was okay.

Chapter 11

I YELLED AND fought the covers to find a way out. My body had twisted beneath the layers, my head no longer at the top of the bed. I was burning up, sweat covered my body with thick flannel pajamas sticking to my skin. The blankets flew off and my father was standing there, dressed for work. I jumped to my feet on the bed and lunged for him and wrapped my arms around his shoulders and head.

"What's wrong, Wes?"

"I saw you driving the truck. You crashed."

My father held my head next to his. "It was just a dream."

"It looked real," I said. "Like the ones we talked about that day. You came down a hill into a wall."

My father pushed me away so he could look at my face. "A wall?" His eyes were wide.

"Yes," I cried, trying to hold him again. "The road ended at a wall and there were no brakes. You couldn't make the turn." It was still clear in my mind, playing over and over even in my now wakened state.

"Why do you think it was me?"

"I... I just knew. I felt like I was you in the dream."

He put me down on the bed.

"Can you stay home today?"

"I have to go to work, you know that." He sat down beside me. "Tell you what, I'm gonna call Grandpa and have him pick you up after school. I have a long day so you'll get to spend the night with him."

The drive from my grandfather's house was more than two hours and not one that was made on short notice, not to mention tomorrow being a school day.

"But the dream-" I said.

"It was just a dream. I'll be careful, Wes," he said. "Don't worry about me."

My father's calmness spread to me. "Okay." There was something about the calm. It wasn't disbelief or even fear, but more like acceptance, understanding.

He helped me stand up then rubbed my head and turned to walk out the door, stopping to look back at me from the darkened threshold.

"All right, Wes?"

"All right," I said. Then my father was gone.

I sat on the bed and waited until I heard the pickup come to life outside then move down the driveway, the eighteen-foot trailer following behind it. There were still two hours until school but I got up and dressed in the darkness, not wanting to be in the glare of the overhead light. A couple of eggs were in a bowl on the counter from last night's chores and I fried them in the skillet, my actions on autopilot.

It was dark as I began the walk into town, the sun only beginning to glow above the trees as I got to the paved road. The small town came to life at dawn. Delivery trucks rolled in and out from the grocery store. The cafe that sat on the edge of Route 66 through the middle of town always had customers whenever the doors were unlocked. I sat on the steps outside the school until they unlocked the doors then went inside to warm up before all of the other kids arrived.

I stared at my books and papers and turned in a test with only half the answers filled in as I went through the day in a fog, the remnants of the dream still banging around in my head. Never one of the noisy students, I floated through the day without anyone noticing or caring that I wasn't really there. I looked up at the clock to see the last fifteen minutes of the day were all that remained and prepared myself for the final clicks then the bell. I'd wait to be the last out of the room and building, not wanting to be run over by the mob pushing their way down the hallways.

Five minutes before the bell would ring, the principal knocked on the door to my classroom. The class quickly became quiet and looked at his imposing stature in the door. "Wesley, please bring your coat and come with me." As he spoke I knew it had happened, the dream had come true. I tried to resist it, tell myself there was still a chance.

He was going to call Grandpa to come get me anyway. It really didn't mean anything.

The usual exclamations came from the other kids, assuming I was in trouble. I knew I wasn't and followed the principal. There were only four classrooms with one long hallway to the front door of the school. The old hardwood floors were worn down from so many generations of school children running over them. My father's own feet had run down this hallway. The principal walked beside me, telling me Grandpa was here to pick me up. He shared no other information and his actions indicated he knew nothing else. At the end of the hall he sent me out into the cold by myself.

Wearing my heavy winter coat I stood for a moment on the front step where I'd sat and waited this morning. I looked around and saw my grandfather's flatbed truck on the street a half block down. I'd left my schoolbooks underneath my chair, not wanting to bother with them, so I walked empty handed and climbed into the truck.

"How was school?"

"Fine." I stared down at my hands. I didn't have to ask but did. "Why'd you get me out early?"

My grandfather sat silently with his hands in his lap with the truck still sitting in front of the building, engine running, a blast of lukewarm heat coming from the vents. "Listen, Wesley. Your father had an accident."

I didn't react. Didn't answer or speak in any way.

"So we need to go to Tahlequah," he said.

Still silent my head moved in a nod with no assistance from me, forcing a response.

The old truck groaned into gear and rolled out of its parking space. I sat upright the whole ride just staring out the front window with thoughts running through my head about the dream I'd had that morning. The morning activity of downtown was replaced with a calm afternoon. No deliveries, only a few cars. In the cold there were very few people walking down the sidewalks. Downtown faded away into the blurred pastures dotted with pump jacks. It was an hour into the trip before I spoke.

"What happened?"

Grandpa was matter of fact about everything he said, and this was no different. I knew he would tell me everything I needed to know without hiding the details I deserved to know. "He was coming down a long hill and lost his brakes," he said. "Or his brakes couldn't handle the load he was hauling, they don't really know."

My vision darkened as I heard my grandfather describe what I'd already seen. The images flew back into my head, matching with his words. I'd begged to him not to go to work.

"He was towing the big trailer and couldn't stop. The police officer who called me said your dad saved a lot of lives by laying on his horn to get people out of the way."

I saw the people. They rushed out of the way, others stood motionless in the oncoming danger. Cars turned quickly onto side streets as the blue and white truck barreled down at them. I saw their faces. A mother holding a bag of groceries, two children younger than me in tow, her brown coat buttoned up to her neck to fight off the cold wind. Faces watched in horror as the truck sped past, hand constantly on the horn. A group of school kids with book bags stopped at the corner just before stepping out in front of the truck, their mouths agape at the sight of the runaway vehicle. Then I saw the wall again.

"And he hit the big white wall?" I said.

"How do you know about the wall?" By the tone of his voice it seemed he knew about the dream and just wanted to know more. It wasn't inquisitive, but analytical.

"Don't know. Just do."

"Your dad was able to jump free from the cab of the pickup before he hit."

The words hung for a moment before they processed, before the meaning came to me. Words and vision were not aligning anymore. "He's alive?"

"Yes, but he's in bad shape. The trailer jackknifed after he jumped out and it struck him hard. We need to see him tonight."

The weight of the information didn't fully register, the urgency of the drive. He was alive, that was all I knew right then. I tried reconstructing the dream in my head, changing the scenario to see him jumping free of the truck. I couldn't see it. It wouldn't change for me.

More was said but not heard. The haze moved in around me and stayed. Lights going past on the highway were blurs in my periphery. Again and again I tried to reset the dream, to see dad jump out of the cab, when I realized what I was doing. I'd taken the dream and was controlling it. I was moving it around, going forward and in reverse, to see every detail. The pull of the newfound skill was addictive as I inspected everything I could, though still all from my father's point of view in the cab of the pickup.

"You know, Wesley," my grandpa said. "He doesn't understand, not fully."

I was startled back to the seat beside my grandpa. "Understand what?"

He looked over at me then back to the road. "The dreams."

A streak of heat traveled through my body, a ripple of sweat formed on my forehead. The short conversation with my father was the only time I'd talked about the dreams, and even then they were veiled in the context of daydreams.

"Do you?" I said. "Do you understand?"

"I do, Wesley."

At once I had so many questions but couldn't find the voice to ask them. It wasn't until the dream about Larry that I had started to think they were anything more than just dreams. It had been coincidence, I thought, about the dog getting hit by a large truck driving too fast down our dirt road, just days after I had seen the exact thing play out in my sleep. Could he understand? Does he dream things like I do?

"Grandpa, are you like me?"

His hand came to my head and rubbed my hair for a moment. "We're family, Wesley."

Chapter 12

THE SUN WAS setting by the time the truck pulled into the hospital parking lot in Tahlequah and the temperature was in the low twenties. Inside the hospital it still seemed cold, the white walls formed a maze that was easy to get lost inside of, hallways followed by hallways and doors everywhere. I followed Grandpa while looking left and right into rooms with people lying on beds, some sitting in wheelchairs, most of them staring at small televisions mounted on walls. Women in white moved from room to room in what felt like slow motion, leaving covered metal trays behind.

Grandpa rang a buzzer at a pair of closed doors marked 'Intensive Care Unit' then a nurse led us through the large room. Beds lined the walls, tables of electronic equipment beside them. Some had people wired to the machines, others were empty and waiting. A few were hidden behind pale green curtains, silhouettes of people moving around on the other side of them cast on the thin material. There was beeping and sounds of air being forced through tubes. In the far corner of the room the nurse stopped and made sure we were still with her, then pulled a curtain aside for us to walk through.

My father lay on the bed, eyes closed. Wires came from his head and chest, there was a mask over his face with a deflated bag hanging off of it and a machine on the table next to him beeped along with his heartbeat. It didn't look like my father, weak and broken. The worst I had ever seen him was the day mom died when the funeral home came to pick her up. He watched them as they worked, following them through the house even though they'd asked us to all stay in the kitchen so as not to witness that final, unmajestic journey she would take.

Grandpa touched my shoulders and urged me to the side of the bed. I could hear my father's breathing, the sound amplified by the machine that was pushing air into his body.

I put my hand on his arm and it reacted to the contact, first by pulling away, then it relaxed and accepted the touch. When I looked up his eyes had opened.

I had a million thoughts come to me at once, so many things I wanted to say. To apologize about the dream as if I had caused this. To tell him I loved him. Before I could say anything, a middle-aged man with a long white coat came in behind us and spoke too loudly. "We're ready to remove the breathing tube whenever you are. You'll only have a few minutes before he's gone."

I turned to Grandpa. "What's he talking about? What's that mean?"

"Wesley, your dad isn't going to make it." He kneeled down to look me in the eyes. "They're going to take the tube out of his mouth so he can talk to you before he goes."

I didn't feel my legs collapse or the impact of my knees on the hard tiled floor. Grandpa caught me just before my head struck the ground. I began to scream and hit, punching him in the chest and shoulders. Two nurses tried to pull me away from him, his voice came out more sternly than I'd ever heard, telling them to get away. He pulled me in close so I couldn't hit him anymore, and held me tightly against his body.

"Wesley, we don't have long," he said. "The more we wait, the less chance there is to talk to your dad."

I squeezed his neck with my arms, my face burrowed against his. A warmth came from his skin into mine, and I thought I felt him speak to me only no words were said, a calming voice inside my own head. His breathing pacified me, his pulse soothed me.

I calmed down enough to stand on my own and held my grandfather's hand. A connection was there that I hadn't felt before with the old man, even with as much as I had always loved him.

We stood quietly as the doctor flipped several switches on the machine that was forcing my father to breathe. As the whooshing sound slowed and faded, the doctor took hold of the tube in my father's mouth and pulled firmly until twelve inches of clear plastic tubing covered in blood and other fluids came out of his windpipe.

My father coughed and choked while the nurse suctioned the excess moisture from his mouth. As he began to breath on his own, it was slow and labored.

"Wes." My father's voice was quiet and rough, barely heard over the other machines in the room.

I moved in closer and took his hand in mine.

"Dad," I said.

"I tried, Wes. I tried to miss the wall. I really tried."

"I know."

The beeping coming from the machine next to the bed slowed. "Your dreams. They aren't just dreams," he said.

"I know." I had never allowed myself to fully accept what I had grown to know until that moment. "The dreams, they come true."

"Your grandpa will help you. There's more I wanted to tell you but I never found the right time. I didn't know how to."

"Don't go away, Dad. I can't lose you, too."

"Wes, I love you. I'm sorry I have to leave you, but grandpa will take care of you now. Better than I ever could."

Grandpa stepped in right behind me and put his hands on my sides to hold me.

"It's coming, Wesley," Grandpa said. "Be ready."

I was confused by my Grandpa's words and held my father's hand tight. The beeping continued to slow and I felt the grip loosen on my hand.

"Don't go, Dad," I pleaded. "Please don't go."

I felt it before I heard it. The life in his skin, in his touch, was gone. It didn't fade away but just ended. The beeping became a steady tone and my stomach tightened as the rest of my body went numb. The nurse pressed two fingers against his wrist then turned the machine off. Everyone was quiet in that moment, even those who did not know the man who had just died.

The enclosed area behind the curtain became a vacuum, the air pulled out leaving nothing to breathe and no words could escape that void. The nurse moved in the silence, her actions mechanical, repetitive motions of a person who sees death daily, performing her job. Sensors were removed along with tubes, all meant to make him look more normal, more like him.

There was a surge, imperceptible to the nurse. But I felt Grandpa tighten at the same moment I felt it.

My father's body seized, his head came up off the pillow, eyes opened wide as he gasped for another breath. His hand bore down on mine so hard it would leave a bruise in the shape of his fingers. He rolled toward me as best he could, reaching out and grabbing my wrist with both hands and lifting his head to look at me, the wires and tubes that would have held him back now gone.

"Your mother…" He had a smile on his face and no sign of fear as he fought for the ability to speak. "Your mother…she loves you so much, Wesley."

Our eyes were locked, the grip on my hands still tight, and it felt as if he were looking into me. Then the light in his eyes went away and the shell of my father's body faded and fell back, becoming one with the bed. Grandpa grabbed my shoulders and held me steady to make sure I didn't lose my grasp on my father's hand.

"Hold on, Wesley."

I tried to let go, to move back away from the table and the body that had been my father but my grandfather wouldn't let me. He held me there, his arms keeping mine where they were, holding my father's dead hand.

Then the lifeless hand held between my own became warm and then hot. For a moment I thought he was still alive, that he was just sleeping or unconscious. Then it came. The warmth, the love. What I would later describe as *the everything*. The heat that came from his dead hand grew hotter and moved into my hands and ran from my feet to my head. My body felt light, as if I were no longer touching the ground. Then in a burst of energy I felt it transfer to my grandfather through his grip on my shoulders.

The three of us were connected in that moment. The thoughts and memories of Joseph Hudson spun into a web that transferred to my subconscious and fused with my own grey matter. For one moment I knew everything about my father, understood him and knew how much he had loved me though he was never able to tell me or show me. I felt the lifetime of emotions that I had never received, an embrace of everything the man was unable to say out loud. I felt all of the pain my father had felt, from the loss of his wife to the flesh being torn off of the back of his hand by an oily tool. I felt his fist strike the sheriff's face when he was told his son had been killed and the silent anguish that haunted him when standing over Larry's grave.

The pain swirled and pulled away then happiness surrounded us. I saw Larry being born then myself as an infant, held in my mother's arms, my father smiling down at me. In the flash of a life going by in the fraction of a second I witnessed fireworks lighting up the sky, the booming of explosions so close they shook my body, as my father and mother lay on a quilt on a hot July night as a young couple in love. I saw my father as I never had, happy and content, in love and loving, a man with a woman at the center of his universe.

Then the memories broke apart as the heat faded to warmth then to the cold skin of a dead man. The feelings would stay with me for the rest of my life, the memories of emotions but not the memories themselves. Those belonged only to my father.

I placed his hand down on the bed beside the still body then reached out and touched the side of his face, a face which now did not look entirely like the man who had raised me, the muscles relaxed as they only can when blood is no longer pulsing through veins. I smiled and pulled my hand back.

"I'm ready to go," I said.

"You can spend some more time with your daddy if you like," the nurse said.

"This isn't my father anymore."

Chapter 13

THE HOUR DRIVE to Grandpa's house in Jay was a blur of dark fields and occasional glimpses of the waning moon. I stumbled from the truck to the tall four poster bed in his house that I used when visiting. As soon as I was covered I was asleep. Even in my rest there was the sense of loss, that something was different now, but I wouldn't fully realize the effect for several more days if not longer.

The dream started, different than the others. There was no sweating or thrashing around. Light faded in slowly, swirling around in my head, then my body. I felt light and began to float above the bed and saw myself sleeping in the darkness, a soft light cast across my face and body as I lay calm and still. But inside I was anything but as my dreams moved into lucidity, colors bright and images in sharp detail as I joined my body again.

My eyes opened and I was in my own twin bed. No sounds came from the house or outside the windows. I sat up and Larry's bed was there, neatly made and smooth. I walked down the stairs and smelled the bacon first then heard the sizzling of the meat in its own grease right before walking into the kitchen.

Then I saw her. She stood with her back to me at the sink, wearing a long blue dress with white polka dots. I knew I'd seen the dress before but couldn't place it. The water was running and I heard her humming as she always did. It was a song I never knew the name of, maybe a song that didn't exist outside her own thoughts, that she had made up and would repeat without realizing she did it. I hadn't seen her in years, and much longer than that since she was healthy, but it didn't seem peculiar to have her here in front of me. The table was set for four people, knives and forks and spoons placed beside clean white plates. A pitcher of fresh squeezed orange juice and another of milk were in the middle.

"Good morning, Wesley." Her voice came from inside of me, surrounding me. "Have a seat for breakfast."

I did as I was told. Once I sat, my plate was covered with pancakes and scrambled eggs, with several strips of crispy bacon on top of them. I turned to look at her but her back was to me again.

"Go ahead and eat, Wesley. Nobody else is here."

I glanced at the other place settings then took a bite of eggs, but found no taste on my tongue. I tried the bacon and it was the same. No texture or flavor, the crispness an illusion. I turned to ask what was wrong with the food but she was gone.

The kitchen blurred and sped past me then I was standing on the front porch, looking out across the yard of bright green grass. There was motion to my right and I saw her blue polka dotted dress in the garden as she walked along the short rows of vegetables she planted every spring.

Walking across the yard I felt nothing beneath me, no roughness from the uneven ground I knew surrounded our house. I stopped at the low fence surrounding the garden and watched her, still with her back to me.

"Mom?" The sound of my voice felt deadened, hitting a solid wall that couldn't be seen and she didn't react so I spoke more loudly. "Mom?"

The earth shook then widened ahead of me from left to right and out to the horizon. Fenceposts spread apart, the barbed wire stretching out in endless spiky strings. I spun around to see everything moving away from me and toward me simultaneously. I put my arms out wide to keep my balance, the motion around me playing with my equilibrium even though I felt no movement and I wanted to be somewhere else.

I closed my eyes and felt the stillness. My breath was fast and I worked to slow it, feeling my pulse coming back down with it. The calmness came to me and my thoughts were clear and I knew she wasn't real, she wasn't there. It had been so long with so much death and I just wanted to see her, needed to see her, and realized my mind had done what I wanted, what I requested. Then somehow, deep inside, I knew that I could control it.

Still in the blackness I moved my thoughts around, sorting them to find exactly what I wanted. An exact moment in time to which I wanted to return. With a deep inhale I relaxed.

Then I opened my eyes.

Long light came through the bedroom window onto the floor in between the twin beds. I sat next to Larry on his bed, my knee touching his, and I felt the emotion I had felt that day but with the knowledge of what would happen. He would be gone soon, off to the Army, then not long after that, dead.

"Do you have to go?" I asked.

"Yeah, I do," he said. "I got drafted, so they're making me go. But I was gonna sign up anyway, just like Dad and Grandpa did.

"Why do you wanna go?"

I was still on script, the same it had been that day. But I wanted it to be different.

"It's a way out of here, out of Stroud, out of Oklahoma," Lawrence said. "I don't want to work the farm, fix oil pumps, just grow old out here. I wanna get out."

"You don't have to work the farm or the oil fields," I said. "You know Grandpa wants you to work with him."

The new words I wanted to say were there, in the front of my brain and fighting to get out, though my voice kept saying what I had that day.

"Fixing tractors?" Lawrence said. "Nah. We both know he'd rather have you there anyways."
"But I don't want you to go," I said.

It moved too fast. Muscles unable to defy the memory.

"I know," Lawrence said. "But I have to. I'll be back to visit when I get leave. Maybe I'll take you with me when I come back."

"You can't go, Larry!" I yelled.

The memory was gone before I got the words out. Space sped past me again, images flashing and disappearing in order, watching myself get older and Larry grow taller. Walking through the pastures and sitting at school. Fighting in the yard with Larry, endless talks with him about nothing in the dark after bedtime. I saw my father covered in blood and oil coming home from the fields after another man had been caught in the machinery, and the rare family dinners around the table. Mom sitting in her chair with a piece of material in her hand, chin to her chest asleep, tired from the disease. Then reaching under the kitchen counter for the red box and pouring it into her teacup. Everything blurred and spun. Then it all stopped.

I stood in the door to my parent's bedroom. The blue

and white polka dotted dress was laid out on the bed along with a pair of white shoes and I knew inside the memory that it was the first time I'd ever seen the dress. There was silence, no floorboards creaking from activity. No voices. I walked into the room and rubbed my hand on the material, running my fingers from white dot to white dot. My father came up behind me, his hand falling to my shoulder for only a moment and words uttered softly, unsure. I have to leave for a little bit, but Grandpa's outside. He picked up the dress, folding it over his arm. It made sense to me but I couldn't place it. The moment was there, stored along with so many others, but it wasn't registering.

Motion again, but not as fast, not as violent, only a short jump in time. When everything was sharp again I saw her.

She had the blue and white polka dotted dress on. It was smooth, freshly pressed. Her hands had white gloves on them that I'd never seen and were folded across her stomach. The white shoes were hidden somewhere in the dark, out of sight of anyone who walked by.

She looked more like she used to than she had the last year or so, her skin smooth and pink from makeup. I kept staring at her, every few moments thinking, knowing, that I saw her chest move, a breath inhaled or exhaled. But every time I looked again there was only stillness. People were gathering behind me now, voices growing and fading with greetings and sadness, tears. I reached out and touched the dress again, my finger tracing from white dot to white dot down her arm.

There were no more images flashing and time speeding past. It just faded from the brightness to grey then to black.

Chapter 14

THE STAIRS IN Grandpa's farmhouse were familiar from many nights spent there, knowing each creak and groan from the old wooden steps after sneaking down in the night to find which desserts were left in the icebox. The house was always a comfortable place, spending weeks out of each summer sleeping until the sun was well up in the sky then staying out all day climbing the hills that surrounded the house. When I was younger my brother would be there with me. Larry would usually lead the way into some adventure with promises of danger and a buried treasure he'd overheard Grandpa talk about late one night to our father when we were supposed to be asleep. We never found the treasure but always came back down to the house covered with mud and the occasional scratched up knee or elbow, exhausted from our day.

Grandpa was in the workshop behind the house, his

hands already covered in grease as he tore down the engine of an old tractor to replace one of the large cylinders that had cracked.

"You're up," he said without turning around.

"Yessir." I loved to watch him work and the smell of the diesel fuel and greasy engine parts.

"I'm guessing you have a lot of questions."

"I do but I don't know what they are yet."

"That's very wise," he said. "Anyone can ask questions, it's knowing the right ones to ask."

He lined parts up and slid them together like a giant metal puzzle. Bolts dropped into holes and got turned into position with a large wrench.

"We going back to Tahlequah today?"

"No. I've already made arrangements for your father to be taken to Stroud. We'll head down tomorrow and stay through the funeral."

I looked off toward the hills behind the house. "Why don't I miss him?" The feeling seemed to be absent, the emotion. Even with the burst of memories fed to me as he died, I felt nothing.

Grandpa set the large wrench down and stepped outside to the water pump that came up beside the barn, turned it on and washed his hands in the freezing water. "You will," he said. The grease came off slowly but the old man was used to not having his hands clean. "Right now you don't completely realize he's gone."

He walked to his red Farmall tractor, rotated the key to turn it on then helped me climb and sit on top of the engine facing backwards toward the steering wheel. We'd done it since I was big enough not to fall off. Grandpa climbed up to the metal seat and put the tractor in gear and we slowly moved off toward the hill behind the barn.

"I was just about your age, maybe a year older." Grandpa spoke over the rumble of the motor. "At first I thought nothing of them, thought they were nightmares."

I looked down at his weathered face as he steered the large tractor around an empty watering trough. "You have the dreams, too?"

"I do."

The tractor began the ascent up the cow trail that was etched into the side of the hill. The motor didn't show any signs of a struggle against the incline, perfectly maintained by the old man for decades.

The land wasn't good for much. He had kept some cows for a few years but never enjoyed tending to them and found them more trouble than they were worth with the little amounts of money they brought in. Once he'd sold them off the last time he never bought any more. He made his living fixing tractors for farmers and loggers all over the area.

"These things come to us. We don't know why and we can't control them," Grandpa said. "And we don't know where they come from."

"Does everyone have them?"

"No, only a rare few people. It seems to stick to family lines, and it skips generations, seems like."

"So dad wasn't, he didn't—"

"No and he didn't believe in it most of his life," Grandpa said. "Not sure he ever really did at all. He always thought I was a bit crazy with my talk of dreams. And my grandfather died before I was born so I didn't have anyone to talk to about it. My dad thought it was all a lie or the work of the devil. More than once he beat me when I'd insist on something I'd seen was true, then he'd beat me again a few days later when it actually happened."

He turned the tractor toward the back pasture on top of the hill and brought it along the edge of the tree line. He dropped it into its lowest gear and let it move along at a slow pace without the need for pressing the throttle pedal down. He turned in his seat and looked out through the trees as we passed, his left arm draped over the steering wheel to keep us moving in the right direction. The tattoo on his forearm came out from under his rolled flannel shirtsleeve.

I watched him stare into the woods.

"What are you lookin' for?"

"I'm not really sure anymore," he said.

"Then why are you looking?"

"Habit. Hope."

I turned and began to stare out into the trees for whatever my grandfather might be looking for. The heat off of the engine below me was keeping me just warm enough and the trees were blocking most of the wind.

"Are they real?" I said. "I mean, do the dreams always come true?"

"Not always. Sometimes you see something before it happens, like you did with your father. Sometimes you see something while it's happening. And in a few instances you see something after it happened."

"Like with Larry," I said.

Grandpa looked at me then back at the woods. "I thought you had. I felt it when you grabbed me at Lawrence's funeral."

We made the turn that brought the tractor past the ledge over where he had been dumping his trash for thirty years. Every so often he'd come up in the morning and set it on fire to burn it down then sit and drink bourbon out of the bottle all through the day and into the night, watching the conflagration of refuse.

My grandmother died when I was a baby so I never knew her. But he kept what photos he had of her in the house and talked to them as he walked by sometimes. I'd heard 'How you doing today, Alma?', 'It's a right cold one today, is that your doing?' and once when he hadn't known I was hiding behind the big leather recliner writing in my notebook, he'd stopped in front of the largest photograph of her, an eight by ten in an oval frame, and touched her face in the glassy image. 'Oh Alma, how I miss you.'

"Your father was a teenager, I guess," he spoke loudly to be heard over the huge diesel engine. "He was never around, always with his friends. It was the talk of the town one day. Cornerstone Bank had been robbed up in Southwest City and the robbers had gotten away clean. State police and even the FBI had been called in to try to find them, but there was nothing to find. They'd just vanished."

"What happened to them?"

"Nobody knows, really," Grandpa said. "The police said they thought they drove south to Mexico. Imagine that, just living it up in the sun on stolen money."

I knew little about Mexico and even less about living it up. I smiled at my grandfather.

"I woke up in the middle of the night, sweat from head to toe," he said. "I'd had a dream. It was far from my first one but it didn't make sense. I didn't recognize anyone in it. Didn't know it at the time, of course, but it was the night the robbery had taken place. I'd seen the bank robbers and watched them like it was a movie in my sleep."

I sat up straight and listened.

"It was like I was there with them, the bank robbers."

"You saw them break into the bank?" I said.

"No, that's why it took me a while to connect it to the robbery," he said. "I saw three men in a car driving down the road in the middle of the night. They were screaming and yelling and slapping each other on the backs and shoulders. They came to a field and a small airplane sat there in the darkness. One of the men questioned how they were all going to fit, being there was only two seats. Then there was a flash of light as a gun was fired, and that man fell to the ground. The other two left him there and took off in the plane after loading several bags into the back."

"Do you know where they went?" I said.

"That's the thing, Wesley," he said. "I saw what happened to the airplane."

I was scooting closer and closer to him to the point I was about to fall off of the tall tractor.

"A bit into their flight, the two men began to argue about where they should go," he said. "One thought they should go to Mexico. Then the other one, who wanted to head west to the coast, to California, pulls a gun out and shoots his partner right there on the plane. And after that, he gathered up those bags and the one parachute they had on board and he jumped out of the airplane and let it just keep on flying with a dead man at the controls."

"How can a dead man fly a plane?" I said.

"That's the thing about an airplane. It wants to fly, they're just designed that way," he said. "So if it has power and everything is set just right, that thing could keep going until it runs out of gas and crashes."

"What about the guy that jumped? Where'd he go?"

Grandpa brought the tractor to a stop. We were at the highest point of his land and just above the tree line so you could see for miles across the county. Grandpa stood up on the right axel holding the large tire and looked around.

"Here."

Chapter 15

THE EMPTINESS STRUCK me as soon as I walked through the door of the house in Stroud. It had never been a loud or even happy place, especially after my mother died. But there was a difference now. A stillness. Grandpa came in behind me and put his leather bag on the floor inside the door. The silence was honored by both of us, standing there without a word, as the house breathed in and out, the subtle whistles as the wind snuck through the gaps in the old window panes, the electric buzzing of the refrigerator coming from the kitchen. I didn't want to move and didn't want Grandpa to move either. The lives that had spent their years in this house were disappearing, only mine left. I wanted the walls to speak to me, to tell me the secrets they held.

Grandpa's hand gently touched my shoulder, a warning to prepare me that the peace was about to be broken.

"I need to go over to the funeral parlor to talk about the arrangements," he said. "Do you want to come with me?"

I stared down the center hall of the old house. Down deep I felt he understood the moment, understood that I needed these seconds and minutes with my former home.

"Can I stay here?"

He nodded with the slightest smile and left. It had only been a couple of days since I'd last been in the house, but I already found it smaller. Moving around the room, my hands touched furniture, walls and the few pictures that were hanging.

Once down the hall to the kitchen I turned and reversed my steps but with more purpose. In the hallway, I carefully lifted the framed family photograph off of its hook, the only one I'd ever seen of us all together. In it my mother was smiling, holding me on her lap. Larry stood to her right and our father behind us. I set it on the floor near the front door. In the living room I went to the straight back chair and carried it to the hall and set it down beside the photograph.

Upstairs I first went into my own room and looked around then turned and crossed the hall into my father's room. The bed was made as it was every morning before he'd leave for work, a habit forced into him by my mom. I wanted it to be messy, the quilt and sheet thrown back from where he'd climbed out of bed two mornings ago, to show a sign he'd been here recently. Instead it looked like it could have been vacant for weeks, months. All that was in the room were the bed against one wall and a dresser against another. I knelt in front of the dresser and slid the bottom drawer open without worry of being loud as I had been the only other time I'd looked in there.

Below a folded quilt I found the only other items I wanted. The silver hairbrush was probably the most expensive single item my family had ever owned, a gift to my mother from her mother on her wedding day. Wound around the bristles were still the slightest remains of my mother's hair, long brown strands from before she got sick. I placed the brush on top of the dresser and looked back into the drawer. The box sat alone now, uncovered and unhidden. It was a part of my brother to me, the only thing remaining. His clothes had gone to the church, his few other possessions given or thrown away.

The stained mahogany was almost soft to my fingers. I'd held it only once before, while my father was out working. I sat it on the dresser then lifted the gold hook and opened the top. Pinned to the inside of the top was the Purple Heart the Army had given to my father at the Air Force base when Lawrence's body came home. Below was the Colt M1911 pistol my brother had carried on his side in Vietnam.

I closed the box and carried it and the hairbrush downstairs and sat them on the straight back chair. The clock began its slow chimes of noon over the fireplace. I figured I had another hour or two before my grandfather got back. I opened the box once again and pulled the pistol out and put it in my school bag then left out the back door.

The wind was at my back as I cut across the Butler's field to the west. The milk cows ignored me as I went past. It took me twenty minutes to make the walk and I stopped outside the old church. I looked up at the orange and red rocks and reached out to feel the ancient stones that had been pulled from the surrounding ground when the church was built.

"I don't know when I'll be back," I said. The building had become a mystical place for me. It was solitude and solace, welcoming and confining. I already knew I wouldn't miss the farmhouse, but the old church was different. It was special.

I stepped around to the opening and went to the sapling and lightly touched the ends of the branches that continued their fight to grow in the cold and dry earth.

Back outside, I put my bag on the ground leaning against the wall of the church and pulled out the pistol. I'd never shot a gun, or even held one, but had watched my dad take shots at coyotes with the .22 caliber rifle he kept inside the back door of the house. He never aimed to hit the wild animals, just scare them off as they worked their way toward the chicken coop. A few times he went hunting with men from work. I'd watched as he backed his pickup into the yard, the horns of a twelve point buck visible over the top of the bed. He dropped the tailgate and those black eyes stared at me. Later he made me get a bucket and rinse the bed out, blood having dried to the scratched and rusty metal. It didn't bother me or make me sick, it was just blood and I would enjoy eating the meat from the buck.

I held the gun in my hands, careful to keep the large barrel pointed away from me and my finger off of the trigger. I turned it side to side as I inspected it, not knowing what I was looking at. I found the safety and switched it off then on again. The magazine release was firm but finally gave and it fell out and slipped through my fingers to the ground.

I picked it up and brushed it against my jeans to clear the dirt off and looked to see the ends of fourteen bullets stacked up inside the metal magazine. I slid it back into the grip of the weapon and I heard the solid and satisfying click as it went back into position.

Looking around for a target, I saw the large maple tree thirty feet away. The top branches that provided some shade for the old church during the summer were bare in the winter cold. Orange and red stones were stacked next to the tree from the part of the wall that had been removed from the church.

The gun felt good. Better than I thought it would. The weight worked against my arms and my fingers barely reached around enough to grasp it, but it was right. Larry had held this gun, shot it. I closed my eyes and tried to feel him, sense his hand on the grip before mine, but all I felt was the cold black metal.

I switched the safety off and brought the pistol up level, both hands holding the heavy .45 caliber gun. I pulled the hammer back to bring a bullet into the chamber, needing both thumbs against the pressure. I closed my left eye and looked down the sights until I was centered on the trunk of the tree, then switched eyes, then back to my left. My legs shook and I lowered the gun to calm myself. I spread my feet shoulder width apart, locked my knees, and raised the gun to took aim once more. For a moment I considered leaning back against the wall for support but stayed a step away from the building.

I took a deep breath in and held it, trying to keep my body still. I saw the tree, a blur at the end of the barrel as I focused on the sights. It was a living thing, I knew that, and I had no right to put a bullet in its trunk. It wasn't food, there was no sport in it and it wasn't trying to harm me. Its only crime was that it was there. I squeezed the trigger.

My head slammed into the stone wall of the church as the explosion from the weapon rang my ears and I fell to the ground. I sat in the dirt staring out across the field then my vision swirled and blackness came in from all around until only a pinpoint of light remained, then darkness.

The hard beating of my heart vibrated my eardrums, thudding out a slow and steady beat in the darkness. Between the beats I heard crying, pleading, then the darkness lifted slowly to reveal a woman, and I was looking down at her on her knees. She screamed as I pulled her head back by her long hair. I felt my own hand reach back and strike her in the face with my fist. Her body fell to the floor and I knelt down, my hand then going to her neck as her eyes accepted the death that would come soon, almost longing for it to avoid feeling the pain. My hand tightened on her skin and I felt her struggling to breathe. The darkness pulled in from the outside edges of my vision until it was black again.

I opened my eyes, the sunlight stinging as if I'd been in darkness for weeks. The woman was gone but the memory remained. The pain hit me and I rolled to my left feeling as if I had to vomit, only spots of spit landing in the dirt. I felt warmth on the back of my head and reached back, feeling the thick fluid running through my hair then saw the deep red blood on my fingers.

"Shit." I'd never sworn in front of my father for fear of the beating that would follow but had heard him use the words often. The blood was dark and heavy on my hand and I thought about it wrapped around the woman's throat and striking her. She wasn't familiar to me but I felt she would be at some time.

I stood up, then fell over onto the wall and staggered forward as the dizziness hit. I leaned back on the wall, keeping my head forward, until I felt like I could move again. I was about to pick up my bag to leave then remembered the gun. It had landed a few feet to my right, the barrel pointing toward me on the ground. I stepped to the side of the pistol and picked it up, put the safety back on then put it in my bag.

The flow of blood from the back of my head slowed as I walked through the fields, my left hand pressing against my hair. Back at home I was relieved when my grandfather's truck was not in the driveway. I went to the one bathroom just off the kitchen, stripped and stepped into the cold shower. The water around my feet was crimson as it swirled and flowed to the drain. I stood and held the shower nozzle over my head until the water was clear again then rinsed the tub out and dried myself off. The headache persisted, a dull throbbing from the back of my skull.

I stepped out of the bathroom with a towel around my thin waist and picked up the dirty and bloody clothes I'd rolled up. As I turned to go to the stairs my grandfather was standing in the hall, the Colt M1911 hanging in his left hand.

"You okay?"

I froze. "Yessir." I could tell he knew.

"Come here."

The old man turned me around and ran his hand through my hair. His rough hands pushed against the wound.

"You cut it up pretty good, but looks like it stopped bleeding well enough," he said. "Let me know if you feel dizzy or like you're gonna get sick."

"Yessir."

"It's just you and me now," he said. "We need each other."

"I know." His words moved through my head and ran alongside my father saying them to me just months earlier. "I know."

"Put this thing away for now. Later I'll show you how to clean it then how to shoot it." He handed the pistol to me.

"You're not gonna to take it away from me?" I said.

"It's your gun now, Wesley."

Chapter 16

THE FUNERAL HALL was filled with the same faces as it had been for Larry plus a few that I didn't recognize. Grandpa told me they were from the oil leases dad had worked over the years. The sheriff gripped hands and worked to ensure re-election while everybody shook their heads slowly while talking about Joseph Hudson and the bad luck that had followed him. Conversations would go silent when I walked by, quiet looks on faces trying to look sad and consoling staring down at me. I was patted on the back more times than I could count.

After escaping the hug of a woman I'd never met, her perfume so strong I thought it would remain in my nose forever, I moved on through the crowd to get to the back wall and with any luck a place to hide until the service. A row of chairs sat along the wall, mostly being used to hold coats and handbags. I felt eyes on me and turned. At the far end of chairs was a woman sitting alone and watching me. Even though I'd seen her nearly every school day for three years, it took me a moment to place her, the context being all wrong. She usually stood in front of me, smiling even while faced with a classroom of children who wanted to be anywhere else. She waved ever so gently at me when I looked at her and I walked over.

"Hi, Ms. Albertson."

She stayed seated, her eyes just below mine so for once she was looking up at me.

"Hi, Wesley." She spoke in a hush but still somehow audible over the people talking much more loudly around us. "I'm so sorry about your father."

"Thanks."

She took my hands and held them between hers, keeping eye contact the entire time.

"I knew your father," she said. "We went to school together in the same classroom where I teach you now."

"You did?" Never in the three years of having her as a teacher had I known that she knew my dad.

She nodded. "You may not believe me, but you're a lot like him."

I thought she must have been thinking of somebody else. There was no way I was like my father.

"He was so nice as a boy, very quiet and kept to himself," she said. "And he was cute. All the girls were sweet on him, but he never knew the difference. He'd just go on about his way even when one of us would try to talk to him, that is until Helen showed up. He had eyes for her the second she moved to town. Nobody else had any chance after that."

Her hands still held mine and I didn't want her to let go. She was a connection to my father that I'd never known and had been in front of me for years. Two days ago I wouldn't have cared, at least not so much. It would have been an anecdote, a funny story to tell when I got home.

"Doesn't sound much like me," I said.

"Why, I disagree, Wesley." I could smell something sweet, her perfume, I guessed, but not offensive like the other woman. "You are the nicest boy I have ever had in one of my classes, and oh so smart."

I shrugged. "But... the girls, they don't..." I dropped my chin.

She tilted her head down to find my eyes again. "Then you are just like your daddy if you don't see it."

"See what?"

"You know, standing in front of that classroom allows me to see everything going on. I know who is cheating on tests and who isn't even tryin' just by looking around. I can easily tell when a boy fancies a girl, they are not too good at hiding it. And I can definitely tell when a girl likes a boy. They may be more sly than the boys about it, but when you know what to look for, it's pretty obvious."

"You mean, somebody likes me? A girl?"

Ms. Albertson smiled at me. "Several, my young man. You could practically have your pick."

My surprise and excitement was short lived as my shoulders lowered and the reality set back in.

"I guess you don't know, then."

"What's that, Wesley?"

"I'm not coming back to school. To your school, that is."

A sad look spread across her face.

"I had wondered but hoped it wasn't true. That's too bad. I'll miss you. But wherever you are, perhaps just look up a little bit more and maybe you'll see what you haven't been."

I turned at the sound of the preacher announcing the service would begin in a moment and when I looked back Ms. Albertson had stood up.

"Take care, Wesley."

"Are you not staying?"

I felt the warmth from her smile, not a consoling or sad, but loving.

"I came only to see you, Wesley." She leaned down and kissed my cheek then she walked away and out the door.

Then everybody around me was in motion, making their way to the wooden pews to be in place for the preacher. I wanted to run after Ms. Albertson and have her tell me more. Grandpa appeared in front of me, a woman right beside him talking. I couldn't hear a word she said but saw her give him a small piece of paper then walk away after an exaggerated handshake.

I sat connected to my grandfather in the front row. The words the minister spoke were almost exactly the same as they had been for Lawrence. That he had been called to a higher place. That his soul was free now. I wondered if the man only had one sermon for funerals as I daydreamed through the service. My thoughts kept going to Larry and I'd force myself to think about dad again.

At the cemetery the number of people thinned as a strong and cold rain fell. A canopy had been put up beside the open grave, just enough room for a dozen people with the chairs left out. Final words were said and people left until just grandpa and I stood staring down into the hole. I picked up a handful of the soil as my father had for Lawrence and threw it in on top of the wooden box.

It wasn't supposed to be like this. So much death following a little boy, I knew that much. But for some reason it was. I'd loved my mother more than anything and still missed her. I guess in some way I missed my dad. The way I see it, parents are supposed to protect their children, keep them innocent as long as they can. It hadn't worked that way for me.

I watched the rolling land out the window as my grandfather drove the old flat bed truck down the dirt road back to the farmhouse. "What are you gonna do with the house?"

"Well, I think you should have a say in it," Grandpa said. "Your father left it to you."

The house became visible through the rain as we got closer and I saw it differently than I ever had. It was no longer my home. I didn't know when it had stopped being that, when my mother had died, or my brother. But I realized for the first time that it hadn't been since before I lost my father.

"Let's sell it," I said. "I wanna give the chickens to the Butlers next door, if they'll have them."

"Okay," Grandpa said. "A real estate agent gave me her card. She said she already had someone interested. Let's start packing up anything you want to keep and we can leave the rest or throw it out."

"I already got what I wanted. It's in the hall," I said. "And my clothes I guess."

The next week at the farmhouse was filled with packing and moving boxes and furniture. The agent had people looking at it within a few days and an offer came quickly, well below asking price, and Grandpa and I took it after little discussion. The house would be torn down and the land used to store oil equipment and I couldn't think of a better use for it. I didn't know if the house was cursed, or if I was, but getting rid of it seemed like removing a source of darkness from the earth. Four people had lived there and only one was still alive. I just hoped I was getting out in time.

I made it back to the old church just one more time in that week. I'd expected to see a red stain on the wall where my head had struck it, but maybe the rain had washed it away. I searched the big tree all over but never found any sign I'd actually hit it with that bullet. There was no writing that afternoon, just sitting inside listening to the air move through the tin roof. The sound had scared me once but now I found it beautiful and would miss it.

Grandpa took me to school one more time to collect my things from the office and formally tell them I'd be transferring over to the school in Jay. It was a few days before the holidays and the anticipation was palpable in the hall. While Grandpa talked to the principal I walked along the worn wooden floors one last time then looked in through the narrow window of my classroom. Ms. Albertson was in there, her ever present smile on her face, talking to a bunch of kids who wanted to be anywhere else. As she looked around she saw me, but didn't stop what she was doing. She knew I wouldn't want the class alerted to my presence. Instead, as she explained something in great detail, as she loved to do with her arms gesticulating wildly in presentation, she looked back at me one more time and winked. Before the few students who saw her do it could turn around to look at the door, I was gone.

Grandpa decided to wait until the new year before starting me at the new school, with only days to go before class let out. I had no complaints about that and we had a simple Christmas together. He hadn't put a tree up since grandma died but went out and found the best evergreen on his hill. We had no decorations so we spent an entire night tearing up pieces of newspaper, shaping them into bows and ribbons and wrapped them around the branches. Grandpa said it was the most wonderful Christmas tree he'd ever seen.

By the time break ended I was settled in, the few things I'd brought with me were placed around the house and it already felt like home. Usually the beginning of school was a source of trepidation for me, but the fresh start had me almost excited. I'd asked Grandpa if I could buy some new clothes with part of the money from the house and

we spent a day in Tahlequah shopping at Hines department store. The worn and faded jeans were thrown away,
too far gone even to donate to another boy. I kept the
hand-me-down boots with holes in the bottom at the foot
of my bed beside my new sneakers, the first I'd ever had.

I put out my best effort at the new school, eager to not
blend into the background. I kept my brother in my head,
trying to channel Larry's ease of being outgoing. I kept my
eyes up and smiled at everyone, especially the girls, to see
if Ms. Albertson was right.

At the end of my first day, the old truck sat on the road
outside the middle school in Jay and I climbed in.

"How'd it go?"

"Good," I said. "I think I have a friend."

"That's great. I don't know about you, but I'd like some
ice cream."

"It's freezing cold outside!"

"I've always thought that was the best time for ice cream."

After picking up two vanilla ice cream cones down the street
we sat in the truck in the parking lot of the Dairy Queen.

"I'd like to start teaching you about the tractors," Grandpa said.

"Whaddya mean?"

"I could use some help, and seems you're the perfect
person to hire as an apprentice."

"You want me to fix tractor engines?" I said.

"Not right off, but maybe build up to it."

I took a bite off the side of the cone and chewed. "I'd
like that."

Chapter 17

OUR SCHOOL WAS small and any boy who tried out made the football team. I didn't necessarily want to play, but I knew Grandpa would enjoy going to the games, even if I never got to play. I spent my first football season sitting on the bench and saw only one play in the final game when the coach rotated every freshman in at least once just so we could say we played. The score was so lopsided for the other team that it could do no damage to the season's losing record. The play lasted all of three seconds. I'd been head on with a senior from Grove twice my size. I was left on my back and he ended up taking our quarterback to the ground.

In the spring we were all required to run track to stay in shape until the summer twice-a-day practices started again. The team was a mix of typical jocks and thin, gangly boys like myself. The coach just needed a head count to fill out the roster. I'd get a letter jacket and something for my college application.

I was on the far side of the grassy field in the middle of a two-mile run when I saw the newest boy in school. He just stood in front of me, hidden from view of the coach by the small chapel used by the younger grades once a week for required bible classes.

"I heard you're an orphan," the boy said. "You're momma and daddy both died on ya' because they didn't like you."

I moved left and tried to run past him but he stepped over and grabbed the sleeve of my tee shirt. He yanked me to a stop, stretching the thin material off of my shoulder.

He had just moved to town and started school the week before in my class. During that time he had beaten up three kids, one of them two years older than us. I could do nothing but stare at the boy. I'd been able to avoid him until now.

"That true? You an orphan?"

He easily had twenty pounds and six inches on me. But I wanted to punch him. I really wanted to punch him. Growing up with an older brother I'd had my share of scraps out in the yard with bruises and blood though I'd never consider myself a fighter.

"Little Wes Hudson, orphan boy. Nobody loves him."

The closest thing I had to a best friend in school stood behind me. "Come on, Wes. Let's get out of here. We got more laps to do." Chris would have my back about anytime but now. Nobody wanted to tangle with this kid.

A few days before he'd started at school I'd seen him in town at the grocery store with his mother. He was dragging behind her, complaining the whole way and berating her while grabbing stuff off the shelves and putting it in the cart. That night I saw him again but as an adult, the dream making no sense to me.

I glanced over my shoulder at Chris then back at the new kid. He stood there defiantly, chest out, eyes beating down on me. A half a dozen other boys had gathered around us and I knew I could run or I could stand my ground. I wanted to run but knew the consequences would be the same either way.

"What's your name? Hicks, right?" If I was going to get beaten up, it would be for good reason, not just for being there. "Are you a hick?"

"What?"

"I'm saying, are you an ignorant farm boy just pretending like you belong in school with kids who are actually smart or do you have trouble remembering your ABC's?"

His face turned red as he went from confused at being spoken to like that to being angry. His fists balled up at his sides and I could tell he was going to charge me at any time.

"You do realize this is high school, right?" I pointed down the field to the red brick building that held the lower grades. "Or should you be over there with the other kids learning their letters?"

"You better shut up, orphan boy, or you'll end up dead like your mommy and daddy."

I stepped closer to him and spoke so only he could hear. "Try it."

Our chests were almost touching, and he was getting out of breath from getting so angry.

"Oh, you're gonna die, asshole." The words spit out of his mouth more than being spoken.

I just smiled at him, which pissed him off more. "Yeah. Someday, but it'll have nothing to do with a hick like you." I stepped in closer. "Do you know how you're gonna die? Cause I do."

He took a step away from me, more out of surprise than fear, then his shoulders rolled forward. I watched his eyes and saw his fury build. Then his right arm came up and out to the side and I saw it in slow motion. I'd learned from Larry never to watch the fist because there was always another one to come at you. It was the eyes that mattered. The punch that could break my nose was preparing to fly in my direction and I saw it play out frame by frame. My eyes never left his eyes but I could see the fist that was starting its forward momentum toward my face. I saw everything I needed to see in his glare. In an instinct I didn't know I had, that my brain and body could process so quickly and carry out with no effort, my hand came to my shoulder and snapped out at him while I turned and leaned in, his body moving toward mine. My fist struck with my arm almost fully extended, stopping solid on his face. His arm was suspended in air beside my head, missing its target by inches and leaving him off balance.

Time played out in normal speed again and it was then that the blood burst from his nose like a shower nozzle, spraying across his white gym shirt and shorts. I stepped back just in time, none of the bright red fluid landing on me.

"Holy hell!" Chris grabbed my shoulder. "Come on, let's go."

I watched the blood drain for a second longer then smiled and walked away.

You never know what will be a waypoint in your life. It could be the decision to sleep in one morning and therefore miss being in a car crash, or simply deciding to have tea instead of coffee at the café. Or it could be smashing the nose of the new school bully. I would never be the most popular kid, but I was certainly noticed more after that. Benton kept his distance from me, likely from being spooked by what I had said to him than from the beating I'd given him, but it worked for me either way. He quit the football team after that and dropped out of school halfway through our senior year to join the Army.

I didn't have the dream about Benton Hicks again for years, not until I was an adult and had once again come face to face with him. It made no sense then either. He was older in the dream. I had something heavy in my hand and struck him in the head with it, his lifeless body fell to the dirt.

Chapter 18

"WHAT ARE YOU doing up so early? You usually sleep in after a game."

I reached down and hit the switch on the air compressor to turn it off. "I'm meeting up with some friends later and wanted to get this motor put back together first."

Grandpa looked over my shoulder. I was fitting the last cylinder into a flat-four tractor engine that was sitting on the bench.

"Looks good, Wesley," Grandpa said. "Mind the rings."

"It's not my first John Deere, Grandpa. How're your knuckles today?"

Grandpa held his hands up and looked at them, bending his fingers slowly.

"Been better, but been worse," he said. "Too many years of working on these damned engines."

"Yeah, thanks for showing me what I have to look forward to."

"You'll be off to college next fall," he said. "You'll be done with your time in the shop."

"It's not that far to Stillwater and I'll be back every weekend," I said. "And when I'm done I'll have my degree in engineering and then we'll start making our own engines."

Grandpa patted me on the shoulder and turned to go back inside then stopped. "Who is this you're meeting up with later?" he said. "Guys from the team?"

"Umm, sorta," I said. "More like from the cheerleading squad."

He said nothing but I saw the slightest grin as he went into the house.

I had quickly learned to love the engines. The pieces fitting into pieces and each performing their one job to the best of their ability. Cleaning parts and removing years of grease and grime until they were smooth again was satisfying. Assembling the engines and then turning the motor over for the first time, to hear it rumble and work as one cohesive unit again, was a reward all its own.

The engine put back into one piece, I showered and dressed in jeans and a button down shirt. I started the engine on the GMC pickup I'd bought after getting my driver's license two years earlier.

"Be careful out there." Grandpa stood on the front porch.

"I will. What are you gonna do?"

"I think I'll fire up the Farmall and take a drive up top."

"Hope you find it today," I said.

"Me too."

I drove down the driveway and onto the main paved road. Once out of sight of the house I put the pedal down further and the truck lurched forward. I'd spent the first three months after buying the truck rebuilding the engine. It now ran better than when it was new and faster than most cars at the high school.

I stopped in front of a house near the school, a two-story brick home owned by one of the two doctors in town. As I began to pull the handle to get out, a girl came running from the house and climbed in the passenger door.

"Hey there." Colleen leaned over and put her arms around me in a tight hug. Her blonde hair was pulled back in a ponytail and I tried not to stare at her.

I saw a curtain swing closed beside the front door of her house. I didn't care that the hug was more for her parents than for me.

"Hey there, to you," I said. "What do you wanna do? We have a few hours until we meet up with everyone."

"Just drive."

The afternoon was a blur of driving and talking. She slowly moved across the bench seat as the day went on until she was sitting next to me, her left hand on my right knee. I circled the town a dozen times, unwilling to stop the truck for fear she'd move away from me. As the sun faded into evening we headed north out of town. The highway ran straight and I pushed the speed up faster than I ever had.

The wind came through the windows and whipped around the cabin of the truck. "I'd take this over my daddy's Cadillac any day." Colleen leaned her head back to feel the air move across her. I stole glances while watching the road, the line of her neck running down from under her hair into the collar of the blue tee shirt she wore.

As the light outside grew darker we reached the bridge over Grand Lake and I let off the gas. The truck slowed quickly, the exhaust releasing a series of pops out of the pipes. I turned onto a side street then a gravel road.

"Think anyone's here yet?" Colleen said.

"Probably not. We'll have it all to ourselves for a while."

"I hope so."

Alone with Colleen Murphy. That was enough to make any boy nervous. She was on the cheerleading squad, one of the smartest people in our class, and more beautiful than anyone I'd ever seen, in person or in the movies. It was only three weeks ago she first talked to me, walking up with her hands behind her back after practice one night. She'd asked if I was sad about my senior season ending soon. It was small conversation for the sake of finding something to talk about. I had tried to ask questions to keep her there longer, to hear her sweet voice and to have an excuse to be looking right at her. But soon she was gone, running to a car with her friends and speeding out of the parking lot.

The trees came up on either side of the truck as the road turned into a cow trail. I slowed and pulled the knob to turn the headlights on and made a left at a fork in the trail. I stopped once we came into a clearing.

"First here," I said.

"Let's swim."

"It's almost dark. And the water's probably freezing cold by now."

"Perfect," she said.

Colleen was out of the truck and ran into the beams of the headlights. She turned and pulled her shirt off and then her tight blue jeans. I stared at her standing in her bra and panties. As I reached for the door handle she ran away from the truck then jumped into the air where the headlights began to fray and fade into the darkness and she disappeared.

"Holy shit." I ran out onto the rocks and stopped at the edge and looked down. The sun was gone but reflections from the clouds gave just enough light to see twenty feet down into the murky water of the lake where Colleen was just resurfacing and treading water.

She smiled up at me. "Jump!"

"You scared the hell out of me." My body shook and I was glad she was too far away to see me tremble. I unbuttoned my shirt and took my jeans off. As many times as I'd been out to the rocks, I'd never jumped. But I'd also never had a nearly naked girl asking me to.

"Here I come," I yelled. I took a few steps back then lunged forward and flew through the air. My fear faded as I fell and the thrill of falling took over. A moment of weightlessness, floating, then the crash into the water.

The lake was even colder than I expected. The instant submersion gave my body no time to adjust and under the dark water I panicked, not able to see which way was up. My body was straight when I entered and cut through the water before I balled up and turned myself around. I was a dozen feet under and kicking my legs, which only took me deeper. Darkness came in around me as my eyes blurred into a halo of light. I no longer felt the cold on my skin, the water holding me in place, comforting me. I wasn't as much submerged as embraced.

I tried to get my bearings to see which way was up, but the water was so dark. My eyes couldn't adjust. Then it grew lighter, a shape coming into focus. My brother appeared in front of me, welcoming me, motioning me to follow. Behind him our mother came into sight, young and healthy and smiling at me. I stopped kicking and looked at them. I knew they weren't real, that they were not there with me in the lake, but it had been so long since I'd seen them. I wanted to talk to them, to have her hug me and tell me she loved me. I wanted a bedtime story like she used to make up while Larry lay in his bed pretending to be asleep but listening to her every word.

My lungs tightened. I opened my mouth and took in a breath. The water entered me and traveled down into my chest before I could even try to stop myself. The lake became hot around my body as I twisted, holding my hands to my mouth. My body wanted to breathe and I couldn't stop it, but in that moment was unsure if I wanted to ever breathe again. Light flashed around me and I saw Grandpa, old and tired in bed then he was gone. I saw Colleen but she was much older and even more beautiful, she was reaching to me, then she faded away, too. My brother and mother were still in front of me and I shook my head and worked to calm myself. They reached and tried to pull me toward them. I kicked hard and my body floated through the water and it felt like I was flying. The heat was still there, burning my lungs and my skin but I kept kicking to my mother and brother. They faded in the darkness, gone once again, then I saw a bubble of air that released from my mouth and moved on ahead of me. I was headed toward the surface. I kicked hard, looking back over my shoulder to see only the dark water.

My face hit the air first and as my shoulders breached I gasped, pulling fresh air into my lungs. My legs and arms circled and held my head above the water and worked to catch my breath.

"Where'd you go?" Colleen said. She was a dozen feet away and swimming to me.

The remaining water in my chest began to come up as the new oxygen came in. I took in as much air through my nose as I could and dropped my head below the surface and allowed the lake water to come out. I wiped my mouth as I resurfaced then kicked my legs to move to Colleen.

"I wanted to see how far down I could go." I paddled my limbs to stay afloat beside her.

"I was getting worried," she said. "I couldn't see you."

"I'm right here."

"You're shivering."

"Water's cold."

"I'll warm you." She brought her face to mine and kissed me gently, our heads bobbing in the water as our arms slowed their circular motions to allow lips to touch. As first kisses go it was pretty memorable. Not a fumbling in the front seat of a car or over the armrest in the back row of the cinema after hands slowly crept toward each other in nervous anticipation.

"There's something about you, Wesley," she said. "You're different."

"Different how?"

"I don't know. Just different. But good different."

The air above us lit up as a pair of headlights shined out from the ledge twenty feet above the water.

"Someone else just got here," I said.

"Too bad."

Chapter 19

GRANDPA WAS SPENDING very little time in the workshop, and even less time out of bed. We'd spend hours in the dim light of his room as he'd tell me stories about growing up in Texas. He started talking more about the war, of standing in the wet trenches of France in World War I, German bullets flying overhead. More than once he'd finish a story then start telling the same one all over again.

We knew what was happening. That was the one thing I didn't want to discuss, but he did. The appropriate appointments were made and trips to the city followed. Hours spent inside large machines. He grew weaker before my eyes. But I never had a dream about him.

I woke up and looked into his room and he was sitting up straight as a board wearing his finest white dress shirt that I hadn't seen since my dad's funeral. It hung loose on him now from losing so much weight and he fidgeted with it to try to smooth it and make it look better. Even with all the extra space inside the shirt he looked uncomfortable.

"What's going on, Grandpa?" The memory loss had become worse. Whole days would be blacked out, forgotten. Entire parts of his life were gone.

"Could you skip school today?"

"It's Saturday."

"Is it? Oh. Well then." He looked around the room. "I'd like you to take me on a drive."

He hadn't left the house in a month, not since the last appointment in Tulsa.

"Where to?"

"Well. I wanna visit my daddy."

I thought about the stories he'd been telling me, the reminiscing of his own childhood and the abuse he'd been through.

"You want to go to Texas?" I tried not to sound like I was trying to talk him out of it. I was supposed to spend the day with Colleen, as I did every weekend and weekday afternoon since the night at the lake.

A small smile spread across his face and he nodded. He knew I would do anything for him but he never wanted to impose.

"We'd better get going then." I packed some food into a small bag and helped him into the pickup. I had no hesitation to take the old truck on a long trip but it was still intimidating. A quick phone call to Colleen and she understood, further cementing my ever growing affection for her.

He slept in the passenger seat, his chin dropping to his chest in chortled snores. I tried my best not to hit the brakes hard and send him leaning forward, only a lap belt to hold him in place. The miles rolled by with only the hum of the tires on asphalt and the occasional mutterings from Grandpa in his sleep. He woke when we crossed the Red River as if an internal beacon went off.

"Are we in Texas now?"

"Yes, Grandpa."

It was another three hours to go until Plainview so we stopped in Vernon and had lunch at the counter of a café in the small downtown then continued on. He was wide-awake and watching the scenery like something familiar would appear. It was flat and dirty and the few towns we passed had nothing in them besides a gas station and a few weather beaten houses.

"Hasn't changed much out here." He'd been quiet since lunch and his low, slow voice almost startled me.

I looked around and saw nothing that could have changed in the half century since he'd left this part of the country. "When was the last time you visited?"

He answered with no hesitation. "When my daddy died. Came down for the funeral."

We saw the signs as we approached Plainview, which was huge compared to anything we'd seen since Oklahoma City.

"It's bigger now," he said.

It took three stops, including one at the police station, to get directions. He didn't remember any addresses so we were going off of landmarks he could recall. We found his old street and stopped at the house first. It was a small A-frame with nothing but a door and one window on the front. I had expected to see it worn down and empty like most things in west Texas but instead it had fresh paint in a light green color with a cream accent and a welded wrought iron star hanging to the left of the front door. A young couple pulled up in a Jeep and went into the house as we sat at the curb and watched.

From his stories I knew there was no love in the house when he was a child. Even his mother thought him strange because of the dreams and kept her distance. His father got close only with a belt.

He waved his hand that he was ready to move on and I followed the scribbled directions south to the edge of the city. The cemetery was huge and sprawling, dotted with round trees. As we got out of the car a small single engine airplane flew over us then landed across the street at the airport. Grandpa watched as it touched down.

"They trained glider pilots there during World War II," he said. "Alma and I would sit here and watch the big planes pull them up, circling and circling until they released the glider. Just over there we saw one go nose down into the ground. The papers said the pilot died on impact, but he'd had a heart attack while trying to land on a solo flight."

I didn't question how he knew about the heart attack. He couldn't remember how to tie his shoes but he knew things that happened fifty years earlier. The pressure in his brain was curious in what it blocked and what it let through.

I walked the rows while he waited in the shade until I found his parent's markers that rested beside each other, then he came over to me. He stared down at the graves. I stood beside him and took his hand in mine. No words were said. I'd of course never met them and all I knew about the two didn't lend me to liking them. But somehow this man at my side had come from them and had led me through life. Clouds traveled with the wind over the large land sending round shadows moving across the ground, sometimes covering us then revealing the sun again.

He squeezed my hand and let go.

"You ready, Grandpa?"

He nodded and I turned and walked slowly down the row toward the parking lot, glancing at the names and numbers on the stones. The most recent dates were still decades old and the names were of other generations, Hazel and Montgomery. There were two Ezekiels within three plots of each other. I stopped when I realized I didn't hear his footsteps behind me. I turned and looked. He stood with his back to me, his head down and shoulders rolled forward, still over his father's grave. I worked my way back to him, cautious not to interrupt his moment, then stepped up beside him.

His black dress pants were unzipped and he had himself out and began to urinate.

"Grandpa, what are you doing?"

"Take that, you son-of-a-bitch." He waved himself around, sending urine all over the dried brown grass. "Told you I'd piss on your grave."

Chapter 20

I STARED OUT my bedroom window to the hills behind the old house that I'd spent so much of my childhood exploring. On the floor at the foot of my bed sat the boxes I'd packed, filled with the various items I felt I needed to make my dorm room feel like home. I turned my attention to the box and began to pull items out, placing them back where they'd lived in the years since moving to the house.

As my hand reached out for the framed photograph of my family a deep red spot appeared on the glass, then another. I sat the photo down and put a hand to my nose to feel the warmth of the blood coming down onto my upper lip. I went across the hall and pulled tissue off the roll and dabbed my nose with my head tilted back. After the third tissue the flow slowed. I walked back across the hallway and to my left saw the shape of a person at the foot of the stairs below.

Colleen stood there, looking up at me. "I was knocking."

"I was in the-," I paused. "I didn't hear you." I took the steps down slowly until I was in front of her for the first time in months.

"How've you been?" she said. Her gaze stayed away from my eyes.

I shrugged. "I'm doin' okay."

"I was going to come to the funeral," she said.

"Didn't have one. He didn't want it, made me promise."

She nodded then looked up at my face.

"Oh my god, your nose is bleeding."

"Shit," I reached in my pocket for the extra tissue I'd grabbed and held it to my nose.

She took my arm and led me into the front room and sat next to me on the small sofa. The bleeding stopped again and I pushed the tissue back into my pocket.

"Are you okay?" she said.

"Yeah, just a lot going on."

Her hand reached over and touched mine. "I miss you, Wesley."

I looked at her hand and wanted to hold it, to take it in mine and feel her warmth against me again. I thought of the one night we'd spent together months before, after the final game of the season. Her parents had been out of town and we'd sat awkwardly on the floor in front of the fireplace in her house. We drank wine from the large collection her father kept, neither of us liking the taste but both needing the edge taken off the moment before us. When I saw her naked for the first time I became frozen as I took in her beauty, the smooth pale skin that was so soft and warm to my touch. I'd been embarrassed to show myself, afraid of how she'd react only to find out later she had been intimidated by me and nervous at the thought of having me inside of her. We held each other for hours that night, naked bodies pressed together, neither wanting the night to end.

"I miss you, too," I said. "But you know I can't."

"Why can't you? We leave for college in a couple of months and can-"

"I'm not going."

"What?"

"I'm staying here. There's too much work to do," I said.

"It was his work, not yours," Colleen said. "He wanted you to go to college, you know that."

I shook my head while still looking at her hand on top of mine. "I can't. I can't go to school. I can't be with you."

"I don't understand you, Wesley," she said. "I thought you loved me."

The dream had come a month after our night together in her home. She'd looked different but I knew it was her, the flowing blonde hair was shorter and her skin not as young anymore but she was still as beautiful as she is now. She was driving a big sedan and pulling off of a side road onto the highway when the eighteen-wheeler hit her car. The driver had spilled coffee onto his lap and looked down, swerving out of his lane just as her four-door Ford pulled out.

It was more detail than I'd ever seen before. The twisted metal of the car wrapped around the front of the big red semi cab and the child car seat that had been thrown out the front window of the car onto the highway, the little girl still strapped to it.

"I just can't be with you," I said. "I can't explain it. You wouldn't understand."

"Try me, Wesley," Colleen said. "Just… try."

I pulled my hand out from under hers and crossed my arms. "You should go."

"I'm not giving up on you," Colleen said. "I'm not."

She stared at me, shaking her head, then stood and went out the door, looking back only briefly, then the door closed.

I wanted to go after her, run through the driveway and jump in front of her car and tell her I was sorry and that I loved her. But I knew I couldn't. The dreams had never been wrong and I had to do whatever I could to stop the future I'd seen.

I listened to the quiet house. My grandfather had made it a happy place to be even in the wake of so many losses. We both found laughter again and I understood what a family was supposed to be like. The ones that had died weren't taboo subjects. We talked about them and laughed about things that had happened and cried about others.

It had happened quickly but both of us were so used to death that we took it like another day ahead of us. The headaches came first then the confusion. The once sharp mind of my grandfather became cluttered and unclear.

Checks he wrote to pay the bills would come back, the numbers unreadable or written backwards.

The doctor in Tulsa said the mass was just about the size of a peanut when we went to his first appointment. A month later it was as big as an egg. It was shortly after that when I woke up one morning to find my only remaining family member out beside the workshop staring at the old red tractor we'd ridden together so many times, a tire iron in his hand and wearing no clothes, his hands bruised and torn up. It was a cold early spring day and a light snow was falling, my grandfather stood there, the white flakes freezing to his wet skin from the shower he'd been taking when he became confused and went out the back door of the house while I was still sleeping.

There were moments of clarity when we would have conversations like we'd had for years. As quickly as those moments came they also went away. I had packed up all the knives and scissors and hidden them after my grandfather just thought his hand needed to be cut off one night and took a steak knife to his wrist while I was out with Colleen. The thought had passed but not until there was a three-inch cut in the old man's skin that required a dozen stitches.

In our long talks in the dark bedroom he told me about the tumor and when he first knew he had it, and how I would have one. I sat quiet, stunned, scared, listening to him. His words were even and calm but far from rehearsed. He'd had nosebleeds when younger, more than were normal. It wasn't until he was in his twenties, after the war, that he knew about the tumor. There had been no doctors visits, or any way for them to even find it back then. It was just something that came to him. A realization, a sensation that something was there that should not be. When the results of the first MRI came back only months before his death, he wasn't surprised at the results. He was relieved he'd been right all those years.

He had many ideas about the growth, but no proof for any of it. But he didn't know if the dreams created the tumor, or the tumor caused the dreams. Whichever it was, they were connected. Over the years he learned to calm the dreams, slow them down and keep from having them as often, and he told me how to do that. I didn't want to believe any of it, of course, not wanting to accept my fate at seventeen years old. After he would fall asleep I'd go to my room and try to sleep. Some nights I ended up crying for him, others times I cried for myself.

"Alma!" His voice boomed louder than it had in so long. It was before sunrise and I jumped from my bed and ran into the next room. "Alma!"

Grandpa was lying there, his arms reaching up into the air as he called his dead wife's name over and over.

"Grandpa," I said. "It's okay, Grandpa."

The empty eyes turned and looked at me and I knew it was time. I sat on the side of the bed and took his hands in mine.

A small spark came back to his eyes when he looked at me. "I saw her, Wesley," he said. "She's waiting for me."

It was impossible to hold back the tears and they fell

freely. "Then you'd better go," I said. "You know how mad she gets when she has to wait for you."

I watched the spark begin to fade and just as it did the slightest smile crossed the old man's lips, then he was gone.

I grabbed his hands tightly. The warmth came again just as it had that night in the hospital with my father, moving through my hands, then my arms, and through my whole body before leaving me. In that heat, the transfer of emotion and memories, I learned more about the dreams than he'd ever been able to teach me.

Through his eyes I saw the trenches and boys dying from gunshots and sepsis. I saw the moment he first met the woman who would become his wife, and then when their only son was born, my father, and the sadness that followed when told they could have no more children. My father grew through flashes of light until he stood tall while the recruiting officer handed him the papers to sign to join the Army as Grandpa watched proudly.

I saw dreams he'd never told me about, dark dreams of faces I'd never seen committing gruesome acts I'd never even considered were possible. These images would stay with me, keep me awake at nights wondering how he had handled them. My always happy and loving grandfather had demons beyond belief in his mind.

Chapter 21

I DIDN'T MIND being alone. It was relaxing not having to worry about anyone else, taking care of someone. As a young boy I'd enjoyed it, sitting by myself for hours in the old church. But there was always an end to the solitude. When I'd get home Dad would be there, and earlier on, Larry and Mom. School on weekdays. This was different. There was no end in sight.

That first winter after Grandpa died, there were three weeks, probably, I don't think I spoke to another person. I had no tractors to work on and the phone wasn't ringing with new customers. I don't know if they'd heard Grandpa had died and found someone else to fix the machines for them, or it was just the cold, hard ground keeping people from worrying about their farming equipment. One man did call a few weeks after the funeral, having just heard. He said he'd come the next week with a trailer to pick up the tractor he'd dropped off a few months earlier to get it to a new mechanic. Its engine was locked up and was supposed to receive a full rebuild. When his Dodge pickup rolled up the next Tuesday with an eighteen foot trailer and two men to help him, I drove the tractor out from behind the workshop and up onto the trailer.

"Did he finish before he passed?"

"No sir. I completed the rebuild myself." I proceeded to tell him everything about the build, issues I'd found with the cylinders, and new parts he hadn't anticipated needing. With a handshake and a freshly written check, he promised me his continued business. Word spread and more jobs came in.

The first storm of that winter was the worst in years. It dropped two feet of snow and stopped everything. The news out of Tulsa showed impassable roads but somehow the reporters got out there with their cameras. Even though I'd have been alone anyway, I felt the forced incarceration in my own home from not being able to get in my truck and drive anywhere.

I spent much of the time going through the drawers and closet in my grandfather's room, putting anything that seemed important in one pile and the rest into a box to take up the hill and burn. The important pile was small, mostly documents like the deed to the house, the title to his pickup, and an old bible. I'd avoided the task for almost five months and for once had no excuse not to do it.

At night I sat in the big leather La-Z-Boy recliner, the only luxury my grandfather had ever afforded himself, a bottle of whiskey on the table beside me as I flipped through the few items I'd kept from cleaning out my grandfather's room. After reading every line of his birth certificate I moved on to the worn out bible. I'd never known anyone in my family to be religious, especially my grandfather. It was thick and worn, the spine showed signs of having once been coated in gold, or something meant to look like gold. Opening the front cover I saw sentences and paragraphs in pencil covering every open space of the first pages. With a magnifying glass I held the book close and read what I could.

There were scribbled dates preceding each section of text, details about the dreams he'd had his entire life. I flipped through and stopped counting when I hit a hundred and hadn't even reached Leviticus. Some of them were very detailed and others were as incomplete as the dream likely had been. Going back to the front I began with the first and read several pages before stopping, my eyes weary from the darkness of the room and the effects of the whiskey.

Sleep wasn't an option that night, or the next. I spent the next few days going over the bible, reading every word Grandpa had put in it. I saw so many names I recognized, friends of his and clients, people in town and even some back in Stroud. The common thread was death. In each one a person was lost. It was not always who Grandpa knew, but relatives of theirs as well.

For years I'd had the dreams, mostly of family and never in great detail. With the bible, in the pasts and deaths of so many people, I saw my future. Thoughts that it wouldn't be like that for me were pushed away quickly with each page I turned, knowing my fate would be the same as his. It would be a life filled with death, an existence surrounded by people mourning and crying. Some would be accidents, others natural. And perhaps those lives that would be taken against their will. I saw more than a couple like that in his writing, one I even remembered from the news. A group of girls on a scouting trip down near Locust Grove. It was reported that a vagrant was suspected and apprehended, an old man living in a makeshift tent in the woods. But Grandpa had seen it and knew the truth, but the murderer was untouchable and a tractor mechanic who'd had a dream wasn't someone the police would ever listen to.

It was late on the third night and I'd forgotten to drink the Irish whiskey I'd poured, when I saw a date I knew too well. It was the day my brother died. At first I closed the book, not wanting to read it. I had my memory of him and how he died and didn't want it altered. But the curiosity was too strong and I found myself flipping back to that page and reading.

My dream of Lawrence had been vague, a blurry reflection of his actual death. Grandpa saw it in detail. Even before I had time to react to it I was thinking about how hard it must have been for him. He saw his grandson die in war and was unable to do anything about it.

In his writing I saw my brother's final moments vividly, and his buddy Bill Johnson right there with him. It was mostly as the soldier had described to us but more violent in how the makeshift booby trap had exploded, Larry's step on the bamboo stalk forcing a nail down into the wax sealed compartment filled with gunpowder.

I remembered the drink and took it down quickly, the melted ice water diluting the flavor and strength, then poured another from the open bottle.

Chapter 22

I SAT IN the cab of the pickup holding the cake in my
hands, the words 'Happy Birthday Wesley' spelled out
on top in curvy blue letters, the number 30 below it. I
closed the lid and sat it carefully down on the floorboard
to my right and smiled the whole way home. The sun
was beating against the roof of the truck so I rolled the
windows up and turned the air conditioner on so high
my skin turned to goose bumps.

The sound from the stereo filled the cab. Music usually just occupied the space between my thoughts and silence, never finding a way any further into my life. It was
just there. I found the stories made up and set to music
pointless and even silly. When an older song came on I'd
sometimes give it a little more attention, a couple of Elvis
tunes and the simpler Beatles' songs before they got too
weird. Today a melody was floating around me, inviting

me to listen. Drums that sounded like they came from another land drove the song forward and the power from the repetition of words pulled me in. I hadn't thought of Colleen in some time and instantly she was at the front of my mind and I wondered how I would look in her eyes.

When the song ended, another began that pushed me away faster than the previous had captured my attention and I turned the radio off.

I'd stared at the cakes with their perfectly formed flowers in different colors lining the edges of the smooth white frosting and couldn't remember the last time I'd even had a cake. Aside from the exotic fruits I'd seen and bought one of each to try, I was drawn to the big bakery department at the back of the big new Wal-Mart in Grove.

When the woman in the blue apron behind the counter asked if I needed anything I'd stood there for nearly a full minute before answering. She must have thought there was something wrong with me or I was just plain stupid. Finally I stuttered out some words and watched her go to work.

It was the solitude I'd chosen. Years went by unmarked, unremarkable, with only Dick Clark to let me know it was time to change the calendar. Business was good and making money, which wasn't too difficult with the house and land having been paid off well before Grandpa died. All I had were the few regular monthly bills. I even got a big new television to replace the small one he left behind. My old GMC still ran well but I found myself at a dealership outside Tulsa one day and paid cash for a new

Sierra in bright red with vinyl seats and air conditioning. But I still preferred to drive with the windows down. Old habits. I spent a lot of time reading, a stack of books from the town library always beside my chair. Didn't care what it was, but preferred the made up stuff. I'd gone through about everything Stephen King had written and had to sleep with the lights on one night, never looking at clowns the same way again.

The last birthday I remembered celebrating was when I turned eight years old. My mother was still alive though already very sick. My father was working more and generally in a good mood. Lawrence was the typical big brother, loving one moment and punching me in the gut the next. The cake that day had been angel food that mom baked herself. In the confusion from her illness she'd mixed up the amounts of some of the ingredients but everyone sat at the table eating that cake and trying to swallow every bite without letting her know how bad it was. She sat and watched us with a smile on her face, unable to eat anything that night. I always suspected she knew how bad the cake was and just appreciated how her family put on a show to make her feel good.

I sat the cake in the middle of the small round kitchen table and stopped to look at it every time I walked past, determined to wait until after supper to cut into it and have my own private birthday celebration even though it was a month early.

I put a small chicken in the oven that came all ready to cook from the store and had a bottle of beer from Ireland.

When I poured the bottle into a glass I thought it had gone bad at first when I saw the black liquid.

When I sat down at the table that evening I looked at the dinner plate and silverware I'd set out and the perfectly cooked chicken and the tall glass of beer and felt embarrassed at such a show, even with nobody but me there to see it. A few minutes later everything was moved to the folding table beside my recliner where I sat to eat every night. I turned on the television just in time for Jeopardy.

The beer surprised me, having not expected to like it, and I ate half of the chicken that I thought would last me all week. I finally went back to the table and opened the cardboard box and stared at the cake again. I cut a slice and slid it over onto a plate then took it with a fork back to my chair. The first bite was halfway to my mouth when I stopped.

Thoughts rushed through my head of all the things that had passed to get me to this point. If it weren't for the one framed photograph I was certain I'd have forgotten what my mother looked like. My grandpa's voice was still in my head everyday as I worked the tools around the big gas and diesel engines out in the workshop.

"Happy birthday," I said.

I took a bite of the rich chocolate cake and looked up at the television as the next answer appeared. "Who is Woodrow Wilson?"

Chapter 23

NOBODY CALLED ME, but no one noticed or seemed surprised I was there. Thirty, maybe forty people were gathered east of town. Almost all of the sheriff's office vehicles blocked the road with blue lights flashing on their roofs. Calls had gone out all over the county for the search party and the disc jockey from the country radio station in Tulsa had even announced it.

A young deputy, likely appointed by senior personnel of the agency, climbed onto the top of one of the SUV's and began to yell out to the crowd. "Becca May Anders went missing from her home last night, sometime between midnight and six o'clock in the morning."

I wanted to correct the deputy, tell him the girl had quietly walked out the back door of the house at 10:30p.m. She had a backpack filled with a random assortment of clothing and toys over her shoulders. Her father was just down the hall in the front room, naked and on top of the babysitter after getting home from the new Indian casino up north. I didn't know if this was the first time but the babysitter hadn't complained and willingly took the drugs offered to her, as well as the fifty dollars the man paid her for her services.

Drugs had become a problem. Each night on the news they reported on another house that had been raided, a car pulled over on a routine traffic stop that turned into an armed standoff, or dead bodies found either from an overdose or a drug deal gone bad. The hospitals had seen their fair share of overdose victims dumped at the emergency room doors, car tires squealing to get away before security came running out to get a license plate number. It had come so fast that the small town police and sheriff's offices weren't trained to handle it. The state troopers helped where they could.

"She was last seen wearing pink pajamas at approximately 8:30 last night when she was put to bed."

The dream had been a calm one, compared to most. I could only guess this was because nobody had died, not yet at least. I half listened to the deputy as I ran the dream through my head, looking for any other details. By now I was sure the father had cleaned the drugs off of the table and flushed the condoms he'd used with the teenage girl down the toilet, the use of which were perhaps the only intelligent choice he'd made that night.

"All doors and windows were locked from the inside," the deputy continued. "Foul play is suspected but not confirmed. Keep your eyes open for anything suspicious or out of place. If you see something, stop where you are and call down the line of volunteers until your message reaches someone with a radio to get the sheriff's office out there."

It was more people than I liked to be around, more than I had seen at one time since school probably. No one noticed me or talked to me which was fine. I kept to the edge of the group and didn't make eye contact, not sharing in everyone's comments of how tragic this was and hoping the poor girl was still alive. I knew she was, or at least was when I'd awakened.

We were ushered into a field behind the house, the long metal gate scraping the ground as two deputies pushed it open. I passed by one of the men in his brown uniform with dark brown tie and the wide brimmed hat replaced with a sheriff's office soft cap for the day. I felt his eyes on me as I passed.

"Wes?"

I heard my name but kept moving. I knew who it was the moment I'd seen him.

"Wes Hudson, that you?"

I stepped to the right out of the way of all the volunteers walking into the field and looked at the deputy.

"It is you." He stepped over to me. "Benton Hicks. We went to school together."

My head cocked to one side. "Benton Hicks?" I remembered how my fist felt when it struck him in the nose, the only time I'd ever hit someone.

"Come on, Wes. We had several classes together."

"Benton Hicks. Yup. Okay." I relented. "I remember you." I'd hoped we could end it there.

"What have you been up to?" Benton said.

Glancing over my shoulder at the people moving into the field then back at him, I did my best to look in a hurry. "Not much. Just working on tractors. I'd better get going."

"Still out past town?" he said. "Didn't know anyone still lived there."

"Just me." I took a step away.

"Hold on." He reached into his shirt pocket then handed me a card. "Let's catch up over a beer soon."

"Sure." I gave him a short wave and headed off into the field.

I caught up and moved through the group to be on the north side, to head up toward the tree line on the ridge and the gulley on the other side of it where I'd last seen her, asleep under a fallen tree.

It was noon and the sun was right above us, no shadows being cast on the ground as we walked. Everyone spread out into a line with fifteen feet between us as we'd been instructed. A few kids from the high school had skipped class to be there and walked shoulder to shoulder, treating the search as day out of school rather than the serious matter it was as they talked and pushed each other around.

Only one person was to my right after we formed the line and I was going straight for the trees. I wished we could hurry up; get them moving so the girl could be found before anything really did happen to her. It wasn't a hot day but too many hours exposed in the bright Oklahoma sun could dry a man out quickly, much less a seven year old girl.

We reached the trees and I veered right to push the man further up. At the lip of the gulley I stopped and called out. "I'll go along the rim if you'll go down through."

The young man waved and went down the hill with ease. I moved slowly around the rim and spotted the tree from above. The girl should be on the other side, blocked by the downed trunk. I watched the man to make sure he went the right way. When he began to turn left back up the hill I had to stop him.

"Check that tree out, looks like there's space under it," I called out.

It was moments later when I heard the man yell. The girl had been asleep and he thought she was dead at first. I turned and alerted the next person in the line, easily fifty feet away now, and the call went down through them until it was radioed in. I wanted to leave right then, get out of the way and not have my name connected to it. But it would be too visible to walk off across the field alone. I needed the anonymity a group provided, so I waited. Everyone was curious and tried to see the girl as she was carried up by paramedics, strapped down to a backboard.

I'd had so many dreams over the years, most ending badly. Some had yet to become real or at least I hadn't heard anything about them. Faces weren't always recognizable, locations unknown. I didn't know how far the dreams reached, if they had a limit. Grandpa had seen the bank robbers when they were still fifty or sixty miles away, but was it because they were coming toward him, his land? I've always felt there had to be a connection of some kind, that they weren't just random people coming into my thoughts.

I watched the coverage on the news that night. I'd been on the road before the TV truck got to the scene to make sure I wasn't on camera. The young man got all the credit, though he did mention the 'man who pointed me in the right direction.' I relaxed into the chair. I was relieved the girl was safe, alive. But she was now back in the house she had tried to run away from.

A dream returned that night, one I hadn't seen since high school. I knew the face but still couldn't see the location, just the dirt that Benton Hicks fell back onto after my hand swung something large and heavy and struck him in the face.

Chapter 24

LIVING IN A small town is like having windows all around you, everyone knowing what you're up to at all times. I had tried my best to stay out of the windows. I left my house for groceries and to pick up tractors from out of town. Most days I figured I was forgotten about, a man older than his years living alone out in the country. My customers came from all over, very few from my own town, or I'd hook up the trailer and drive to them. Conversations were short and stayed focused on the work they needed done. I'm sure some of them thought me a rude man, or simple minded, when I'd ignore questions that would lead to longer talks.

I looked forward to the drives. Oklahoma would roll past outside the windows of the pickup and I took it all in. I never knew what Larry didn't see, why he wanted out so badly. It wasn't perfect, I knew that. But it was real. I wouldn't mind seeing the ocean some day. Something about water was calming. Driving over the bridge at Grand Lake always relaxed me. Would be nice to have a boat, maybe a pontoon with chairs and even a place to cook out. I could spend all day out on the lake. No people around, just me and the gentle swells of the water.

Moments strung themselves together into minutes then hours. Days flew by quickly in the workshop, hands deep into the grease and steel that made up the big engines powering the farm equipment vital to the Oklahoma landscape. Putting the last bolt onto an engine brought a sense of accomplishment. Occasionally I wished I could create something new, something unique, rather than just rebuilding the same things over and over, but then the next tractor comes in and I'm addicted to the cylinders and gears once again, checking and rechecking to make sure everything is lining up and working smoothly.

I caught myself mimicking my grandfather. Though I'd bypassed the old man's tradition of throwing trash out up on the hill, I still liked to drive my truck up top, light a campfire and sit under the stars in the middle of the seventy-five acres of hills and woods. Sometimes I had a bottle of whiskey with me, sometimes a thermos of hot black coffee.

I'd bring the old bible and read through my grandfather's dreams until the sunlight faded and it grew too dark to see the words. After so many years I'd been through them all so many times but continued to read, finding comfort in them. Even though he was gone, just know-

ing someone else had been through this, experienced the
dreams and the deaths, and came out some semblance of
normal, helped me keep going.

Many nights I thought of Jake, *Pyothopi* of the deer
clan. I knew him only a few hours but his memory stayed
with me. I'd never been one to question the universe or
the gods or whatever makes everything move in some sort
of harmony, but I did often wonder why I met him. That
one random and hot summer day that we sat at the old
church and talked about the walls that surrounded us and
the world on the other side of them, then he was gone.
A perverse harmony, distorted and cruel at times. In order for one thing to happen, one person to live, a dozen
other things have to go wrong. We accept that death is
certain but try to ignore the fact that in every moment it
is also imminent. I have seen these moments more times
than I care to, so many that they are not much more than
clutter, mental detritus thrown around and mixed in with
my thoughts of what to have for dinner and why the fuel
injectors on that Farmall aren't working. There's nothing
I can do to help the people I see, to save them. I learned
that early with my own father. The only time I've ever felt
I did something good with the dreams was the young girl
with her backpack.

Lying in the meadow on top of the hill and staring into
the darkness with the formations of glowing dots, con-
necting them together in my mind into new and different
constellations was like a meditation. Often I wished I still
had a notebook and wrote stories down, but that had left

me long ago. More than a few times I'd fallen asleep on the grass only to wake up in the middle of the night, the fire long burned out. On one of those nights I stirred when I felt something touch me. I opened my eyes and saw the dark shape at my feet then heard the quick raspy breaths. The clouds had moved in while I slept and blocked all of the stars, only the slightest glow from the moon created any illumination. The animal moved up toward my head then the eyes of the grey wolf locked with mine. They held for what seemed minutes but was probably seconds, or less. I knew the wolf could have my throat out before I ever raised my arms to try to stop it. What were you supposed to do when confronted by a wolf? Was it make yourself big? Walk slowly away? The instinct of the wild animal was to kill quickly. But there we stayed, staring each other down until the beast finally took a few steps back and walked away, fading into the darkness.

Except for the one day I took Grandpa to Texas, I'd never been anywhere. If the Arkansas, Kansas, and Missouri state lines weren't so close I might never have crossed those borders. I liked the feel of Oklahoma, the understated sense of belonging somewhere that didn't pretend. You know what you're going to get and that's exactly what you got. Amanda at the bank will always call you sweetie. Shawna will always make sure your coffee is filled up over at Beasley's. And blue jeans and overalls Jared Walker sells at the Delaware County Mercantile and Hunting Supplies store downtown will cost you a couple dollars more than at Wal-Mart.

I hadn't even noticed my hair going from dark brown to salt and pepper, it happened so slowly. The men always go grey early in my family. One morning I raised the cutthroat razor blade to my cheek to work through the thick stubble that grew overnight and stopped when I looked in the mirror and saw my own grandfather staring back at me. In some ways I wished I looked more like my father, so every morning I'd have something to make me think about him. I loved my father in death as I did when he was alive, in the only way he would allow and be comfortable with. The contrast of how I had felt about my grandfather was strong.

Grandpa talked about his time in the war a lot near the end, but I wanted to know more. Through documents left behind, I'd traced his path through the Army during World War I, and into the trenches in France. Reading books and watching documentaries I understood why he never talked about it. So many young men didn't return. Those who did felt they had the weight of all their fallen friends on their shoulders.

Barely a day went by I didn't think of my mother, the few memories I had were watered down with time, remnants from three decades earlier. At times I couldn't tell if I was recalling real events or ones I'd created in my mind to help me remember her. Her silver hairbrush, now wrapped inside a plastic bag, a few strands of blonde hair wound around the bristles, still lived in the bottom drawer of my dresser.

On a cool spring morning I stepped out of the back of the house and looked at the red tractor my grandfather had loved, that we had ridden together so many times up top to look for the windfall of cash from the bank robbery that had been forgotten it was so long ago.

I stared at the tractor and thought of the old man who had lovingly cared for me, had shown me what I knew about the dreams. The memory came to me of my grandfather standing beside the red machine with the tire iron in his hand, naked as can be in the falling snow. It had been one of his last days on earth.

I looked at the tractor that had now sat for years in the same spot up by the road, a sign hung from it reading, 'Tractor Repair.'

Chapter 25

THE WORN BURGUNDY and beige linoleum floor of Beasley's Cafe was a time machine of boot scuff marks and coffee stains. The chrome trim around the edges of the tables was battered from years of abuse. The place had been here since before I was a kid visiting my Grandpa and he'd bring me for pancakes on Sunday mornings. It had sold a couple of times but nothing ever changed. The waitresses wore the same blue dresses with white aprons that they had for better than fifty years. It defined our small town. Just friendly enough, just clean enough, didn't cost much and never too busy. The steak was gristly, but not so bad to not order it, and the baked potatoes were always just right.

It was the only restaurant in town, so it was the best one, too. You had to get up to Grove to have any more selection, but it was good enough as long as you didn't mind seeing everyone you know there.

What had started mostly under duress had turned into a near weekly event, and one I grew to not dislike over time. When he first showed up in my driveway in his Crown Victoria cruiser a few weeks after the little girl was found safe, I did my best to give him the cold shoulder, to show little interest in catching up, conversation in general, and least of all having a friend. He'd been resilient in his pressure, almost to the point of intimidation. I didn't know why it meant so much to him but in the end I relented and we rarely missed a Thursday night after that first time. Benton Hicks sat in the booth in the front window of the restaurant, the same booth we'd sat in for nine years now.

"Happy 40th, buddy."

I'd hoped he wouldn't remember. "Damn, we're getting old," I said.

"Don't I know it, but at least you'll always be older than me."

"How's work, and Becky?" His wife had been a year behind us in high school. I had known who she was but didn't recall ever sharing a word with her. She hung out with the football team and was a cheerleader one or two years with Colleen. She was a little plain then, but pretty. Just cute enough and outgoing enough to make the cut for the popular crowd. She'd turned into a fine looking woman, better than Benton deserved. And he knew that. They'd dated before he dropped out of school and went into the Army then married when he was back on leave. The first baby came nine months exactly from his final day at home.

"Becky's good. Still pushing to do dinner at our house. I think she's just jealous. Work is the same ole' shit," Benton said. "The sheriff is being a real bastard, but I guess getting voted out of office will do that to you."

I nodded. "Must be kinda hard to spend your last days at work with the guy who destroyed you in the elections working right there. So what big plans do you have once you're the boss?"

"Hard to believe, isn't it?" he said. "I have some ideas for the office. Sheriff Brewster really let a lot slide."

It hadn't been much of a race. Brewster was in his late 60's and didn't have his heart in it anymore. Benton ran a good campaign and everybody always seemed to like him. He was young enough that he could be around quite a while, too, and people around here didn't like change so once he's in, he would be for a long time.

"I hear drugs are becoming a pretty big problem around here."

"Not around here. Not on my watch."

"I've read that meth is becoming common. Been several houses raided down south." I scanned the menu though I always ordered the same thing.

Benton shrugged it off as the waitress came and we ordered dinner. He was extra friendly, asking her questions about different items on the menu even though he could probably go in back and cook it all himself he knew it so well.

After flirting with the waitress he continued to talk about work and I tuned him out. It was the same complaints every week, either about coworkers or residents with absurd calls to the sheriff's office. I'd just listen and sip on my beer, give the occasional nod and 'Mmm hmm'. We were friends by default. He certainly had a lot of people around him, but I hadn't even cared to get close to anyone. The only thing we had in common was that we'd spent a little time at the same school. I figured over time that he didn't recall me busting his nose open or he was too embarrassed to ever bring it up, so I never did.

"Oh, hell. Did you hear about Colleen Murphy?"

Her name brought me back and my body tightened up so quickly I was sure he saw it. I didn't want Benton to keep talking, to hear what news he had about Colleen. The images of the demolished Ford sedan from my dream had never left my thoughts in over twenty years. I knew Colleen had married and moved to St. Louis but nothing past that. Her parents were both dead and she had no other family in the area.

"No." I kept my eyes on the glass. "I haven't."

"D-I-V-O-R-C-E-D," Benton spelled it out. "And I hear she's moving back to Jay."

My eyes were still locked on the beer as I took in the news. The tension that had built up so quickly in my neck began to release just as my gut seized at the different emotions hitting me.

"What?"

"I was with a gal I know in the prosecutor's office a few nights ago in Oklahoma City. Colleen's gonna be doing some work for them, helping with the backlog of cases in our district," Benton said. "You two sure had a thing back in the day."

"That was high school, and it lasted all of a month or two." A day didn't pass without me thinking about her, the weeks of spending every waking moment together and the one night in front of the fireplace in her home.

"So? Not like you're doing too great on the socializing. Except for Thursday nights here with me when do you ever get out of that old house of yours?"

"I go grocery shopping on Saturday mornings," I said. "Anyway, I like being in that old house of mine."

Benton laughed, his hand slapped the table, spilling some of the fresh beers that the waitress had dropped off. "Look at that, you're craving being around people. You can go anytime you want but you go to Wal-Mart the same time everyone else in town goes?"

"Just always gone on Saturdays," I said. "Not going to change my routine cause everyone else is going out."

The seed was planted and the rest of the evening's conversation was a wash. I'd nod and grunt a 'yup' or 'sure is' at times but my brain was wrapping itself around Colleen once again. I thought of how her naked skin had felt beneath my fingertips now rough from callouses and scars. I couldn't recall exactly how her voice had sounded, or her laugh, but knew I'd recognize it anywhere if I heard it again.

Chapter 26

THE MEADOW WAS in late bloom. A cool snap in the summer had confused the seeds and when the temperature went back into the 80's again they sprouted and created a field of magnificent colors all across the hilltop. Blues and yellows, greens and purples. The menagerie attracted the honeybees and they flew low, bouncing from petal to petal to drink and inadvertently leave pollen behind, continuing a cycle that had been going on forever.

I took my steps carefully through the growth, trying not to step on any of the blossoms and disturb nature at work. Time gets away and I hadn't walked the hill as much as I used to, for exercise and the foolhardy idea of finding the bank robber's money.

This was a day I needed the solitude for a few hours, to be somewhere I knew I wouldn't run into anyone else and be forced into a mundane conversation about nothing.

My mind and my soul needed the respite, the centering, before that evening.

Sleep wasn't coming as easily lately. A dream had been recurring, a pattern I wasn't used to, as it was usually a single dream then done. But I kept seeing the young girl, hidden in the back bedroom of the drug house. It would be different now and then, showing me more about her. She stared at her closed bedroom door, not understanding the sounds that came from the other side. Once she had gone out to see what was wrong, who was hurt and crying out in pain, moaning, but she'd been grabbed too hard and dragged back, the door slammed. A sliding bar lock was installed shortly after and when her presence was unwanted she'd be locked in, several times missing school the next morning because her father would sleep late and sometimes even leave without remembering to let her out.

I started my own logbook, a variation on grandpa's bible. If he had felt it important, or cathartic, or why ever he did it, then I felt obliged to try. I used to love writing and couldn't even recall when I fell out of the habit. Starting with the more recent dreams, I then worked backwards and filled in the blanks and was surprised at the detail I recalled from decades earlier.

As I walked back down the hill along the path carved into the side by Grandpa's tractor, I stopped and looked down over the house and workshop. It was the very spot I'd stood beside Larry one day as children after hours up top exploring. We'd both stopped to look, a moment still

belonging only to children, before we entered back into
the world of adults. I'd felt the warmth on my lip and
wiped it with the back of my hand. The deep red streak
across my skin confused me for a moment and I looked up
at Larry. When he saw me there was a look of concern on
his face. It was far more blood than it should have been.
He held my head back as I pinched my nose, the flow
slowed then finally stopped.

"I'm scared."

"It'll be okay. Let's just get down the hill."

"I don't want to. Dad'll be mad."

He'd looked at my shirt and understood, then he pulled
his tee shirt off and told me to do the same. He took mine
and rolled it up so the blood was hidden and tucked it
into my back pocket, only the clean white back of the
shirt showing. We ran past Dad and Grandpa like we were
playing chase and right into the house. Larry sent me upstairs to get a fresh shirt and he went into the bathroom.
He spent an hour in there scrubbing my white tee shirt
until every bit of blood was gone.

I drove up past the high school and parked outside a
brick single story home. The big white Chevy Suburban
SUV with Delaware County Sheriff markings on the side
sat in the driveway, a new Chrysler sedan beside it. He'd
been sworn in as sheriff a few months earlier and got the
new truck with the title. I'd put the dinner off for longer
than I could. It took long enough to get used to the weekly meals with Benton at the café, being around his wife
was going to stretch my socializing patience.

Becky Hicks opened the door and smiled at me. "Wes Hudson, I can't believe you're actually here."

"I know," I said. "I hope you didn't take it personal."

As I went to step in she sprung forward and hugged me and I awkwardly put my hand on her back. She spoke quietly into my ear. "I'm so sorry, sweetie," she said. "It wasn't my idea and there's no stoppin' him. You know how he is when he gets a thought." She turned and disappeared into the house, around the corner and out of sight. I stepped in and swung the door shut.

The motion caught my eye as she stood up from the sofa in the far corner of the room. Except for the one time I'd seen her pass by in a car while I sat in the bank parking lot it had been nearly two decades, longer since I'd been in a room with her. She'd come to see me one last time the week before leaving for her senior year in college. We'd sat on the front porch of my house and talked for hours. Whenever she was looking the other way I'd gazed at the side of her face and the line of her jaw and neck. I'd memorized her look, her voice, her scent.

"Hi, Wesley."

"Colleen. Didn't know you were gonna be here." I tried not to move, fearing I'd forgotten how to. Walking seemed an impossible task.

"In all fairness, I didn't know you were either," she said. "Looks like our sheriff is also a bit of a meddler."

"Yeah, he's good at that." I tried to laugh and it came out as a stifled cough. "Also seems he and his wife have made themselves scarce at the moment." I felt like I was talking too loud or too fast. Was I slurring my words?

Colleen moved through the room easily with the motion I remembered, the same fluidity and poise she had as a teenager. She was even more beautiful now. Gray speckled her dark blonde hair and the gentle lines on her face added even more charm to her smile than she'd already had. She wrapped her arms around me. The scent of her hair and skin overloaded my brain, like when you go so long without your favorite food then the smell of it hits you and it's all you want, all you crave. Then she gently kissed my cheek. It was warm and soft and a little wet and sent synapses flying open and shut in a frenzy of memories.

The evening turned to night as we ate dinner then a failed crème brûlée for dessert. We moved out onto the back patio with our drinks and Benton carried an extra six-pack of beer with him. Becky sat to the side and smoked a cigarette while drinking gin on the rocks. Colleen and I had a bottle of red wine she'd brought and I wondered the entire night if she was thinking of the wine we'd had from her father's cabinet that night on her living room floor.

I tried not to look at her but was unsuccessful. She was a magnet. Whenever I did look she almost always glanced over and caught me, the hint of a grin, the tease of her lips separating slightly, her tongue touching her upper lip as I'd seen her do so many times back in school. The years looked so wonderful on her.

Benton talked and I nodded, stories I'd heard a dozen times at our weekly dinners. Becky interjected her versions of events and he'd wait her out then continue with a "like I was saying." When Colleen talked I casually listened to keep from staring, while hearing everything, absorbing her voice. She brushed off most talk of her years in St. Louis and ended the questions about her ex with "all I'll say is he's a pig" and I hated him for making her feel that way.

When she finally said she had to go, I made my excuses as well and walked her out. She was parked across the street and we stood at her old Mercedes sedan and spoke for another hour, bodies getting dangerously close but never touching except for her occasional hand on my elbow when I'd say something she took as funny.

I don't know what we talked about. It was a whirlwind of conversation going from high school memories to how the town had changed. We teetered on the edge of personal thoughts and topics, our voices getting lower, softer, then one of us would yank the wheel back to the mundane, the grocery store checkout banter that filled the time while the bread and peanut butter moved down the dirty black conveyor belt. I didn't want the night to end. I wanted to be standing here talking to her when the sun came up. I wanted to hold her.

She looked up at me after sitting down into her car, a grin that should be a criminal act on her face. "So, will you call me?"

Chapter 27

I STAYED IN bed and listened to the morning arrive outside. A few acorns fell on the roof and rolled down, some ending up in the gutters, others going silent as they made their two-story fall to the ground. A large truck went by on the road at the end of the long driveway, the rumble from the engine as the driver let off the gas in a low gear vibrated my bedroom windows.

So will you call me.

I'd looked at her wrapped up in that grin and was left speechless. The conflicts that kept me from her for so many years came back and invaded my brain, taking over any rational thought. I'm 40 years old and alone, goddammit. An old 40. Not one of those late in life fathers out running around with their children in the yard. Colleen's the only woman I'd ever been with, the only one I'd ever wanted. Thoughts of her skin against mine still invaded my thoughts regularly, memories of the touches we'd had and dreams of ones we hadn't.

I had work to do but mostly I just stared. I stared out the window. I stared at the front of the newspaper long enough to have read the entire thing but never took in a single paragraph. It was impossible to focus on anything other than her.

So will you call me.

Grandpa hadn't said a word when I broke up with Colleen in high school. He noticed she wasn't around anymore and I was home all the time. He asked only once what happened and I just told him she broke up with me. It was dropped and he never asked again. He would push me to get out, to go hang out with friends, but his health was fading and I needed to be with him.

For so long I'd convinced myself I was living exactly as I wanted to, as I needed to. I liked being alone, having no one to answer to or disappoint. No one to worry about being in one of my dreams and then seeing them die, once in my sleep and again when it happened. It was a necessary exile, self-imposed solitary confinement for my own good.

I could travel if I wanted. I had thought about visiting France one day, to see the remnants of trenches that Grandpa had stood in. I knew most are gone, only a few left over and preserved as relics, but it would be close enough. Or Vietnam where my brother pulled his final breaths. But I was happy here. The rolling landscape of Oklahoma was all I needed. Just driving into Tulsa raised my blood pressure so there's no way I could handle a flight across the ocean. The unused passport sat in a drawer in my bedroom, renewed several times, no stamps inside.

After one night of watching her move and smile and seeing it line up with my memories of her, all of my convictions were questioned. A day ago I looked around my home with contentment, today I felt only sadness at being alone. Her touch was so long ago and any memories of it were surely faded, the sensation on my skin forgotten. Her light touch on my arm last night making me desire more. We are older now, well beyond the age in my dream. No children would come from us. What harm could there be?

So will you call me.

It was a simple question complicated by a lifetime of isolation and fear. An answer could be verbal or a motion, a simple nod to affirm or even the slightest frown to let her know that no, I would not be calling her. But I did neither. I stared. I drank her in.

As her car pulled away I'd felt the warmth go with it. I turned to walk to my truck and saw a curtain in the front window of Benton's house fall back into place. Damn you, Benton.

The walls pulled in on me as I walked through my own house, the house that had been my grandfather's before me. A few photos still existed of him and my grandmother, Alma. Faded sepia memories of another person. She had died shortly before I was born but had been a part of my life through his stories. With each image I got closer to the back door, the pressure of silence pushing me toward the escape route, and I found myself in my truck driving into town.

I had never been to Beasley's alone. Sitting in a corner booth with a view of the street out the dirty window, I felt people were staring at the man eating alone. But they were all too busy ordering and dining to care about me.

"You alone today?"

I looked up at the young waitress that regularly served Benton and me on Thursday nights. She held two coffee pots, one with a black lid, the other orange.

"Yup. Just didn't feel like cooking."

"That's what we're here for," she said. "Regular or un-leaded?"

"Hmm? Oh, right." I turned the upside down coffee cup over on its saucer. "Regular, please."

I ordered pancakes and bacon then sipped on my coffee while watching the cars on a slow Friday morning move through town. Each time the bell on top of the door to the cafe rang I turned to see who it was and each time felt silly for hoping it might be her. Food came and I ate then sat some more. The cafe wasn't busy and the waitress kept my cup full of hot coffee.

"Slow day?" she said on her next time past with the coffee pot.

"Plenty to do, just not terribly motivated," I said.

"You look like you gotta lot of thoughts today."

"Good way of putting it." I sipped the coffee and she continued to stand there and I found I didn't mind. "You can sit if you want."

She glanced around the room then practically collapsed into the bench across from me. "Thank ya. Been here since five and my dogs are really barking, if you know what I mean."

"I do." She was even prettier than I'd realized on my weekly visits for dinner, and younger than I thought she was. Twenty-five, twenty-six at the most but the stress lines and overcompensating makeup made her look in her thirties. Her name tag was worn and showed signs of past employees names beneath the thick red tape with her name punched into it. Shawna.

"How long have you worked here now?" I said.

She pursed her lips and exhaled loudly as her eyes pointed upward in thought. I felt the hint of her breath on me from across the table and caught the slightest scent of the mint gum she was chewing on. "Going on three years now."

"You like it?"

"It's fine," she said. "Long hours on your feet but the customers are all pretty nice. I get to eat a couple meals a day for free which saves me a lot of money. Gary, the cook, seems to accidentally make a bit too much when I'm working so I have something to take home to my daughter."

"You from Jay?" I could tell she was but asked anyway. She probably graduated the high school then moved in with a boy and got pregnant then he'd left her. It was a story told too often here. It's a small town, almost incestuous in nature by the mere fact that there were only so many families that lived in the area. There was always someone to be with if you wanted to marry, as long as you didn't mind dirt under the fingernails or that his or her relatives may be married to one of your relatives.

"Born in Grove and grew up here."

I nodded. The other waitress walked by and tapped the table in front of Shawna as she passed, a signal to get back on her feet. She was much older, late fifties probably, and I wondered if Shawna knew that would be her one day.

"Guess I better get back at it," she said. "Coffee cups ain't gonna fill themselves."

She reached over and put her hand on mine for a moment. "Thanks for letting me sit for a minute, sweetie."

I felt the heat from her hand pass into me and watched her walk away.

Chapter 28

AT SOME POINT over the last twenty years a few restaurants and marinas had been built up on the north side of the lake, each with lavish names that evoked far more exotic locations. The Grande Copa Marina and Nightclub was two doors down from the Wild Parrot Taco Shop. In the space between them were the public bathrooms. Beach front property had been developed to the point there wasn't much beach anymore and land that wasn't occupied by stores and eating establishments was covered with parking lots and boat ramps. There was a sign at the turnoff for the cliff we'd jumped off of as teens offering that land up for sale, too. The sign had been there several years and was covered in spray painted swear words and the barrage of bullet holes collected by anything that sat too long in Oklahoma.

Change comes slowly to this part of the country, but once it does it blends in quickly and soon nobody remembers when it wasn't always that way. At some point you just know you ate there once, or bought that thing that sits on a shelf in the kitchen at that place. A building with a Mexican restaurant in it was a drug store last year and before that a gift shop selling aquatic themed souvenirs like seashells with googly eyes stuck on them to make funny looking faces, even though seashells don't come from lakes.

"I'm glad you called." Her voice was soft but somehow still audible over the sounds around us.

We sat on the patio of one of the cafés overlooking the water. I picked up my beer and took a long drink, unsure how to respond or if I even needed to. She looked amazing and caught me staring again just as she did at Benton's house. The sun was low and cast a warm glow across her skin.

"Lotsa boats out today," I said.

She turned to look out at the three fishing boats floating on the large expanse of water and laughed. "What happened to you, Wesley Hudson? In high school you were not this awkward. When did this happen?"

"I don't recall the exact date."

Colleen shook her head. "I know you're still in there somewhere."

"I don't know," I said. "Been a long time. People change. Everything changes. Last month this cafe was a frozen yogurt shop."

"Not you," she said. "You may not be much of a talker

but you still have the same eyes. I could always lose myself in those eyes."

I took another sip of beer. She wasn't making it easy for me to stay disconnected. Every word she uttered pulled me in. I wanted to just tell her how I felt, how I'd always felt. I wanted to take her home and push her up against the wall and kiss her. Sitting across from her I could almost feel it, her lips on mine, my body pressed against hers.

"So, why did we meet 20 miles from Jay?" she said. "You embarrassed to be seen with me?"

I shrugged. "I have a reputation to maintain."

"What reputation, a hermit?"

"Sounds about right."

The late afternoon turned into evening and we walked along the rough shore of the lake. Each time Colleen tried to ask a serious question I would counter with a random fact about the lake, tractors, Oklahoma, or I'd simply pick up a rock and throw it into the water then keep walking. She was right, I had become awkward. Having little interaction with people had changed me. Even the dinners with Benton didn't prepare me for having real conversations, much less with the woman I'd dreamt about for so long. It was the short conversation with Shawna the day before that convinced me to call. The few minutes with her had been comfortable and gave me hope.

Two men stood on the gravel shore, worn tackle boxes on the ground beside them as they cast their lines out into the darkening lake. One line had just barely hit the water when it tugged back. The man wound in the line quickly to draw it taut, then would lower the rod to give some distance then pull back up. Finally he wound slowly until the fish began to bounce on the surface, then it was floating in the air, suspended by a metal hook through its mouth.

"I miss that," she said.

"Fishing?"

"My dad used to take me when I was little. I don't know if I enjoyed the actual fishing or just being with him."

The fisherman dropped his catch into a white cooler and closed the top.

"My dad and brother used to go," I said. "I'd sit with them sometimes, but I usually stayed home."

"We should go sometime."

I had no interest in fishing but would do anything she wanted. We continued walking, nods given to the two fishermen as we passed. Her hand would bump mine as we walked, her not so subtle way, I thought, to try to get me to take her hand. I didn't, though I wanted to, my skin longed to touch hers in any way. Prompts for conversations of anything other than the most benign topics were met with silence from me. Small talk didn't come naturally. I could tell she was getting frustrated as we got back to the edge of the parking lot where her car sat two spaces down from my pickup.

Decisions are made quickly, not over time. You may deliberate and rationalize and list pros and cons, but when it comes down to it, a decision is made in an instant. You can't take hours to choose 'yes' or 'no'. It just happens. Anything leading up to it is fabricated by your own fears of making the wrong choice. I looked down at her face and could tell she knew to listen, that I was going to say something and that it wasn't easy for me. She cocked her head to the side and showed me I had her full attention with the most subtle of a smile that invited me to begin.

"I don't know how to do this," I said. "I don't know if I want to do this, and I really have no idea why you'd want to have anything to do with me after how I treated you."

The smile remained but her silence was loud as her eyes searched mine. I wanted to kiss her and at the same time I wanted to run, just jump in my truck and drive away.

"That's the most words in a row I've heard you say to-day," she said. "I didn't understand it. Still don't. Part of me has always belonged to you and I feel part of you has always belonged to me. And that was a thousand years ago. We were just kids. But it was always you. I did my best. Got married. We knew it wasn't right, or at least I did. Something just wasn't there and it ended."

I stared at the ground then began to bend over.

"If you throw one more god damn rock into the lake then I'm throwing you in there with it."

I paused, then stood back up with a rock and rolled it over in my hand. I held it out to her. "This one looks like a heart."

She looked at the rock then up at my face. I didn't turn away and try to hide my gaze.

"What are you going to do with it?" she said.

I shook my head then took her hand and placed the heart shaped rock into her palm and folded her fingers around it.

"Be careful with it. It's not as strong as it looks."

Chapter 29

SHE BEGAN TO scream but I was too strong and tightened my grip around her throat, bare hands taking what little life she had away from her. The more she struggled the tighter my hands squeezed.

My body shivered under the thick blanket even as the temperature outside was still in the eighties in the middle of the night. Behind closed eyelids my eyes were rolling back inside my head as the images flashed past in my sleep, some familiar from so many years before, the brown haired girl.

The dream had started as I walked in through the back door of a small house, one I'd never seen before. It was messy, unkept. Toys spread out everywhere. I could see only my hands covered with smooth black leather gloves and occasionally my feet if I looked down as I worked through the rooms. I pulled drawers open and moved clothes and books out of the way, unable to find what I was looking for.

Then I heard the sound from the other room, the front door slamming shut from the tight metal spring, a sharp cracking noise as the cheap wooden frame hit the house. It reminded me of my own door back in Stroud, a sound that doesn't leave you easily. I held still and waited, somehow knowing she'd come back to her bedroom.

The floorboards creaked as she came closer then stepped around the corner. She jumped back with a stifled scream then reached out and slapped at my face. My hand blocked hers.

"What the fuck are you doing here?" she said. She looked at my gloves then her dresser drawers all open, bras and underwear hanging out of them. "What the hell? What are you—"

My hands were around her throat before another word could come out. "Where's the necklace?" I said. I finally recognized her. I knew who she was and it hurt me to be hurting her. She'd been so sweet, so open with me recently. The blue waitress dress smelled of grease from the cafe as I continued to strangle her.

She gasped for air as her face contorted and she tried to claw at me with her long fingernails. Her brown hair was pulled back in a ponytail and for a moment I remembered thinking she was pretty once as she sat another beer in front of me. Her face was turning red, blood vessels bursting beneath the skin.

"Where's the goddam necklace, Shawna?" I released my right hand, pulled it back and slapped her face.

Her hand pointed and I turned and dragged her with me to the tall vanity between the two windows. I wrapped my left arm around her neck and began to pull open each drawer and throw it onto the bed. The fourth drawer made a clunking sound as it hit and I looked in to see the small wooden jewelry box. After flipping the lid open to see the rings, earrings and necklaces I picked the whole box up and slid it into the deep pocket of my coat.

I was in constant motion as the sweat began to pour out of me. The dream wouldn't end. Through the eyes of the man, I saw everything. I felt everything. I knew everything, except for who he was. I saw the fear in her eyes, the desperation of just wanting me to leave, of wanting him to leave.

I dragged her into the living room and threw her to the floor then sat on top of her, my hands back to her throat as her face grew more and more red. Her hands went from clawing at my face to trying to pry my hands away and back again. There was a moment when I saw in her eyes that she realized this was it, she wasn't getting out of this alive or seeing her daughter again and she just let her hands drop to the floor.

My grip loosened and I looked at her. In the dream I tried to take control, to move my body and leave that place but had no effect. I was only a passenger, a voyeur. The dream could be something happening in this moment or was still months away. There was no way to know. But it was vivid and real, bright in my mind and his touches registered with my brain as real physical contact.

"Don't have any more fight in you?" I let my hands move from her neck down to her chest and began rubbing her breasts. "That's a good girl. No need to struggle. Gotta say, I finally see why he was drawn to you. I always just saw you as a little slut not worth the time of day."

I pulled her blue dress up over her waist and tore her panties in half and let them fall to the side. After loosening my pants I pulled myself out and pushed inside her in a violent motion as she lay there and cried. Once or twice she raised an arm and tried to hit me, to push me off, but I was stronger and she had no energy left.

As I was thrusting on top of her I put my hands back to her throat and tightened the grip and watched her eyes as life left them. I finished as her final breath was drawn and never exhaled and I remained there just looking at her before removing myself from her. I refastened my pants and stood up over her and looked around the room then down at the oval rug her body was lying on. I rotated her sideways after moving the small coffee table out of the way and kicking some toys across the room and rolled the rug until her body was wrapped up inside.

I checked my pocket to make sure the jewelry box was still there then stepped to the mirror in the hallway. She'd gotten a pair of fingernails down the side of my face and I was bleeding.

After checking outside to make sure no other cars were there, I dragged the rug through the kitchen to the back door to where my car was parked, out of sight from the front of the house and the road. I rolled the rug and her body into the trunk and closed the lid quietly then drove off.

I sat up in bed. My tee shirt was soaked through and the blanket was on the floor. I wiped my face with my hands and looked at the alarm clock, 3:15 in the morning. I was used to the dreams, as much as one can be, but had never seen anything like this. For a moment I tried to tell myself it was just a nightmare but I knew it wasn't. I'd seen it before. The images had never left me since the day beside the old church.

I knew I wouldn't sleep again tonight so I got up then realized the front of my shorts were wet, his actions having taken over my own body and impulses. My body still covered in sweat, I stepped into the shower and turned the water on, the cold blast shaking me fully awake. I wanted a drink, needed one. The violence I'd witnessed couldn't be forgotten or blocked out and I knew that it would be with me forever, haunting me.

I dried myself then pulled a clean pair of boxers from the dresser. Downstairs, a double shot of whisky poured into a glass, I sat in the recliner and stared at the ceiling and allowed myself to go through the dream, moving it slowly through my mind as I'd learned to do.

"Who are you?" I remembered the cuts across the man's face and the moment of looking in the mirror. It took only a second to realize I knew that face.

Chapter 30

I HAD THE windows down, my left arm hanging out. I had no errands to run or things to buy, I just needed to get out, to get a look. I made the small curve on Highway 10 where it became Main Street in downtown Jay. Letting off the gas pedal in third gear, the pickup slowed as I passed the long single story building on my right, a red canvas awning lining the entire front of the store. I pushed the gas again once past the building and made the left turn then three rights to wrap around the roads surrounding the big gray county court clerk's building then slowed as I passed the store now on my left.

Jared Walker. I was sure I saw him in there, standing behind the counter as he always did. But I also knew my brain might just be telling me he was there. After the curve back onto Highway 10 I sped up and kept going away from downtown. I could have stopped and gone in. I'd known him since I was a boy shopping in his store with my Grandpa. But it was different now. I'd seen what he had done, what he was capable of.

I heard the siren behind me and glanced in the rear view mirror as the white car was speeding up behind me then quickly slowed and turned onto 1st Street. I watched it disappear in the mirror and I kept going. The second car came toward me from north of town and the pitch of the siren changed as it passed me, the sharp, bright tone turning to a dissonant reflection of itself. I'd learned about that in school once, the way a sound changes as it passes you, but couldn't remember what it was called.

I checked my mirrors then slowed the truck and made a u-turn in the road and went back the other way. I made the right onto 1st Street. Another sheriff's vehicle came up and sped past me on the wrong side of the road. I wanted to turn around, to leave the area. But I was drawn to follow them.

I could see the flashing lights up ahead and tried to not slow, but wouldn't everyone slow down? Looking to my left I saw the police cars all pulled onto the lawn of a run down house, the sheriff's deputies going in and out of the front door. Just as I went past the house I heard the screen door slam shut to the frame. The cracking sound repeated in my head as I matched it to my dream from only a few hours earlier.

The sweats hit instantly and I felt dizzy. I accelerated enough to not draw attention and drove three streets over and stopped. After turning the engine off I leaned my head back as my vision began to pull in, darkness coming from all around until I blacked out and began to dream again.

I knew who he was now and dreamt from a different perspective, seeing him, watching him. His face was clear to me now. He was driving the car, black leather gloves still on his hands. The chrome Buick logo shone in the middle of the steering wheel. The headlights barely threw enough light in front of the sedan as it barreled northwest of town then many miles later veered left onto a smaller road. The terrain on the right side began to rise, the trees elevated on the small hill. Then there was water on the left, the pooling of the Neosho River. Several large homes, expensive for the area, sat on the far side with personal boat docks and tall garages to hold luxury RV's.

The car pulled off the road at a gas station, the lights out and pumps locked up. He got out and went to the payphone on the side of the building, deposited a quarter and pressed the buttons to dial.

"It's me."

The words came from everywhere, echoing around me. I spun in the dream, my mind searching for the voice on the other end of the phone as Jared Walker listened, but the sound didn't come.

"It didn't go like we discussed, like you told me it would."

He was silent as I strained for the other voice to be heard.

"I don't know what to say. She got home while I was there and she attacked me."

The words didn't line up with what had happened, lies covering up the truth.

"It just… it just happened. I had to shut her up, she was screaming. She's dead."

He paused and listened then turned and looked at his car. *"In my trunk."*

No matter how hard I tried the other voice wouldn't come.

"No blood. I just gotta put her somewhere, somewhere far away from me."

My head began to hurt inside the dream and the sweat drained from me.

"Yeah, I know where that is. You can make sure nobody looks there?"

Back in the car he drove another fifteen minutes then finally turned onto a small dirt road on the left that wound through the woods until it passed a small marshy area at the edge of the lake. He got out and opened the trunk then pulled the rolled up rug out of the back and across the dirt and gravel until he was at the edge of the marsh. He unrolled the rug to reveal Shawna's body, her skirt still up over her stomach, one shoe missing and her eyes still open. Without a moment's thought or even looking around he picked the body up by an arm and a leg and swung it out into the shallow marsh. He picked up a long branch that had fallen to the ground and pushed her further out and under until she was submerged and obscured by the tall grass.

With the rug rolled up and back in the trunk, he pulled away onto the road and retraced his route back toward

town. He stopped again at a house that had seen its better days thirty years earlier, and even then was nothing to
look at. The outside was lined with torn tarpaper and no
windows were left in any of the frames. The front door
was broken in half and swung open.

He pulled the rug out of the trunk and carried it up
onto the cement block step and pushed it through the
open window beside the door until it fell to the floor
inside.

Chapter 31

I SPENT TWO days inside the house, shades pulled and doors locked. I didn't answer the phone. At one point I became worried that Colleen would drive over to check on me, but I knew she had a lot of work to do at the courthouse in Tulsa so maybe she was preoccupied. I didn't want to see anybody, or talk to anybody.

The television was on nonstop and I switched between the channels from Tulsa and Oklahoma City for any news about what had happened. It wasn't until the late news the second day before it was even mentioned, although briefly. A young woman from Delaware County was missing, her mother and young daughter very worried about her. Foul play is suspected based on the condition her house was found in. They said her name. Shawna Tate. Then they showed an older photo of her where she looks much younger, happier. I looked down at my hand and thought of her warm skin touching mine so briefly as she stood to walk away from the booth where I'd sat alone that morning. She'd been sweet, pleasant. Even through the saturated smells of grease and old coffee, I'd inhaled the slightest hint of her shampoo, lilac, I thought.

I knew nothing more about her than what the news was now reporting. Raised in Jay, worked at the diner for a few years now. But I did know what had happened to her, and that was something I could not call in to the tip line and report. They say it's anonymous, but what if it isn't. What if a state police cruiser showed up in front of my house. What if they thought I did it.

The third day I finally ventured out to the workshop to figure out where I'd left the latest rebuild project. The tools felt good and helped to distract me from Shawna Tate. I spent most of the day working through the parts, cleaning and organizing them, seeing which were reusable and which needed replacement.

At six o'clock the house phone rang, which also rang the old receiver in the workshop and I answered.

"You comin'?" Benton's voice boomed through the line.

"What's that?"

"Dinner, old man. It's Thursday."

"So it is." The days had slipped past me and I couldn't even say on what day the dream had come, only that it had been the morning after my day at the lake with Colleen. Was it a date? I didn't know.

"So, you comin'?"

I stared at the motor then the grease covering my hands.

I had the easy out. But I also saw opportunity.

"Yeah. Gimme fifteen. Maybe twenty," I said. "Wait a few and order my usual."

The line clicked as he hung up without any farewells as was his custom.

With the abrasive Lava soap I washed my hands as best I could then went into the house and changed clothes. Not much longer after that I was sitting in the booth facing Benton just as my chicken fried steak and a tall glass of beer were brought out to me.

"You forgot?"

"Yeah. Was into a rebuild on a New Holland and time got away from me."

"It happens. You're old."

"True."

We ate as I planned my chess game, the subtleness I would need to try to get information out of my only friend. I feared it would be suspicious to blatantly ask about the investigation.

I was about to begin, to ask my opening question in the vaguest interrogation ever when the waitress walked over to the table and filled our waters.

"You trying to find our Shawna?" she said.

Benton sat his knife and fork down and turned in his seat to look up at her.

"We're doin' everything we can, Daisy," he said. "Ain't much to go on but the forensics guys out of Tulsa came in and went over everything. No prints that didn't belong there. Only weird thing was a missing rug from the living room."

I wondered if my jaw was hanging open or if it only felt like it.

"Her mom is going through everything with the detectives to figure out if anything is missing but it's such a goddamn mess in there, don't know if she'll be able to tell."

"Got any suspects?" Daisy said.

He shook his head. "It's an open investigation, Daisy," he said. "But I'll tell ya we don't have any names yet. Hell, until we find her and know what happened I don't know if we can come up with a suspect."

"Well you boys just keep doin' the great job you're doin'. And tell ya what, next round is on me."

The waitress walked away as Benton turned back in his seat and continued eating his gristly steak. She had done my work for me.

"So no suspects, huh?"

"Just heard me, didn't ya," he said without raising his head from his food.

And with that I abandoned my interrogation.

Back at the house I was too wound up to relax and didn't want any more beer. I went to the workshop and continued cataloging the parts. I'd been at it for over two hours and never heard the tires on the gravel driveway in front of the house and jumped when someone walked in through the partially open door to my right.

"Didn't mean to scare you."

She looked amazing but would probably roll her eyes if I told her. Blue jeans and a loose white v-neck tee-shirt, a brown leather jacket over the top of it. She could have stepped out of 1956 but fit right here in 1996, too.

"Was worth it," I said.

She glanced back through the door then walked over to me and I knew to put the tool down and face her. There was a seriousness in her expression, but still warmth. She stopped right in front of me, inches away.

"There was something I wanted to do the other day at the lake," she said.

"Was there?"

A gentle nod. "Or that I wanted you to do."

I could only look at her, drink her in and smell the sweetness off of her skin so close, my body frozen.

Her hands came up to my face and I felt them against the roughness of my stubble. Eyes met after she worked her gaze slowly from my chin to lips, nose then finally looked at me, into me. My head was cloudy as if I'd drank too much but I knew I hadn't.

It could have been seconds or hours we stood there. It was a game of chicken only with lips instead of cars on an empty road. Who would give first, pull to the side to avoid being hit.

I wrapped my arm around her back and pulled her into me as I'd dreamt of doing for more than twenty years, as I'd wanted to outside her car two weeks ago and again at the lake. Then I kissed her, our lips touching for the first time since high school. A second first kiss. It was familiar and new at the same time, less fumbling and uncertainty. No fear of parents walking in the front door.

Her body gave in to mine and I held her as we kissed. Lips parted and I felt her tongue on mine, taking her into me as wet met wet, moving around in their odd but beautiful dance.

I wanted her. More than I'd ever wanted anything. Any cliche you could think of was appropriate and would be rendered original and creative by the desire I had for her. With her body against mine, she noticed my desire and her eyes opened wide as her hand moved to the front of my jeans and we both felt my body tremble as she touched me through the thick denim.

She pushed away from me then turned and walked out the door, and I followed. Through the back door of the house she began taking clothes off every few steps, her jacket was left on a chair in the kitchen, shoes in the living room. The tee-shirt was on the bottom of the stairwell railing and the jeans were gone before we got to the top. She walked into my bedroom then turned to me while releasing her bra behind her back and let it fall off of her left arm to the floor.

As I unbuttoned my shirt she moved to me and took over, releasing each button then running her hand beneath the fabric across my chest until it hung loose and she pushed it off of my shoulders.

I had feared that I would compare every move, every kiss, every touch, to that night so long ago but everything was new. The memories weren't replaced but added on to. We made love, held each other then made love again. I couldn't get enough of her. It was the darkest hours of the night before we relaxed into each other, my arm wrapped around her holding her tight to me. Bodies were spent and exhausted and sweaty. There was a natural silence in the room, only the sounds of our breathing amplified in the darkness.

Her fingers gently scratched my chest in small circles.

"I love you, Wesley."

The words moved slowly through the air and into my mind. At the same time I smiled and had a flashing moment of fear.

"You're not supposed to."

Chapter 32

I PARKED MY pickup halfway off the dirt road and we looked out the side window at the old church. The building hadn't changed much over the years other than a couple pieces of corrugated tin from the roof were gone.

"Tell me all about it," Colleen said.

She sat in the middle of the seat, her hand on my knee as she had back in high school. It had been three months since that first night together again and barely a day went by without seeing her, or at least talking on the phone if she was stuck working in the city.

"It was my private place, a safe haven," I said. "Whenever I had a few minutes to get away, this is where I went."

Out of the truck, I took her right hand and helped her across the rutted ditch that ran between the road and the pasture. Indian Paintbrush grew everywhere and I smiled but saved that story.

"Was it like an imaginary land for you?"

"No, nothing like that. It was just a place away from everything else. I never pretended it was anything it wasn't."

I pulled the end of the long gate open then closed it again after we'd stepped through.

"Things weren't great at home most of the time, so I'd come here."

"Would your brother come with you?"

"No." I thought of the hot day spent with Jake at the church. "Nobody's ever been here with me before."

I stepped around to the side and looked into the large opening. The tree was still there. The top pushing against the roof and had likely caused some of the tin to fall off. The trunk was now more than a foot around.

"You're smiling," she said. "I don't see that too often."

"This was a sapling last time I was here. Wasn't sure it would make it."

"Looks like it's doing fine." She took my hand. "But what about you?"

"What do you mean?"

"You know what I mean," she said. "I don't think we drove two hours to see an old church." I knew she didn't intend to minimize what this place meant to me but she was right. I needed somewhere I felt safe to talk to her.

I stepped into the darkness away from the opening, to the corner where I'd sat the night I found out about my brother. Away from the sunlight outside I felt more comfortable, more hidden. My stomach was tightening and I was sure my heart was beating faster as the nervousness overtook me. It was something I needed to do if I was going to make this work, if I was going to be with her.

"I began to have dreams when my mother was sick," I said. "They weren't normal dreams."

They'd been my secret my entire life except for the brief time with Grandpa. Even my father never knew the extent of them. As scared as I was to share it with someone I was relieved to have someone to talk to about it. If she stayed, at least. If she ran, or even just pulled back the slightest bit, I'd know my mistake and return to my hibernation.

"What do you mean?" she said.

The three feet between us stretched to feel like twenty then a hundred as my mind tried to wrap itself around what I was preparing to tell her.

I shook my head. "I didn't figure it out until years later. When I asked Grandpa about it he told me the truth," I said. "The first dream I had, at least the first I remembered, was of my mother making tea in the kitchen at our old house. She could barely walk at the time. The disease had torn her apart. But I saw here there, standing at the sink with the kettle and her favorite cup."

Colleen stepped around me inside the church so she could see my face, my eyes distant and damp. The air felt like it had chilled though I knew it hadn't.

"I remember everything from it," I said. "The way she dipped the tea in and out of the water, her precise movements even in a deteriorated condition. I'd seen her make tea a thousand times but I never thought about that box. That damned box."

"What are you talking about, Wesley?"

"She poured from it onto a spoon then mixed it into her tea, then put the box back in the cabinet under the sink." My voice was staggering, fading. "I was too innocent to realize it then, that night as it was happening. And I was too stupid to understand why my father reacted the way he did when I told him about it years later." I stepped forward and leaned my forehead against the wall of the church. The cold sharp stone felt good as it jabbed into my skin, my penance.

"Larry found her," I said. "I was still sleeping. By the time I got up she was lying in bed. Dead, cold and stiff."

"Wesley-" her voice trailed off.

"The rat poison must have acted faster than she thought it would. She wasn't able to get back up the stairs to bed and died on the bathroom floor. I can't even remember what the last conversation I had with her was. Something small and meaningless, I'm sure."

Colleen didn't speak and didn't move for the longest time. The silence wasn't uncomfortable, though. I felt she could sense the moment and what I needed. At just the right time she stepped to me, her arms going around my body in the most perfect embrace as I told her more. My dream about Larry and Baby Lily. I told her about Grandpa. I didn't know how much she understood or even accepted but she didn't run. She didn't pull away.

The sun was sending splashes of light across the outside of the old church by the time we left, filtered through the trees across the gravel road. I had told her more than I had even planned, getting easier with each story.

Back at my house I pulled out the bible and watched as she flipped through the pages, her right forefinger occasionally running along a line of my grandfather's writing. She would ask questions sometimes, and other times just shake her head and continue.

The fireplace was warming the living room as we sat on the sofa, the bible now put away. She sipped from a glass of red wine and I had a thick, dark beer.

"How can any one person handle that?" she said. "The knowing, the pain?"

I put my arm up for her to move closer to me and I wrapped myself around her and pulled her in even closer. "I've read that bible more than a dozen times and have no idea. Somehow he learned to deal with it."

"Not just him," she said. "You've been having these dreams for most of your life."

My mind went to Shawna Tate. It was the most important story and the one I hadn't told her. It was hard enough for me to know who had killed her. I didn't want her to know. It was too real right now. All the other stories read like history.

"It's difficult sometimes," I said.

The fire popped and a spark floated up into the air and disappeared. I moved back and forth between feeling relieved for having told her, a first in my life, and concern that she'd get scared and leave.

Her hand reached up and held mine as I stroked her hair.

"Thank you," she said. Her voice was soft and sweet and

exactly what I needed to hear at that moment.

I felt my body tense, as I knew what I was about to say and felt I couldn't keep myself from it. "That night we had on your living room floor."

"I remember," she whispered. I was certain I saw her blush but it might have been the reflection of the fire on her skin but either way it made her even more beautiful than she already was.

That night was more than twenty years earlier but I could trace every moment in my mind, how we lay on the floor in her home and made love for the first time.

"It was maybe a week after that night," I paused.

"What?"

"After the dream I knew I couldn't be with you, I couldn't take that chance."

Her body tightened beside me and I could feel her fighting to keep from sitting up and looking at me.

"I loved you so much," I said. "I loved you too much to let it happen." I inhaled deeply and looked up at the ceiling, looking for my next words in the plaster cracks above though I'd been rehearsing them for a week if not years. "You were older and even more beautiful than when we were teenagers. You were driving a car with the windows down, the wind blowing your hair. And a baby girl was in the back, strapped into a car seat."

She began to sit up and I applied just enough pressure to her with my arm to let her know not to.

"You never saw the truck coming," I said. "You, and our little girl-"

She pushed against my arm and sat up. As she turned to me I saw the tears streaming down her cheeks.

"How do you know about that?" she said. "How could you know about that and not tell me?"

I stared at her. "I-" I couldn't find my words.

"I haven't told anyone here what happened," she said. "It was just too painful. How do you know?"

"What are you saying... you had a girl?"

"Yes, I had a girl. She wasn't yours and mine," she said. "She was mine. Until she was eight months old and we were leaving home to go to the grocery store. The red truck came across the center line as I was pulling out."

"Colleen—"

"I was unconscious for hours. When I woke up Bryan was there, just sitting in the chair beside my hospital bed," she said. "His face was pale. I was barely awake and he told me our little girl was gone, she was dead."

She leaned forward into my arms and I held her. Feeling her body against me made me wonder how I had gone so long without her.

"We didn't have anyone to tell here," she said. "My parents are gone. I never even planned on coming back."

"Why did you come back?"

Tears rolled down her cheeks.

"For you."

She gently kissed my lips and I was lost in her.

Chapter 33

I SLEPT IN the recliner, the living room being the warmest room in the house. An old quilt my grandmother had made before I was born was covering me. My arms became heavy as the sweat coated my skin.

"I need your help."

I was outside the man this time, watching Jared Walker make the call instead of seeing through his eyes. I struggled inside the dream, forcing myself to control what I was seeing and hearing.

"She's dead."

I knew the call was short and pushed my mind forward, trying to get closer to the phone, to hear the voice on the other end before it was over.

"In my trunk."

"...the hell..."

There it was, the voice, but too muffled to hear everything it was saying.

"No blood. I just gotta put her somewhere, somewhere far away from me."

"... dump the bitch in...Neosho...the marsh on the..." it faded out and I leaned into the dream. *"...where that is?"*

"Yeah, I know where that is. You can make sure nobody looks there?"

"Not your..."

I sat up in the chair, hitting the wooden handle on the side to bring it upright. I'd had the dream several times since that first night and had never been able to hear the voice or what it said before.

I hadn't been in the store for years. From what I'd heard I wasn't the only one. Wal-Mart had pulled customers away from the local shop and left it hurting. The small downtown area of Jay had become a collection of empty storefronts mixed with a few small businesses still clinging on, always hoping for that next customer to come in. Paint was faded and peeling on the buildings, awnings once bright and colorful were worn pastel pieces of canvas. Except for the Delaware County Mercantile. The awning was bright red and the lettering along the edge crisp white. Windows were clean and current merchandise was displayed in the windows.

I watched from inside my truck as a man I didn't recognize came down the sidewalk and stopped at the door to the store. His hair was greasy and his clothes looked like they hadn't been washed in months. After looking each way he went into the store. I waited, wanting the shop owner to myself. A few minutes later the dirty man came out and turned down the side street away from the square, his steps having more purpose now, a small paper bag held in both hands.

Stopping at the door I read the sign, Delaware County Mercantile and Hunting Supplies and then pushed through.

I heard the voice before getting sight of the man.

"Wes Hudson, is that you?"

Turning I saw him as he stood up from unboxing items behind the counter.

"Sure is, Jared," I said. "How's business?"

"Oh, could be better. I've cut back on a lot of the perishables cause everyone's going down the street now. But I still get some regulars through for clothes," Jared said. "The hunting supplies keep me open, really. The big stores don't carry a lot of that so it brings people in."

"Good to hear," I said.

"If it weren't for the diner doing good I'd probably have to shut the store down."

"What's that?" It was a small town. How could I have not known what he was talking about.

"Beasley's. I own that, too, you know. Bought it, oh, fifteen years ago now."

Small pieces clicked.

"Anything you lookin' for?" Jared said.

"Just thought I'd stop in. Been way too long," I said. "I find myself holed up in the house and never get out."

I wandered through the aisles of home goods and around the circular racks of camouflage shirts and jackets. One corner was devoted to the hunting equipment. I looked through the glass counter at the rows of rifles and shot-guns and on a lower shelf the sleek black pistols and silver revolvers. Hanging on the wall behind the counter were bows and crossbows and the head of a large buck with an arrow right through the head.

"Nice gear, ain't it?" Jared came up behind me. "A lotta guys gettin' into the crossbows now. I don't understand it. Give me a good thirty-aught-six any day."

"Never been much into guns." I thought about my brother's M1911 sitting in my drawer at home that I cleaned once a month. "That crossbow is pretty nice though."

As I roamed the aisles I stopped and stared at the tall fishing rods lined up. Before I could give it another thought I called out. "Jared, you know what, there is something I've been wanting."

He helped me pick out a pair of rods and everything I'd need to get started. I knew I could go out to Wal-Mart and buy the same stuff for cheaper, but felt the need to be here, to be with him and absorb what I could.

I paid for the gear and as I was picking up the bags in one hand paused. "Say, didn't a waitress from Beasley's go missing or something?"

It was probably my imagination, just me wanting to read more into every movement the man made, but I was sure I saw the slightest hesitation, a fraction of a second of reaction from him.

"Yeah. Shawna Tate. Happened a few months ago."

"What do you mean it happened?"

There it was. Another glimpse of a pause.

"Just that she went missing is what I meant," he said.

"Mmm hmm. Damn shame," I said. "She waited on me and Benton quite regularly there."

Back in my truck I sat and held my hands on my lap, trying to slow the shakes from spending so much time talking to the man I knew had taken the life from the young woman. I glanced over at the long green fishing rods sticking up from the floorboard and out the passenger window of the truck. If the sheriff and state police couldn't catch him, I could.

Chapter 34

WE'D BEEN DRINKING for two hours on the front porch of
my house. It was always my house. I didn't think she had
anything against me going to hers, but we just never did.
I would probably clash with her interior design. An old
farm boy always with grease under his fingernails, more
comfortable in overalls than khakis, contrasted against
what I imagined to be a clean modern home with prints
of famous paintings on the walls and the good knives in a
wooden block on the counter, not thrown into a drawer
like mine. I'd wondered several times what it would look
like, me standing there in her house. I pictured white
carpet with white walls and white furniture. My presence
alone would cause a disturbance in the feng shui that
could lead to a natural disaster.

I felt I had enough of a buzz, just enough to loosen me
up, but hopefully not so much I slurred my words or ram-

bled on and lost my train of thought. Sometimes I thought I caught her looking at me like I was a curiosity, a piece of kitsch on a glass shelf in an otherwise normal home. But when I'd look again she was just smiling at me.

She would ask about the dreams occasionally, always a little hesitant like she was intruding into a world that wasn't her own. It would take me a while to get used to talking about them again, and sometimes I just wasn't in the mood. I expected her to ask about Shawna Tate but she never did. Perhaps she never thought about it, or maybe she just didn't want to know about something that recent, that ongoing.

There weren't many nights we were apart. She would drive into Tulsa or Oklahoma City to meet with other lawyers about cases she was taking on, sometimes not getting back until late. Even then my phone would usually ring. 'I'm coming past your house'. And I'd always say to stop and come in, usually waiting up just in case.

"You ever want to travel?" She'd asked me the same thing back in high school. I hadn't wanted to back then. I hadn't seen the point in it.

"Maybe."

"Where?"

"France. Normandy."

"I can see that," she said. "I've been to Paris but haven't been to Normandy."

I could tell she wanted me to say 'let's go', to commit to something larger than I'd ever done before while sitting on my small town porch, drunk on grocery store wine. And I almost did. I wanted to but something inside me still kept her at a distance where I could. It was a push and pull of physical and emotional consciousness. I wanted her and I loved her and at the same time I still felt I couldn't be with her. That every moment with her was putting her in danger.

"Grandpa was in the trenches in France in World War I," I said. "And Dad was supposed to be on Omaha Beach. His buddies from high school who enlisted with him died on D-Day running up the sand. Grandpa had dreamed that Dad would die on that beach and tried to keep him from going but Dad never believed in the dreams."

I thought I saw that look from her again. The sideways glance at a strange item in a glass case.

"Dad was at Fort Hood finishing up basic training and was preparing to head to Europe," I said. "There was an accident on a ropes course when one of the lines broke and sent Dad and another boy falling thirty feet to the ground. Dad broke his leg. The other boy broke his neck and died a few days later."

"Oh my God," she said.

"After a few weeks in recovery, Dad was given an honorable discharge. His buddies went to Normandy and never came home. It was maybe a year later that he found the bible and was reading through it. He found where Grandpa had written about seeing him and the other boy die on the beach. After a lifetime of not believing in the dreams, he couldn't forgive Grandpa, like he'd somehow kept him from going over, or maybe thought he'd known about the accident and didn't warn him. It was like he wanted to die on that beach, that it would have given his life meaning, or maybe he thought he could have made it, even saved his friends."

"Did you ever talk to your Dad about it?"

"No. Grandpa told me most of it shortly before he died," I said. "So I've wanted to see where Grandpa was in the trenches, and for some reason the beach that my Dad wanted to go to so badly."

"Then you should."

We talked about where she'd been. It wasn't a lot of places but far more than I had ever dreamed of going. Some of the travels were with college friends, then a honeymoon in Italy later. Work had taken her to Toronto several times when the firm she'd worked for had a client with offices in Canada.

The drive into Texas with my grandpa shortly before he'd died was the furthest I'd been from Delaware County.

We moved inside when the chill in the air went from comfortable to cold and she took her usual place beside me on the small sofa. She curled into me, her face in the nape of my neck and I inhaled her warm red wine breath.

"I'm doing my best." I spoke softly but the words were still too loud in the noiseless room.

"You're doing great."

Being alone had felt natural because it was all I knew. I would imagine what it would be like with someone else in the house, and believed it would be oppressive, but it was probably my own psyche working to rationalize the decisions I had made. The months with Colleen now had fractured those thoughts and each day with her, each night with her, the spiderweb of cracks spread but hadn't yet shattered and fallen to the ground. There was still a hesitation in my actions that I felt and was sure she could see and feel as well. She always instigated anything physical and I would follow, happily.

She knew what she was doing with the physical, the sex. By comparison to me anyone would, though. I never asked and she never offered any information about her past. I knew of her husband, of course, and always believed she had boyfriends in college. I had been her first, I knew that at least. Several times she'd rented movies to watch and it didn't take many for me to notice a theme in her selections. I didn't know if she was trying to give me subliminal instructions or just enjoyed the films.

There were no movies tonight, just her and me. I could feel her body move with her breath as she was wrapped up in me and I wanted to kiss her. Then as if she had heard my thoughts she raised her head and took her lips to mine. Every time we kissed I felt like that high school boy in front of the fireplace again, with the wonder and awe of having a girl who wanted to touch me.

Her face pulled away from mine and she looked at me, our faces inches apart. The moment had weight and lingered, never feeling too long in her eyes.

"I love you," she said.

She had said the words before but I had never repeated them. It wasn't for a lack of feeling the emotion but for fear of expressing it.

"I love you, Colleen."

Her lips were on mine again. Of course I loved her. I always had.

Chapter 35

I WOKE UP with only a sheet half covering my naked body and looked over to see Colleen asleep beside me. The sheet was wrapped around her, her knees pulled up almost fetal. It was a moment I wanted to live in, to stay in all day or longer. Mornings waking up next to her were the best mornings. More than once I'd opened my eyes to find her head on my chest, her still asleep. Other times she was already awake and stroking my skin, waiting for me to wake up and make love to her.

Her eyes opened with a few blinks and she smiled when she saw me staring at her.

"What." She didn't pose it as a question.

"You're gorgeous."

She blushed and rolled her eyes. "I'm old."

"Yeah. But you're also gorgeous."

She was on top of me a moment later and lips connected

again. Then I was inside her. It was fast and rough as she moved her body against mine. She rolled us over and pulled me tighter, harder, moving her body more quickly beneath me. Our sex had been soft, it had been making love as I had imagined it in my naive world. This morning it was different, primal.

"Harder," she said, her breath getting short.

I tried to follow her, to keep up. As I thrust I felt the darkness come into my eyes and then could see only Shawna Tate, held down on her living room floor with those black leather gloves. Jared Walker on top of her, forcing her, choking the life out of her.

I pushed away, to try to get off Colleen and she grabbed me, pulled me in closer. The dream stayed with me and I was unable to break away, her legs wrapped around me. In the same moment I wanted to stop and I wanted to stay inside her and I let the darkness win. I moved with more strength as the sweat formed and dripped from our bodies. My hand moved up her naked chest to her neck, my fingers spread out around her throat and pushed down and held it for a moment as her body constricted then I pulled my hand back and went to her face, my fingers going into her mouth. I raised her left leg up to my shoulder to push in deeper as she was driven to climax and I finished with her.

I rolled off her and out of bed, pulling on a pair of boxer shorts then leaving the bedroom. Downstairs in the kitchen I poured a glass of water from the sink and stared out the back window. The two worlds had never crossed before and it frightened me. I didn't think I was able to hurt her, to hurt anyone, but I had hardly been able to control myself, stop myself, when my hand went to her throat just as Jared Walker had done.

"You okay?"

I'd heard her come down the stairs softly, cautiously.

"Yeah."

"Anything you want to talk about?"

"No." I still could not tell her about that dream, about Shawna Tate.

"If you ever do."

She filled the kettle and put it on for coffee as I forced my mood to change, to come back to the moment. Eggs were made along with toast, and we sat and talked about nothing, the dream still present in my mind. After we cleaned our plates off the table I took her arm and pulled her into me and held her. It was a silent apology for my abruptness, my lack of sharing, and one she seemed to understand.

"Thank you," she said.

"I have a surprise for you."

"Oh?"

"Let's get showered and dressed. Nothing fancy."

"You don't own anything fancy."

"True."

Thirty minutes later we were in my truck, her still wet hair hanging loose with the wind blowing it around. I wanted to watch her but had to drive. The fishing rods were in the bed of the truck along with the tackle boxes.

I pulled to a stop outside a gas station and she ran in for a box of bait. I sat in the truck and looked around then at the pay phone on the end of the building. I hadn't been out this way since the dream, since the murder, and never noticed the pay phone until I'd seen Jared Walker use it.

Colleen climbed back in the truck and I pulled onto the road. A few minutes later we passed the tar paper house on the left. I felt like a hypocrite, refusing to tell her about the dream but bringing her into it anyway without her knowledge.

"Where we going?" she said. "There's some great fishing closer to town. Or we could go to the lake."

"Didn't think about that." I tried to play it off. "Grandpa used to go out here so I thought we'd give it a try."

"I didn't know he fished. You not have any of his old gear?" She turned in her seat to look in the bed of the truck at the clean new plastic boxes and unused rods and reels.

"He got rid of them when he got older and couldn't go anymore." Grandpa never threw anything away.

I pulled off the road and down the trail as if I'd driven it a hundred times, the way mapped out in my mind from reliving it over and over.

"Here?" She grabbed one of the rods and tackle boxes and looked out over the marshy water. "Doesn't seem like great fishing."

"He swore by it, but maybe he didn't actually like catching them," I said.

She showed me how to tie the line on and then handled a worm like a pro, poking it then winding it onto the hook. Once our rods were ready, we cast out into the water, trying to avoid the roots and grass. Her hook was only in the water a few minutes when it got a tug then she was pulling a smallmouth bass out.

"Guess your grandpa was right," she said.

I was just as surprised as she was. "Yup. He usually was."

She put the fish in the cooler and got her hook ready again. I was working my line over to the right, winding it in and sending it out again. I knew my chances were low, but I wanted to try. To see if I could find her. Find anything that would lead to her.

Two more were caught on Colleen's hook while I continued my blind and secret search. Several times she tried to get me to move away from the tall grass but I persisted. "Fish like to be in the grass," I told her.

I cast again and let the hook sink deeper before beginning to pull it back in. I turned the reel with its soft clicking sound. It made three rotations then stopped. I tugged on the rod and the line went tight, caught on something under the water. My heart raced and I began to sweat.

"You stuck?" Colleen said.

"Yeah. Think so." I kept tugging, trying to pull something up, my mind going crazy thinking about what I might pull out of the water.

Colleen kept her calm with her own rod, lightly casting it back into the water while still watching me. "Give it some slack, let the line move in the water to free itself."

I didn't want it to free itself.

"Seriously, Wesley. Let some line out or just cut it and start over. There's too many roots over—" She stepped forward to the water when her line went hard. "Got another one." She began to work the pole to bring the fish in.

I kept pulling on my line, finally letting some out to try and loosen up what I hoped was on the hook from its dark watery grave and come to the surface. I wound the line in then gave a gentle tug again and finally felt movement, the slightest give to offer hope.

"This one's really fighting," she said. Her fish still wasn't out of the water. It would be her fifth.

"Keep it up." More movement from my line. I pulled then let loose a little and pulled again. I was thinking about how I'd react, not knowing what it was at first then shock. One of us would drive back up to the gas station to make the phone call and we'd wait for the police to arrive. Another tug and whatever it was moved a couple of feet. I stepped closer to the water, my boots getting wet. More movement then a big give and for a moment something dark appeared above the water then sunk below again, taking my hook with it.

I was in up to my ankles now, releasing and pulling, trying to not break the line. I didn't know what this would mean, what evidence they could find to catch Jared Walker. But it was something. My chest was tight from holding my breath.

I pulled again and it gave way. It didn't bounce on the water like the fish did. It flew out with the tension of the fishing line and landed at my feet just below the shallow water I was standing in, hidden from sight again. With the sounds of Colleen still fighting her fish off to my left I leaned over and reached into the water that had been disturbed, dirt floating around, obscuring what lay beneath.

I followed the fishing line until my hand touched it and I pulled the line up, hesitating for a moment before bringing it above the water then raised it up. On the hook was a rubber bicycle inner tube. All my emotions began to bubble up from inside, from anger to frustration and finally I just laughed.

"Wesley, look at this," Colleen said.

My attention left the inner tube and I looked over at her to see the fish she'd reeled in.

At the end of the line she held dangling in the air was a piece of a light blue material. I dropped my rod where it was and walked over to her and looked at it without touching. Somehow, still attached, pinned to the cloth was the white plastic name tag with one word on it.

Shawna.

Chapter 36

IT WAS SILENT in the pickup. Colleen stared out the side window until I stopped in my driveway.

"You're awful quiet."

She got out and walked to her car.

"They asked us both to stay here until Benton comes to talk to us."

I could see her shoulders drop as her chin fell and I stepped over to her and put my hand on her back. "Are you okay?" She pulled away from me.

"What were we doing there, Wesley."

"What do you mean? We were fishing."

"No. What were we doing right there." She turned and her eyes were red and wet and the anger was building up.

I shook my head. "Just fishing."

"You better goddam tell me right now why you chose that spot. Your grandpa sure as hell didn't fish there and I don't think he even fished. We were there to find that girl, weren't we?"

I was stuck and didn't know what to say. I'd wanted to protect her from that dream but needed her to help me at the same time.

"Yes."

She walked away, her hands going to her head as if trying to hold all of the thoughts in, then she turned back to me. "Why didn't you tell me? You've told me everything already. But you let me go and find a dead girl in the lake without any damn warning?"

"I'm sorry."

"That's not good enough, Wesley," she said. "That's just not good enough."

Tires on gravel interrupted us as we saw Benton's SUV come up my long driveway.

"Let's just get through this then we'll talk more. I'll tell you everything."

The SUV stopped and Benton climbed out and walked over.

"Wes. Colleen." He tipped his wide brimmed sheriff's hat at us in a more formal act than I was used to, but then I wasn't usually being questioned by him about a dead girl.

"Benton. Thanks for coming."

"Sounds like you two had some morning out there."

"You could say that." Hurry it up, Benton. Get this over with.

"So can you tell me what happened?"

"We decided to go fishing. Colleen here was doing great,

had four or five smallmouth already in the cooler, when she hooked something under the water."

Colleen looked up and was different. "Oh, Benton. It was horrible. That poor girl."

The sheriff nodded. "It must have been pretty shocking, if you aren't used to that sort of thing." Right. Used to it. Two deputies vomited when the body was pulled out of the water and a third almost passed out.

She leaned into me and I wrapped my arms around her. "She's pretty upset about it, Benton."

"I can understand that." I could tell he had more questions, wanted to know more, but a soft spot of compassion was holding him back. "Colleen, would you want to go in and get some water and rest while I finish talking to Wes?"

Without a word Colleen turned and went into the house and we watched until the door clicked shut behind her.

"It's gonna be a rough day," I said.

"Want me to send Becky over so she has, you know, a woman to talk to?"

"No, I think we'll be okay."

He walked over and leaned on the bed of my truck and looked across the side yard that led to the hills out back. "That's an odd choice for a fishing spot."

"Is it? Was my first time."

"First time fishing, and you choose the dirtiest, weediest part of the lake possible?"

"Like I said, I didn't know better."

"Mmm hmm." He nodded, still watching the hills like they would put on a show for him. "But why right there?

You coulda gone a hundred yards down the road to the bridge where everyone fishes."

"I wanted to be alone with Colleen." I wasn't sure if he was buying it or not so I tried to change the conversation, take it off of me and Colleen. "So, was that really her?"

"Yup. We'll get dental records to be sure, but it was her uniform. Hair color seemed to match, too."

"Damn what a world this has become. Who'd do something like that?" I wanted to tell him. Jared Walker. He killed her.

"I don't know. But we're gonna do our damnedest to find out. And having her body now is a huge step forward."

I watched Benton leave and once he turned and disappeared down the main road I went inside to find Colleen sitting in the kitchen. "You okay?"

"No, I'm not okay. Start talking."

I had allowed her into my world but not granted full access. I'd kept things to myself and now paid the price. I told her about the dream, of Shawna Tate and her resting place in the marshy edge of the lake until our actions helped her body to be found, some slight closure for her mother and daughter. I described the whole thing to her as she sat at the table, trying to hide her reactions to the story I was telling. I could see her skin tighten as each detail more horrid than the last was revealed. But no words could persuade me to tell her who I had seen, the face and name of the man who had taken a life so violently.

She asked again and I said no. The story was unfolding and hopefully within time the truth would be known. We sat quietly. It was an uncomfortable silence, no noise to fill in the empty space. Then suddenly she was up and walking to the door.

"I need some time. I think you do, too."

And she was gone. I didn't chase her, didn't beg her to stay. And I didn't know if she'd be back. I had no experience with this, nothing to go by except television shows and country songs.

The excitement I had from the small victory of finding Shawna Tate was gone. A hit of a drug that wore off, and I had no more to inject into my bloodstream, to bring me up to that high again. And now I was crashing, the one woman I'd loved had left.

Shawna Tate was found. Her mother and daughter could find some solace in that, have a body to bury and mourn for, rather than just not knowing. It changed nothing for the girl, she would still grow up without a mother just as I did.

But Jared Walker was still free. I had no villain responsible for the deaths in my life. I could be mad at the disease that took my mother, the enemies in Vietnam or faulty brakes in an old truck. There was no one to make accountable for them, to hang up and point fingers and scream at. Shawna's daughter had that villain. She just didn't know who he was yet.

It was a decision without thought. I filled a thermos and threw a couple of apples in a bag and left in the truck. As I pulled into downtown I saw the red awning then the reflection of sun off of a window as a vehicle pulled up in front of the store and parked. Benton Hicks got out of his SUV and walked down the sidewalk as I rolled past, his attention not on me so I went unnoticed.

I made the series of turns around the county clerk's office and parked at the corner, spaces open on the Saturday afternoon. The sheriff was in the store for twenty minutes and finally left in his truck. He had likely made the rounds of telling Shawna Tate's mother, then Jared Walker, her former boss at Beasley's Cafe.

Even with the windows down on the early fall day it was getting warm in the pickup. Every few minutes a breeze would push some cooler air through then it was still again. But I didn't have to sit long. Maybe ten minutes after Benton left, Jared came out and locked the store, then disappeared around the corner. His dark brown Buick appeared and sped up as it hit Highway 10 and I pulled in behind him, leaving a large space in between.

He was driving fast. I had no problem keeping up, but didn't want to get stopped by the police or have him brake and come up on him too quickly. Red tail lights lit up and the Buick made a fast left turn. Six houses down he pulled into a driveway and went into a large brick ranch style house.

Chapter 37

I PARKED DOWN the street and watched his car and the house. It was his home, I could only guess, never having known where the man lived. It was the nicer side of town and he owned two businesses. Not many cars came or went off the road but I slid down in my seat anyway to where I could still see through the top of my steering wheel.

The sun went down early this time of year and the dimming sky turned the air cooler. I rolled the windows up and sipped on warm coffee. An hour after nightfall Jared appeared, this time backing a Ford pickup out of the two car garage. I kept my distance again and followed as he headed back out toward the lake.

Headlights on a dark country road stand out quickly, so I kept my distance and let him get a curve or two ahead. As we got closer to the lake I thought about turning off and heading back, not wanting to go to that place again and having no idea why he would go there. I didn't know if the police would still be set up, looking for more clues in the swampy water.

In pursuit of the killer that had occupied my thoughts for so many months now, my mind wandered as it did when fishing just hours earlier. How could I get proof? What would it take to catch him? Every few thoughts were stopped by a sense of futility, unable to see how I could end it.

I came around a curve and the tail lights were gone. My breathing stopped. I let off the gas momentarily then put it back on, not wanting to look or sound like I was slowing down in case he had stopped to see who was following him. Then a slight reflection off to my left and I saw the shape, something that didn't fit. As I passed the old tar paper house, the back end of the Ford was just visible on the far side, pulled as far off of the road as it could be. I took another curve then slammed on the brakes and pulled off of the road, out of view of the house. Before I knew what I was doing, I was on foot, running down the side of the road. I had no plan and felt I had no control over my actions. It was impulse, action without thought. My lungs got tight as I ran, trying to see rocks on the side of the road to keep from falling on my face. I moved further off the road to the tree line as the road curved back toward the house and I went slower from tree to tree.

No other cars went by on the dark road. The sky was clear but no moonlight was illuminating the land. Just the natural light that somehow comes in darkness, reflections stacking up on top of each other through the air, enough to show what I needed to see.

Shadows moved on top of shadows, and sounds carried easily in the night air. Jared Walker was there. He came out of the tar paper house, the stitched oval rug over his shoulder. He moved slowly, an older man and I could hear his heavy breathing. He threw the rug into the bed of the truck then leaned forward onto the tailgate for a minute before getting back in the cab.

If he headed out of town he'd see my truck on the side of the road. I began running again, glancing over my shoulder every few steps to watch for him. He never came and I got to my truck and climbed in, chest in pain. On the road I U-turned and headed back in. Passing the old house, his truck was gone. Not having passed me, he must have gone back toward town.

Why would he go back for the rug? Why would he risk that?

I went back through town then rolled slowly onto his street again. Just the car in the driveway. But he could have parked the truck in the garage again. He wouldn't take the rug there, to his own home, would he?

Continuing down his road I watched the house as I passed, no lights were on that I could see.

I spent half an hour driving through town, watching side streets for signs of his pickup but never found it. I'd lost him. I drove home and took a few beers from the fridge and sat on the front porch. He had the only piece of physical evidence I knew of, the only other thing that could connect him to the murder. I drained the first then opened another beer.

Thoughts turned to Colleen in the quiet. It was the first night in weeks I'd been home alone. I'd tried her home number and got the answering machine.

Two beers turned into six before falling asleep on the porch, the blanket from the living room dragged out with me after my last run to the refrigerator. It was a restless sleep as I saw the murder again and relived finding Shawna Tate's body. I woke up early and began drinking again, reaching for the harder stuff on the shelf above the kitchen sink. I didn't want to be drunk, just loose, and paced myself. A sip here, a bigger sip there. The edge was fading and it felt good. I wanted to not think about Jared Walker or Shawna Tate. I wanted a normal life for a few hours. For a day. No dreams.

Another try of Colleen's number and her answering machine again. I wandered around the house and looked at the symbols of my solitude. A single chair, two coffee cups to rotate when one is dirty. When I walked into my bedroom I was saddened as I remembered my father's room when he died and mine was no different. A bed against one wall, a dresser against another. And in the bottom dresser drawer, as it was then, the mahogany box with my bother's army pistol.

Where did he take the rug?

Sip. Push it away.

My head spun a little when I bent over and pulled the box out, then held the heavy metal weapon in my hand.

The first time I pulled the trigger hadn't gone well but I'd done it many times since then. I'd throw a hay bale in the back of the truck and drive up top then shoot from different distances, shredding the bale until it was scattered all over the field. The gun felt good in my hands now. The weight gave it purpose, implied the danger. Grandpa had taught me well, how to clean it and shoot it. I thought about taking it up the hill and firing off a few rounds then thought better.

That son-of-a-bitch is still out there.

Another drink, then another. Not today. Give me one day.

But I couldn't stop them. He was a part of my everyday thoughts. Finding the body made it worse, knowing he was walking around free while Shawna's mother was planning a funeral.

The buzz was wearing off. I dialed again, no answer. Hung up as her cheerful voice came on to tell anyone who called that she wasn't home.

He deserves to die.

Another drink. Television didn't help to distract. Can't focus on the motors in the workshop right now. I pulled my yellow pad out of the top shelf above the refrigerator where it lay flat and hidden from sight. Flipping page over page, I scanned the notes I'd written, many late at night, eyes blurry from lack of sleep. Ideas, thoughts. Plans. I started from the beginning again and read every word, my pen underlining and circling some lines, crossing through others.

There was something there, vague ideas that came together into something solid, something possible. Possible in theory, in pencil on paper. In reality it was something else. I was becoming the one I hated so much in order to stop him, to end him. The police couldn't do it. Even with the body in front of them they couldn't figure it out.

They can't do it. You can.

I moved the pieces back and forth. It was possible. Doable. A machine came to life in my head, the parts fitting together, roughly at first then falling into sync. The risks were there, but what there was to risk is so low, meaningless. My life was stagnant, so little had changed in the years since grandpa died. Colleen was gone, maybe for good. That was for the better. She was distanced from it, protected.

I had an escape plan, an option to leave and never come back, but it was the last resort. I looked out the kitchen window at the Farmall tractor and thought of grandpa with his tire iron, standing naked in the snow.

Chapter 38

A FLATBED TRUCK rumbled past as I sat in my old GMC pickup outside the Delaware County Mercantile. The newer truck was left at home, feeling the need to connect to something from long ago. There was a familiarity with the truck, like an old friend. Companionship I required right now.

I felt like my entire body was shaking but when I held my hands out they were steady. The drink had worn off but the machine was still moving, gears grinding as it drove forward. I could still stop it. Just start the engine and drive away. Find Colleen and talk to her in person. Things could be normal again, whatever normal I'd known. I had my escape plan and could take her with me. But the machine didn't want to stop. It had found a rhythm, a pulse. The machine pushed forward on its own, I was a passenger.

The bell connected to the top of the door jingled as I entered the store, nobody behind the front counter. I walked through the aisles, watching for him to appear. Stopping, I looked at the rack in front of me, rows of gloves hanging on metal hooks. I felt the leather in my hands, each pair different. Some softer, some firm. The patterns in the hide varied. Then I held the pair with the wrist strap and silver button to hold it in place.

"Wes, is that you?"

I looked up to see Jared Walker walking behind the front counter with a box in his arms. His voice cut through me. It was more tired, grittier, than it was in the dream that continued to haunt my sleep, the phone call that I spent almost every night trying to decipher. It sounded weak. At least I wanted it to be weak. I knew he still had the strength to kill a woman.

"Sure is." I walked to the front, each step heavier than the one before. I felt like I was moving so slowly but suddenly I was at the counter, face to face with him.

I could end it here. He was twenty years older than me and I was still strong from working with the engines, certainly much stronger than Shawna Tate had been. I could reach across and grab his thinning hair and slam his face into the glass counter.

"Anything I can help you find?"

"No."

I wished I'd had one more swig from my thermos at home. The edge was back. I was close to crossing a line that I couldn't come back from, set events in motion that

I had planned for as best I could. Notes on yellow legal paper now charred at the bottom of my wood stove at home. Now I was just standing at the counter, waiting to push the first domino.

"Wes?" His voice pulled me back and my resolve strengthened.

I placed the black gloves on the counter. The heaviness blew away from me. I'd imagined this moment so many times that I knew it was up to me to control it, to steer it the way I wanted it to go.

"You wanna buy those?"

I shook my head. "They look more like your size." He had followed my script.

"I'm not following, Wes."

Don't hesitate. Stay on the chase.

"These are like the gloves you wore that night." The first domino fell and struck the second.

The air between us expanded as he stood silent, looking for what to say. He was confused but in there somewhere, in his tone, his body language, I could tell he knew.

"What are you talking about?"

It had been months to this point. I'd waited and hoped, watched for the sheriff and state police to go in the right direction, and had become more and more frustrated as time went by. Now I watched his every move, the lines on his face as he went from one emotion to another. He was against the ropes, arms dropping.

"The night you killed Shawna Tate." It was out, free. My heart pounded so hard I was sure he could hear it.

Jared took a step back, his eyes locked on me. He stumbled on his own words. "I don't know where you got that idea, Wes, and I don't appreciate being accused of such things in my own store."

"But you did it, Jared," I said. "You threw her to the floor and strangled her, wearing gloves just like these. Then you raped her while your hands were clutched around her throat."

I could see the blood drain from Jared Walker's face, unable to even argue the truth that was being put in front of him. It was everything I'd wanted to say. It was all that needed to be said. The seed was planted, watered, and would grow quickly now. But it just wasn't enough. I wanted to be sure, to know he would do what I needed him to do.

"Then you took her to the lake, Jared. You dumped her body into the water. Her daughter, her mother, had no idea what had happened to her until a few weeks ago."

"I think you should go now. I don't want to ever see you back in here again." His voice was quiet and wavering. He was bested, beaten. His options were limited.

"You won't." I walked to the door and the bell jingled again as I opened it, an inappropriate levity.

"You're lucky I'm not calling the sheriff."

The door closed behind me.

I let the air rush around me as I drove. Maybe my last drive in the truck I built at seventeen. I wanted another drink but knew I needed to stay straight.

I parked at the edge of the cemetery and sat for several

minutes watching for other cars or people. I got out and walked between the rows of headstones, something I'd done too many times in my life. I reached the marker I was looking for then glanced around again and knelt in front of the stone.

"I'm sorry about what happened to you, Shawna."

The headstone was simple, with only her name and the years of her birth and death. Nobody had thought to add that she was a mother, a daughter or anything else.

"I'm making it right."

Chapter 39

I'VE LIVED WITH death my entire life, either the loss of my own family or the dreams that showed me the final moments of people I didn't know. I wasn't callous toward death, though. I respected it and even feared it, knowing one day it would be me and that the secluded life I'd chosen would make it a quiet death. Maybe I'd be that story on the news about the old person found in his home, dead at least three weeks. I don't have a cat to eat my fingers off or anything, so the story wouldn't be as gruesome as they prefer for the ten o'clock report. There's always the six o'clock news.

The evening had gone more quickly than I'd expected. I did my normal routine to not leave anything suspicious behind, a pattern that didn't fit. I had dinner in my recliner watching Jeopardy, not answering any of the questions or even hearing them at all. I wished I'd gone over to Stroud one more time to sit in my old church, feel the stone against my skin. I wanted to see the tree one last time. The fire was dying down in the stove, the last remains of yellow paper had turned black, curling up and collapsing under its own weight. The machine was still grinding, though silently. It was impossible to stop it now.

I fell asleep with the bible on my lap. Flipping through the pages and rereading the dreams Grandpa had was relaxing, comforting. It reminded me I wasn't alone. In the minutes or hours that I slept I dreamt of him. I saw Grandpa as a young man, standing in the trenches with water up to his ankles. Another boy stood to his side and they were talking, then fragments of helmet, skull and brain sprayed onto the dirt wall behind them. But then other images came to me of my grandfather. Flashes of his life I could never have seen otherwise, from well before I was born until when I did know him as an old man. He was never alone, always surrounded by people. Talking, laughing, cracking jokes. I relived the moment at the feed store when he tried to sell me off to the shop owner, and the police roadblock searching for a prisoner that had escaped from the prison down south and he tried to convince the trooper I was the one they were searching for, a twelve year old boy in overalls and worn out boots. There was always someone with him.

The sound of wood scraping on wood woke me up, the back door being pushed open. It was never locked. Nobody locked their doors in the country. I felt a sudden release of emotion that had been building for months and fought back the tears that tried to force their way out. I wanted to be clear, focused. It was my moment, the only person who could end this. I waited in the dark as the footsteps worked their way through the house. I'd expected to be nervous but was calm, my pulse steady.

The blurred shadow moved into the room as the figure walked toward the foot of the stairs, only the reflection of something metal visible in the darkness giving sign that the shape was more than just an apparition or my eyes playing a sleight of hand game in the absence of light. The shadow turned to take the first step up toward the bedroom.

I turned the light on beside me.

Jared jumped, turning toward the brightness behind him.

"I thought you'd be earlier."

"I had to make sure nobody saw me drive out here." He took steps toward the big recliner where I was sitting, a quilt covering me in the cold room. "So how did you know?"

"You wouldn't believe me if I told you. But there's one thing, before you do what you came to do."

"What's that?" Jared came closer.

For the first time I clearly saw the gun Jared was carrying as he let it come out into the open down to his side, his hands covered with black leather gloves. It was a small weapon, a .22 probably, and old. It didn't look well maintained, not like something a man who owns a hunting supplies store would own.

"Who did you call?"

"What?"

"That night. You stopped at a gas station and made a phone call," I said. "Who did you call?"

He paused in his steps for a moment then kept moving toward me.

"Don't know what you're talking about."

"Figured you wouldn't tell me," I said. "So I guess we should get this over with."

"I guess we should." Jared's gun was in front of him now as he made the last steps to the chair, trying to move further over to my side. "You not going to fight? Is this it, your last act?"

"My brother was the fighter."

The machine in my head came to a stop, quick and smooth like an engine I'd built and oiled. For the first time in a day, in months, my mind was silent. He wanted to make it look like I killed myself. An old, untraceable gun and a loner in his house. I'd surprised him by being awake and he'd had to adapt.

"Have it your way." Jared raised the gun to aim at my left temple. He was too far away, both for the short barrel of the weapon to be accurate and to look like a suicide.

"You better move closer," I said. "You don't want to miss, do you?"

A hesitation and then motion, his steps still landing lightly to avoid making sound though we were the only two people who could hear them. The barrel of his gun was a foot from my head.

I leaned forward, changing his shot, looked up at him and smiled. "This is for Shawna Tate, you son-of-a-bitch."

Jared paused at my words and tilted his head before

pulling the trigger on the small calibre weapon. Then I saw his finger move.

The blast of the gun was softened slightly by the quilt that covered me, a hole no bigger than a quarter burned through it by the bullet that travelled the short distance from the barrel of my brother's M1911 army pistol, through the quilt, and into the left shoulder of Jared Walker.

Jared stood there, his arm still raised with the gun in hand as the blood came out of him, instantly soaking his shirt and the grey wool pea coat he wore. I was worried a reflex would pull the trigger, sending a shot into me as well. I pulled the blanket back with one hand, raised my gun, then took aim and put another shot right through his heart from a foot away. The force of the second projectile pushed him backward onto the floor as a puddle formed around the body from the large exit wounds on his back.

Two bullets. That's what it took to end him, to end the story. I'd sat with the gun for an hour that afternoon, a box of shells beside me, then loaded it. Two bullets. That's what I gave myself to kill Jared Walker. I didn't want him to over-power me and shoot me with my own gun. The rest of the ammunition was back in the bottom drawer of the dresser upstairs. If I'd failed and my shots hadn't struck their targets then I would be the one with blood pooling around my body.

My house was a few hundred feet off of the road just past the edge of town. I could have fired the gun on the front porch all night and nobody would have heard it, or cared. Still, I sat frozen with my ears listening for any sounds to pierce the air in the middle of the night.

Chapter 40

EVERYTHING POURED OUT and left me crumpled on the floor below the wall phone. It would have been an award winning performance if it had not been real. Blood streamed down my left arm from the wound I'd put there myself with Jared Walker's gun, another small detail in the story. Shooting myself in the arm had proven much easier than I expected and far more painful. My call to the sheriff's office had been manic, confused. The young sounding deputy on the other end was panicking, not having taken a call like that before.

The phone was above me on the wall as I sat on the floor with the receiver in my hand, unable to stand and hang it up. After a while it started buzzing, then a loud alternating tone meant to alert you that the phone was off the hook blared out of it. My left arm was red from the blood and I couldn't move it.

In my arrogance and desire to make something right, I'd let him get much closer than I'd planned, than I'd wanted. I was able to feel him near me, smell him. But I'd been surprised it was no different than when he stood next to me while I bought two fishing poles. Both times I smelled his cheap cologne, probably a gift from his wife or daughter. I guess I'd expected the scent of something else, something more evil. Something desperate. When planning to kill a man you need them to be evil to rationalize it. I knew he was. I had seen what he did to Shawna Tate. Perhaps that is what made him evil, that he can rape and murder a young woman, then splash liquid from a $4 bottle of cologne onto his neck and smile at the customers.

Pain grew inside my head, pounding and pushing against my skull. Blood dripped down onto my shirt and I was unable to reach to my nose, my arms not responding to requests. It was ten minutes, or maybe twelve, before I heard the first siren. The bleeding looked bad, red covering my chest and arms and for a moment I was afraid I'd hit a major artery and would end up in the morgue beside Jared. Wouldn't that be something? I grew cold and the shapes of the first responders were fuzzy as they came through the kitchen. A woman in a blue polo with a logo embroidered over the heart kneeled down and her hands went straight to my wrist and face. Martha Henry, I think it was, Jim Henry's daughter. He ran the feed mill down south. She'd been a pretty girl growing up.

I wanted to see my mother and I tried so hard, but she wouldn't come, neither would Larry. Other images flew through my consciousness. The small girl on her pink bedspread locked in her room, the baby being rocked too hard in the vision at the cemetery when I was so young. I couldn't push them away, they kept coming, swirling around. The lives of everyone I'd seen wanted to be seen again, once more perhaps before I was gone, before I joined them. A shiver went through my body, starting from my core and working its way out and I was left frozen, unable to move.

Then the pain came in my head, a pulsing and squeezing of precious life giving blood. I could feel it, alive in there, the tumor just like Grandpa had. I'd thought before that it was a byproduct of the dreams, a foreign body that grows and lives, thriving on the visions of other people's deaths, but always pushed those thoughts away. But now I knew it was true. I knew my fate and had seen it with Grandpa. He'd survived many more years but had also learned to control the dreams more than I had.

As soon as I stopped trying to find them, everyone was with me. I couldn't see them, but I felt them. I felt my mother holding me tightly to her chest and Larry walking beside me up on the hill. I felt the emotions my father had passed on to me in his touch as he died. Grandpa was there above everyone, loving us and caring for us. I was back at the church, the orange stones surrounded me and the sapling was now through the roof, thirty or forty feet tall. I stepped to it and felt the bark on my fingers and looked up to see the high branches blur against the bright summer sky. Turning I saw motion, brown hair against the dry brown grass. It was a young buck, barely two nubs atop its head.

"*Pyothopi?*" The buck looked at me then turned and ran off.

The feelings disappeared and I felt alone again. The cold came along with movement and shaking, darkness then bright artificial lights in an enclosed space. It felt like days, but was told it had only been thirty minutes when I woke up in the back of the ambulance, still sitting out front of my house. Martha Henry was there with me, a smile on her face as her hand stroked my arm in a simple act of caring.

"I'm not in the hospital?"

"No, sweetie. The wound wasn't that bad. The doctor will probably want to put a few stitches in but I have it patched up for now."

I tried to look down at my shoulder then dropped my head back onto the pillow. "Then why do I feel like shit?"

"Could be because you've just been through a traumatic event in your own home, hon. You're in a bit of shock but doing better now."

I smiled at her. Been probably ten years if not more since I'd seen her. It was one night at Beasley's with Benton, I believe. She was there with a young man.

"How's your dad doing, Martha?"

"Wasn't sure you remembered me. Better than you, right now, Mr. Hudson."

A small laugh stirred in my belly and I held it back to keep from hurting. The things nobody knew, that they could never know. She'd been only twelve or thirteen when I saw her in a dream. She had been crying beside an old man on a bed, her grandfather I later found out. He was fit for his age and still worked his farm every day, which had been his undoing. Nobody was with him out in the field when the hay baler got jammed and he went to fix it himself.

"Of course I remember you, Martha."

When I thought they were about to take me over to the hospital in Grove, I was helped out of the ambulance. A sheriff's deputy took me by the other arm and led me to his Dodge Charger, the blue lights still flashing on the roof.

"What's going on?"

"Sorry, sir." He was apologetic in his words and his manner. I could tell he didn't want to put me in the car. "Sheriff Hicks wants you taken in until all this business is sorted out."

I knew that and had expected it. Benton was thorough and certainly didn't want to be accused of handling his friend any different than he would a stranger. But I also knew I had to object. It's what everyone did when they were being put into the back of a deputy's car.

Even in the early hours of morning there were cars out on the road. Some were headed to work in the cities an hour each direction, others probably just heard the sirens and came out to see what was happening in our quiet town. Eyes locked with mine as cars rolled past slowly and before too long the rumors would be out about Wesley Hudson getting hauled in to jail, and shortly after that the truth would spread even quicker.

Cell number two was empty and I took my seat quietly when sent in. In the cell to my right was a greasy haired man curled up on the floor twitching, heavy breaths coming from his restless sleep. Nobody was in the cage to my left.

It was morning before Benton Hicks came into the station. I'd heard his voice a couple times over the dispatch radio, calling in from my own house. I was still awake on the cement bench, unable to sleep and also knowing that sleep would have made me look guilty. Benton made the rounds of the room before acknowledging me. He poured a cup of coffee then talked to the deputy that had been on duty through the night. After stopping in his office to check the messages on his phone he finally came over to cell number two.

"Wes."

"Benton."

"I got a call from the district attorney on my drive over." He took a long sip from his coffee mug, the faded logo of the sheriff's office shield printed on the outside. He relished his position and enjoyed playing the role, letting the important parts of sentences linger behind slowly before catching up.

"What did she have to say?" I had never seen this side of him, the law enforcement officer. I was surprised at how different he was. His shoulders rolled back and voice deepened. Every word he uttered seemed meant to trap you.

"Said it sounded like self defense to her. Unless we have some reason to contradict that, she isn't recommending charges."

I looked down at my work boots, for the first time noticing the specks of blood splattered across the old leather. The quilt had been pulled up to my neck, leaving my feet exposed.

"You have any reason to contradict her?"

"I don't. A man came into your home with a weapon and you protected yourself," Benton said. "Reads like an open and shut case."

"But?" I said.

"But…this wasn't some meth head looking for cash or something to sell for another hit." Benton looked over at the third cell, the drug addict still passed out on the bench. "This was a prominent man, a business owner who has spent his entire life in this county, in this town. He owns one of the nicest houses in the area, drives a new car every few years. What purpose did killing you serve him?"

I sat silently, ready to let the sheriff, my oldest and only friend, work through this himself.

"We've had deputies and even some troopers out asking questions, trying to find out anything they can," Benton said. "We've had a couple people say they saw your pickup outside Jared's store yesterday afternoon."

My stomach tightened. "Yup. Stopped by there to buy some gloves." The weakest part of my story came out early.

"Gloves?"

"Don't have any, except my work gloves, thought it would be nice to have a pair," I said. "Been spending time with Colleen and wouldn't mind looking a little nicer."

"With gloves."

I shrugged. "It was a thought."

"So where are these gloves?"

"Didn't buy any."

"Why not?"

"Weren't any that fit," I said. "I found a pair of nice black leather gloves and took them to the counter to see if Jared had any other sizes. He looked at the gloves and just acted weird, said he didn't." I improvised.

Benton stared through the bars at me, the coffee mug hung down at an angle dangerously close to spilling the contents onto the floor. "You're a piece of work, Wes."

"Been told worse. Usually by you."

The sheriff turned and walked away as he spoke to the deputy. "Let him loose."

Chapter 41

THE CAR PULLED into the driveway and the same deputy who'd taken me to the jail got out and opened the back door for me. Even though the morning air was below freezing and the sun was hidden behind a thick layer of clouds threatening rain, I stood outside and stared at the house as the vehicle backed down the driveway then sped off once on the road.

Let him loose.

The words rolled around inside me.

Time slowed as I stood and thought about the two tractors I had waiting for engine rebuilds, the stack of bills on the kitchen table needing to be paid, and then of Colleen. I didn't know if she was aware of what had happened, that it was over. My efforts to protect her had been wasted, her power over me too strong to hide anything from the green eyes that looked through me and saw everything. So many times in the months since she'd returned I wanted to run away from her but the feeling was always betrayed by my desire to run away with her.

But now she would know, once a friend called her or she turned on the television and saw the news out of Tulsa that was already reporting on it endlessly. And still only the two of us would know the full story, the death that lead to the death. The dead man Jared Walker was still innocent of Shawna Tate's murder.

I walked through the house, every item that could be moved had been by the deputies and investigators from the state police. White dust covered surfaces with voids of clean rectangular strips where the tape had been pulled up to capture the fingerprints that were hiding. They would find only mine and Colleen's. Jared Walker's time in the house had been short and his gloved hands avoided any prints.

Let him loose.

It kept coming back into my conscious thoughts. Perhaps the three words relieved me from my sentence, an informal acquittal. The words held a tangible weight in my mind, refusing to leave the space around me.

I stood in the living room, the pattern of blood on the floor reminding me of the leaves from the Japanese maple that I'd walked across only a day earlier, a memory that felt weeks old. The deputy had given me the card for a company that cleaned up these kinds of messes. I'd wondered at first if there were enough shootings in Oklahoma to support a business that cleans up blood until it was explained that they did all kinds of clean up from natural disasters and pipes freezing and bursting, flooding kitchen floors and destroying hardwood. I didn't want to call them now and was already sure I wanted to clean it up myself, an act of atonement for the sin I'd committed against a god I didn't believe in.

I knew now was not the time and felt the walls of the familiar house closing in on me. The house, the world, felt smaller. The urge to be free of this place, my work, my life, swelled over me.

Grabbing my keys from the hook on the end of the kitchen cabinet, I left the door unlocked and drove away from the house. The field just past my land was still covered in a thick white layer of frost, the sun not yet coming over the low tree line to spread its warming glow. I'd turned toward town without thinking then wished I'd gone the other direction, away from any people that might see me. As I neared the town square I thought about turning the truck through the residential streets just to avoid driving past the Delaware County Mercantile and Hunting Supplies store that now sat closed, probably for good, but decided to just get through town and keep driving.

The engine in the old GMC was steady as always as I passed the courthouse and the sheriff's office I'd been released from less than an hour earlier. It was only then I noticed the flashing blue lights ahead from the roofs of the sheriff's SUV's and several cars with the Oklahoma State Police markings on the sides. They sat at different angles around the Mercantile building, a steady flow of officers and deputies walking in and out through the double glass doors that had been propped open, their arms full of boxes.

On through town the thoughts came fast. I'd never considered the idea that they might search Jared's store. I was tempted then to drive past the dead man's house, to see if police were there as well, but I kept moving. Best not to be seen stalking the business and home of the man I had just killed.

Town turned to open two-lane highway headed northeast toward Grove. I opened up the engine, feeling the pull of the big V8. Heat poured through the air vents and from the firewall separating the cabin from the engine bay enough that I lowered my window a couple of inches to let some cold air in. As the cold hit my face I rolled it down until it was wide open, the already freezing air made colder by being forced into the moving truck.

Let him loose.

It was there again, no matter what I tried to get away from the words. They held no meaning to me other than my freedom from the eight hours I spent in jail, but they continued to follow me.

A few cars were headed the other direction and I only came across one headed toward Grove, which I easily passed in the left lane. I had nowhere to go but just wanted to drive, to be anywhere but my house or even my town right now. It was a freedom I hadn't felt in so long, the years of dreams and death and self confinement in my home. The months of planning and waiting, hesitating and talking myself out of becoming like the man that had haunted me.

I came to the bridge and let off the gas, the stuttering report from the exhaust making me smile as it had since I was sixteen. I glanced both ways at the lake as I crossed it. Only one boat was out on the water, way off to my left, the air and water too cold to enjoy fishing for most people. As the far end of the bridge came into view I hit the brakes without planning to, slowing the truck down then turning sharply onto the trail that shot left off of the road just past the for sale sign.

I made the turns through the brush as if I'd done it often, though it had been more than twenty years since the last time, then pulled to a stop on the cliff overlooking the water. Out of the truck I walked up to the edge and looked down. I stood where I'd seen her stand that day, her white bra and panties the only clothes left on her. The twenty feet felt like a hundred to me and I was amazed I'd ever made that jump, even though it had just been that once, that amazing once where she'd first kissed me. That once where I'd gone too deep and couldn't find my way up, finding instead my mother and my brother down in the darkness of Grand Lake. That had been the last time either had come to me in a vision.

Let him loose.

The words would ricochet back into my mind, taking me away from whatever I had been thinking about, but the water below was lulling me, drawing me closer. I took another step toward the edge, my toes inches from the crumbling rocks.

The soft voice surrounded me, entered me. "What are you doing?"

What am I doing? I wondered to myself, the voice not registering as coming from anywhere other than inside of my head. The water swirled below, always in too much motion to ever freeze over even in the coldest days of winter. What am I doing? The water pulled me, thoughts of Larry and my mother in the darkness.

"Come to me, Wesley."

As the water below me called, a hand fell on my shoulder and gently guided me back away from the edge. Everything hit at once from the hours and months that led to this moment. I dropped to my knees and broke down, allowing the tears to come. I didn't have to turn to know she was there with me. I didn't know how or why, I just knew she was. She was beside me, her arms wrapped around me and holding me tightly.

"Are you okay?"

Her car was warm but I could still feel the heat from her body, even through our clothes and our coats as she held me in the front seat, my head resting on her shoulder. I'd spent my life trying not to be like my father, cold and stoic, avoiding contact with anyone, but knew at this moment it was exactly what I'd become. I'd tried over and over to push away the one woman who'd ever cared for me, loved me, and she'd come back. She was the only one who saw through the wall I'd built and wouldn't let it stop her.

Colleen's hand stroked my greying hair. "Jared Walker." I could feel her shake her head as she said his name. "Of all people."

"You're not disappointed in me? Scared of me?"

"I could never be either of those things," she said. "Nobody has died as many times as you have. Nobody could ever understand. I try to, but mostly I just accept you, and love you."

I turned my face to hers and took in her green eyes and saw the emotion behind them, the love she felt, and for the first time let myself go and kissed her. We'd kissed before, years ago and recently in my home and bed, but I'd been reserved, nervous to open up in such a physical way. As our tongues met I felt her lose her breath as she understood and sensed me let go of whatever had held me back for so long. My hands grabbed at her coat, pulling it apart as two large buttons were flung from the threads that held them in place. She pushed herself away from me and took the coat off, dropping it into the back seat as I raised her shirt and pulled it over her head along with her lacy turquoise bra. Fingers fumbled across buttons and zippers as lips stayed connected, tongues moved and danced around each other.

She climbed on top of me in the wide passenger seat of the old Mercedes, her blue jeans now hanging off of one ankle. As she slowly lowered herself onto me, I entered then pulled her down hard, my arms wrapping up her bare back to her shoulders. We remained still with only the pulsing of my blood giving motion and heat inside her, and then she gently brought her hips forward and back.

My face was buried into the nape of her neck as chests slid against each other, the fine layer of sweat forming a bond between our two bodies. I could feel her pulse quicken as she tightened around me, movements slowing, bringing me along with her, controlling me. As her fingernails broke skin across my shoulders I brought my hand up to her face and pulled it in, my teeth taking her lower lip, her body gave in to the sensation and it shuddered. I thrust and released myself, unable to breathe for several seconds, and she arched her back as we both felt me flow into her.

Bodies collapsed onto each other as I wrapped my arms around her, unable to tell if I was feeling my own pounding heartbeat or hers. Her face worked its way back to mine, lips finding lips again in a lingering and wet kiss.

"That was..."

I kissed her again to keep her from finishing her words. We sat as one, connected, inside of her, as pulses slowed and breathing became shallower again.

My head next to hers, I whispered. "How did you find me?"

"I was driving to your house and you passed me going the other direction."

"Didn't see you."

"You were easily doing 80 through town."

"I was?"

She kissed me again, her tongue sliding into my mouth and meeting my own, her hands holding my face.

I lightly brushed up her sides with my fingertips, and to her small, beautiful breasts. I brought her left nipple between my fingers then leaned my head down and took it in my teeth, my tongue darting across the tip.

Still inside her I felt myself become firm again. She leaned back and looked at me.

"Really?"

Chapter 42

I WOKE IN her queen-sized bed, a smooth white ceiling above, windows dark behind sheer shades. Colleen lay asleep beside me. The clock on the table read 4:16. I had followed her back to her small rental house where she made dinner and we didn't talk about what had happened in the front seat of her car, only grinning and letting out stifled laughs in quiet moments when we'd catch each other's eyes. One bottle of wine turned into two and then a reenactment of our first act from high school in front of her fireplace, hands more sure of where to go and bodies more comfortable with being naked and together. She had been my first kiss, my first everything. I had never wanted anyone else. I knew she was the one then, and had resolved myself to having only the memories of that one beautiful, clumsy evening together.

Her slow, quiet breaths were barely audible even in the quiet room. Her chest was halfway uncovered, the loose fitting white tank top she wore to sleep in showing the rising and falling as she inhaled and exhaled. The frailty of life played out before me, in and out with her breathing. The delicate nature of the human body contradicted our rise to the top of the food chain. So easily a life can be taken, not just struck down violently as I had done myself, but slowly over years from the inside out.

I got out of bed quietly and found my boxers on the back of a chair. Down the hall the fire had faded but the embers glowed red below the surface once the poker stirred them. With another log put on top I had the flames working their way into the dry wood. The heat built up and washed over my mostly bare skin.

Her home was sparsely decorated and simple. It was comfortable. I was used to the faded walls of my house, photos and old paintings in place from before I was even born. I felt good here, refreshed. When we left the lake she didn't even ask if I wanted to go to her home rather than mine, she just drove and I followed. And it was right. It was what I needed.

Watching the fire catch, I thought of the swirling black water of the lake far below, then her voice behind me just hours earlier. I hadn't been startled at her presence. It had felt right, necessary.

I don't know what I would have done on that cliff, if anything. I hadn't gone there to kill myself or to cry or scream at the water. My truck just ended up there with me at the wheel. Maybe I was drawn to where I'd last seen my mother, my brother, way down below that dark water.

He was dead. It was as simple as that. Just yesterday he was walking and breathing, taking up space on this earth that he didn't deserve. Shawna Tate was still gone and her daughter still without a mother. Nothing could change that. But that girl didn't have to grow up coexisting in the world with her mother's killer. Nobody may ever know he had been responsible, but there was at least no chance of them passing each other on a sidewalk or speaking to each other. She was safe from him without ever knowing he had permanently altered her life.

The words that had haunted me the day before, chased my thoughts all the way to the lake, were no longer fighting for attention. In the warmth of the fireplace I sat on the floor, a glass of wine from an open bottle left on the kitchen counter in my hand, and I conjured the words up myself, controlling them this time. I rolled them around my brain and across my tongue.

Let him loose.

They didn't hold the power over me that they had less than a day ago. I moved them through my thoughts easily now, keeping them tamed and simple. Somewhere in the manipulation of them, breaking them apart and putting them back together, their meaning came to me. The emotional absolution I'd received at the hands of Colleen had freed me. The time I'd spent planning to take a life had added weight to my already burdened mortality. Mine was a life of chasing death. My mother, brother, father, grandfather. Shawna Tate. And so many others. With the stroke of a pen on carbon paper copies I'd been released from jail for a murder I'd committed, planned, and carried out with full will of consciousness. And with those three words I'd been released from the guilt of the murder, as well as the ballast of all the other lives lost during my own that had been the confines of my life up to this moment.

A spark popped from the fire, shooting up into the air above the flames, then fizzling and fading into nothing within the blackness surrounding the conflagration. My body felt light and my head free to think about whatever I wanted at this moment, no longer tied to analyzing the architecture of taking a life.

And in that my solitude was broken. My lifetime spent pushing everybody away was over, and a new one was born. A new me. A new life.

I could think about her now. I could think about a life with her, happiness. Waking up with her each morning and falling asleep with her in my arms, lightly stroking her skin with my fingertips. After so many years of thinking of her, dreaming of being with her again, I was able to do just that. For my whole life I'd let the dreams control me. I'd pushed everyone away for fear of knowing their fate. Somehow my grandfather came to terms with this early in life, reckoned with the spirits and the deaths and had chosen to live his own life. I guess he let the dreams free him rather than imprison him, not taking any joy or even solace in other's deaths, but knowing that he was there to receive those dreams, process them however he could.

Little things about Grandpa had been fighting for attention for so long and began to fall into place with resounding clicks. Stops at a couple of different houses on holidays throughout the years with a plate of food for a widow and her teenage daughter, the headstones with names I'd never heard that he left flowers on. He'd never turned his back on the dead. He'd invited them in.

Colleen's footsteps turned my head toward her. "What are you smiling about, Wesley Hudson?"

I exaggerated a scowl that forced itself back into a smile. "I guess I'm just...happy."

"I like it. It's a good look for you."

"Maybe I'll try it more," I said.

"You might tone it back in public a bit. You don't want to scare the locals."

She sat down beside me and picked up my glass of wine, then looked up at the clock on the mantel. "Is it too early to drink or too late to drink?"

"I think it's just the right time."

Chapter 43

THE BLOOD HAD soaked through the rug and stained the wood floors by the time I got back to the house and began to clean. After several hours of scrubbing I retreated to my workshop and took the belt sander back to the house, plugged it in, and took off several layers of wood stain and the dried blood with it. The work felt satisfying and I began moving furniture, sanding the floors from corner to corner.

Even in the room where I took Jared Walker's life, my thoughts stayed on Colleen. Not only the last two days together but also something I had never allowed myself to do much in my life, think about the days to come. I'd always worked day-to-day, week-to-week, focusing on the tasks at hand. The future was too much of an unknown for me to bother with. I knew today I'd have a tool in my hand, an engine in front of me. Perhaps there would be another tool and another engine tomorrow, perhaps not. I would worry about that then.

Colleen hadn't wanted me to leave her home, her bed. She had received a phone call and was needed at the courthouse in Tulsa for a case she was working and I watched from her driveway as she drove off before I came home. I knew the tasks ahead of me and wanted to get them done. I glanced at the clock on the wall and counted the hours until I would drive back to see her and I grinned. The sun was already down but she was probably still in the city.

The house had been my home for so long but I was having a feeling that it was time to move on, let it be a home for someone else. I didn't need all the space and had enough money put away that I didn't need to work as much. For the years I was there with my grandfather it was a happy house. And I knew from the stories he told and the ones written in the borders of the old bible, that he'd loved my grandmother, Alma. That saddest part of their time together was being told after my father was born that they couldn't have any more children.

The room was empty of furniture and the hundred-year-old hardwood floors were stripped down to how they'd looked when the house was first built, well before my grandfather had even lived there. I carried the sander and worn pieces of sandpaper I'd gone through out to the workshop. With the compressor, I sprayed air over the sander to clear any dust and debris out, then put it away.

I turned the compressor off and jumped at the voice behind me.

"Wes." The sheriff stood in the doorway.

"Jesus H. Christ, Benton."

"Sorry about that," he smiled more than he should for an apology.

"What brings you out here tonight?"

Benton walked around the workshop, stopping and looking at the tools I kept clean and organized on the walls and lined up in drawers. "I'm lucky to remember where I left my gun each morning and your wrenches are in order of size."

"My grandpa taught me to keep the shop clean. Much better to know right where a tool is without looking than to go hunting for it in the middle of a job."

"Sounds like he was a wise man."

"He was."

The mood was different than it usually was with Benton. We'd had our weekly dinners at the café for years now, and the historical bond taking us back to high school, and he was always jovial, joking. Just his demeanor seemed serious, almost confrontational.

"You clean that blood up?"

I watched the sheriff, out of uniform now in blue jeans and a thick work shirt with the tails out. I'd seen him like this before, somewhere. "Just finished," I said. "Went ahead and sanded the whole room. Thought a new coat of stain would look good."

Benton stopped and looked at me, giving the air of thinking through what I had just said, then nodding and continuing on his self guided tour of the workshop.

"Jared Walker was a good man," Benton said. "I'd even call him a friend."

I just listened and watched.

"A lotta calls coming in from concerned citizens. If a man like Walker was capable of breaking and entering and attempted murder, what else was he capable of?"

"People are strange creatures. I know in your years in law enforcement you've seen good people do bad things."

Benton's hands ran across the surface of a tractor engine that sat in several pieces on the workbench, the metal free from any grease and grime from its years in service. "That I have. Did you and Jared talk any before he shot you?"

I shook my head slowly. "Not much. I woke when I heard him come in the back door. I asked him what he was doing there. He didn't really reply before coming at me."

"And you just happened to have that gun in your lap?"

"I have it more than you might think." I had the story queued up, notes detailing it sitting in burned black remnants at the bottom of the pot belly stove in the corner of the room. "It reminds me of Lawrence, my brother. It was his army pistol."

"And you sit around with it loaded? Sleeping with it in your lap?"

"I never claimed to be brilliant, especially about guns. He was carrying it when he was killed in action in Vietnam. I guess I just feel him near when I have it with me." The questioning was what I'd expected back at the station, not later at home after being cleared by the state's Attorney General.

Benton grew quiet, stopping on the far side of the workshop in a shadow, leaning against the bench and just looking at me. "State Police were out, you know."

"Think I saw them in town."

"They took over the investigation," Benton said.

"What's to investigate?"

Benton leaned forward slightly to step away from the counter and walked slowly around the workshop toward me. "Turns out they found some jewelry in the safe at Jared's store."

The dream flashed through my mind, freeze framing at the jewelry box Jared had taken from Shawna Tate in her bedroom. I tried to keep from looking frozen. I had hoped that something might come to light after Jared was dead, but it was far from a sure thing.

"Jewelry? His wife's?"

"Funny thing is, it isn't. Mrs. Walker didn't recognize any of the pieces." Benton now stood under the hanging light with the open 100-watt bulb, his features exaggerated from the direct overhead glare. "When they checked out the jewelry box they found an inscription on the bottom. It was light and faded. They almost missed it, but those state police, they're on top of their game."

"What did it say?"

"That's the craziest part. It said, 'To my darling Shawna, Love Mom.'"

The connection had been made and my head spun. When Jared had moved the rug from the deserted house I thought all physical evidence was gone.

"The only Shawna we could think of was Shawna Tate, so I drove out to her mom's house with the state police and showed it to her. Wouldn't you know she collapsed right there on the floor? Had to call in the damn ambulance. It was quite a scene."

"It belonged to her?" I dropped my head and stared at the floor in disbelief. It wasn't fake or an act. I was frozen from what was taking place, that it was happening. I looked up at Benton then I said the sentence I'd wanted to say for so long.

"Jared Walker killed Shawna Tate."

Chapter 44

"SURE AS HELL looks that way."

I rode the line of appearing surprised and being too surprised. "Never woulda thought."

"Nope. Don't think anybody would," Benton said. "But I guess you're relieved, at least, to finally know who it was."

"I'm sure we all are."

"But you especially. It was pretty much the first question you asked me every week at dinner, if we had any leads."

I shrugged to play it off. "Nothing that big had ever happened around here before. Definitely catches your attention." I wanted to move on, switch topics.

"And you went fishing out in that marsh, right where she'd been tossed," Benton said. "Colleen even told you it wasn't good fishin' there and you tried anyway. Then you were putting a line in and came up with that girl's apron out of the water."

"Well, Colleen did. Don't have to remind me about that." I searched my brain for answers and distractions, weaving around the stories I'd made up to keep things in line and to try to move the conversation somewhere else, but Benton continued.

"And you went to Jared's store the very day he decided to come and try to kill you." The sheriff stared at me, I could sense it was not as a friend, but as law enforcement, looking into my eyes and watching my expressions, my movements.

"What's this all about, Benton? Feels like you're interrogating me."

The stare continued for a moment then eye contact was broken and Benton gave a small chuckle. "You're right. I'm comin' on a bit strong. Just had the biggest case ever in Delaware County broken wide open and I'm questioning the one man I knew couldn't have done it. I'd say the one man who could never kill someone, but that sure isn't true anymore."

"That'll be with me to the end of my days," I said.

"Say, remember that young girl that went missing a couple years back?"

The drilling continued, striking another plate deeper under the surface.

"Sure do. Was more than a couple years, though. She was lucky to get home in one piece."

"And you were there on the search, weren't you?" Benton said. "Not only were you on the search but you were right next to the man who found her."

I just nodded. I had no script for this questioning.

"You seem to be around a lot when big things happen."

"Well, two times," I said. "Don't know if you can call that lucky or unlucky." My palms were getting wet with sweat and I jammed them down into the pockets of my overalls. "Didn't you get her father on child abuse, lots of drugs and such at their house?"

"We did. Held him a couple days, but we chose not to pursue it. The evidence was circumstantial and they'd only lived in that house a couple months. We couldn't prove the trace amounts of drugs we found were his. So we let him loose."

My head felt like it slammed into a brick wall at a hundred miles an hour.

Let him loose.

My vision went black and I saw Jared Walker standing at the payphone outside of town. I turned the scene on its axis as I'd learned to do, but was always unable to with this dream, until Jared's mouth and the telephone receiver filled the screen in my head, the audio finally coming through as if the movie theater attendant had finally flipped the right switch.

"It's me."

"Why're you callin' me?"

"It didn't go like we discussed, like you told me it would."

"What do you mean? You talk to her? Did you let her loose?"

My vision snapped back to full color with Benton standing in front of me. The final piece that I was never able to put into place had just flown through time and space and slammed down like an unwanted gift.

"It was you." I didn't intend to speak, it just came out.

Benton cocked his head as he stared at me. "What are you talking about?"

"On the phone, the payphone at the gas station. Jared called you, told you what had happened." It was a knee jerk reaction, the words coming out of shock.

I saw the blood drain out of the sheriff's face and his arms appeared to hang from his body as useless appendages.

"You knew. You've known all this time. You knew where her body was, who killed her."

"How do you-" Benton stammered for words, caught wrong footed. "He told me you knew but I didn't believe him. Even after you'd killed him I wasn't sure."

I had no plan for this. It was off the books. I'd been close to the one person I felt would be able to give me information, to help me on my mission. And all along he'd been complicit, as guilty as Jared Walker.

"Why?" I pushed while I had the advantage. "Why did he kill her?"

Benton lowered his head and stepped back, his will broken, if only temporarily. "I was screwing her. Shawna Tate. Wasn't anything serious. It was just the spoils of the uniform."

"You were cheating on your wife?"

"Don't be so fucking naive, Wes. You sit alone in your house here for decades, you have no idea what it's like to be with the same damn nagging woman night after night. Shawna was young and cute and she flirted with me when I'd go in for coffee. Gave her a ride home after work once when her car was in the shop, and things just went down right there in my cruiser. Didn't even feel like I could stop it if I'd wanted. She wasn't the only one, either. Just the only one to threaten to tell my wife if I didn't get a divorce."

In the time of following the case, in making my plans, I never considered anything like this. I always thought it was Jared having the affair with her.

"So you sent Jared Walker to do your dirty work? To kill her?"

Benton's voice was low. "He wasn't supposed to kill her. That was an accident. I'd given her a necklace identical to one I'd given Becky. It was a stupid thing to do. I was just trying to get that back and he was gonna tell her it was over." He squinted at me. "How…how did you know?"

"Did Jared ever tell you exactly what he did to her?" I worked to regain high ground before his interrogation began again. "Did he? Did he tell you how he beat her, threw her to the floor and raped her?"

"What?"

"He choked her while he was inside her, until she died with him on top of her," I said.

Benton shook his head slowly. "No. He didn't… He wouldn't have…"

"He did, Benton. But why? Why would he do your dirty work? Why would he kill for you?"

The sheriff looked up at me. "You don't know?"

I felt the tide shift quickly away from me as I recognized what was happening, where we were. The dream

I'd had as a boy then again when meeting Benton as an adult was about to play out before me, with me in a starring role.

"You know all of that, and you don't know why?" Benton stood straighter. "You're even dumber than I always took you for."

The momentum spun around once more and was rushing straight at me.

"I've owned Jared for years," Benton said. "I caught him selling meth out of that shit store of his and made him mine. Hell, I more than quadrupled sales and made him do all the work, barely giving him anything off the top."

The frames in my mind were running on top of the live action in front of me, the dream playing out in more detail, stretched out to parts I hadn't seen before, but were now overlaid on reality. Occasionally a movement would stray slightly causing a blur, two pieces of film not lining up just right, then in focus again.

"And the runaway's dad," I said.

"Now you're getting it."

"That's why you didn't charge him. You made him work for you, too."

"Damn straight. Dumb as rocks, but the boy can cook. He supplies me everything I need." Benton stood tall, shoulders back, proud of his accomplishments. "Hell, I took pity on you, having dinner every week, getting you and Colleen back together."

"Don't you even say her name," I said.

"Colleen? Dammit, Wes, you have no idea what you're messing with here. Why do you think she's off in Tulsa today? Think that was just chance?"

"What are you talking about?"

"I wanted to talk to you alone and you two were holed up in that shack of hers for two days. So I got another girlfriend of mine in the prosecutor's office to call her in over some misfiled paperwork, after she purposely misfiled it. I'm pulling all the strings here, Wes." Benton stepped closer. "I don't know how you know what you do, but it don't mean shit now. I was just gonna talk tonight, find out why you really killed Jared, friend to friend. Started thinking you had possibilities, bring you into the business, maybe."

Stuttering of motion, dream on top of real. My head began to swim. From an arms length away I saw Benton's hand move up under the tail of his work shirt. As the barrel of the snub nosed silver revolver came into view still pointed at the ground, the dream snapped into place and I knew it was time. I knew exactly where the large wrench was without looking, my hand ached to reach out and grab it, to feed the dream, give it what it wanted.

I knew he was going to move toward me, come closer with the small weapon, and that was when I would act. The anticipation grew and I feared I wouldn't be able to do it, to grab a weapon and kill another man.

The silence broke with a loud pop and static as the radio on his belt sounded, the sheriff never truly being off duty. The dispatcher's voice came through loud.

"Sheriff, what's your location?"

The moment hung as he stared down the short barrel revolver at his side. I could tell his finger was itching. I was now no more than a loose end to him. But if he was as smart as I thought he was he knew this wasn't the right way, not here, not in my own workshop. It was too messy, even with a throwaway gun. The sheriff's best friend, the same guy that killed Jared Walker, just came up dead? Still his finger hovered, already on the trigger.

"Sheriff, where are ya? State police just gave us a courtesy call, they're raiding a house just outside of town in one hour."

The gun didn't move but his eyes narrowed to thin slits.

"Benton, are you there?"

Finally his other hand moved behind his loose shirt and pulled the radio out and to the side of his face and pressed the button.

"Copy. What's the location?"

"It's on 468. House number is 14984, right at the curve by Beaty Creek."

I saw his hand drop an inch, the revolver swinging to the side for a moment, then brought back true to aim.

"Sheriff, you copy? You got the address?"

"Copy. I know the house."

He put the radio back on his belt and stared at me, then suddenly took a fast step toward me, the gun jamming into my head.

"Dammit, Wes." His voice was strained. "What the fuck have you done to me."

I knew the house, too. It was where the little girl had run away from. I kept my eyes locked with his. His finger moved up and down on the trigger. The dream was off track, changing. The original was rolling off to the side, stuttering and slowing.

"You caused this, Wes. This is on you."

The gun pushed into my scalp and I could feel blood ooze into my hair. But no gunshot, no bullet.

His eyes left me for the first time, moving to the door, then back.

"Fuck me." He was yelling now. "Those idiots will ruin everything."

It was unraveling in front of me, Benton's little empire. Soon the state police would arrest his accomplices who would likely tell them everything they wanted to know for a reduced sentence.

"I'm nothing, Benton." I saw a way out. "Who would ever believe my story."

His head cocked to the side and I saw him struggle with my words, his body now moving, twitching, finger still on the trigger. I had to get rid of him. The dream was still there, skipping back and forth, waiting to be played again. I knew that I could reach to my right and my hand would land on the large wrench, just as I'd seen it. The dream could be played out. I could kill him right here.

"I saw it in a dream, Benton. That's it. Nobody would believe me."

He took a half step away from me, the gun finally off of my skull. "What?"

"A dream. Really. I've had them all my life. But nobody would listen. Why would they? Would you have listened to me if I told you I'd had a dream that Jared Walker killed Shawna? Or where to find that little girl?"

Benton ran his free hand across his face, sweat now running down his forehead. Watching a man that is always in control lose all sense of it was terrifying, the crumbling of an ego.

"How? That's impossible." He stepped away from me and turned to look out the door. My hand went to the handle of the wrench without needing to look and I gripped it, dropping that hand down behind my leg. I was ready in case he came back at me, to give the dream what it wanted.

"You have to go, Benton. You don't have long until the state police arrest him. He'll talk. They'll listen."

Without facing me the gun came up again then his head turned.

"I can't let you—"

"Benton, don't, please."

"I can't let you go, Wes. I can't let you go and I can't let Colleen go."

"Don't say that." My voice cracked at the thought of anything happening to Colleen. "She's not involved in this, Benton. She doesn't know anything."

His head shook. "Can't take that chance. I can end you both."

"You can't kill me here. You know that." I brought my voice down, forcing him to calm and listen closer. "I won't tell anyone, Benton. Nobody would listen to me. You have to take care of them, not me. I'm your friend."

His finger pulled and the hammer started to move back.

"State police are on their way to that house right now, Benton."

There were no signs of life in his eyes, no rational thinking or logic. He was broken.

"Go." I spoke softly.

Seconds passed as we stood quiet in our standoff. The one window in the workshop rattled as a truck went past on the road down my long driveway. Then slowly Benton's shoulders dropped.

Chapter 45

I HAVE WATCHED death from a distance my whole life, but being so close to dying twice in a week was nothing I ever prepared myself for. How could you. Two guns, two different men. The odds aren't in your favor when that happens, but here I am.

Everything about my workshop felt normal. The air was cool and there was the occasional scramble of tiny feet on the roof when a squirrel would drop down from a branch then run across and jump off again. It was so normal I thought about picking up where I'd been. I could have the floor stained by morning if I worked all night.

But that wasn't to be. Instead I was speeding down the driveway in my pickup. I didn't know what I was going to do or why I was going, but it was better than sitting at home waiting for Benton to come back. I'd sat and waited for my killer once and wasn't going to do it again. It was a reflex. He had threatened the one person I loved, the one person who loved me. The mahogany box with my brother's pistol inside was beside me on the seat but didn't know if I could actually use it again on another person.

I kept expecting to see a row of state police cars but the streets were empty. As I worked through the county roads the night got darker. The curve came up and I slowed and pulled over, my headlights now off. In the distance I could see the back of Benton's SUV sitting dark, and beyond that the worn out house. I hadn't seen it since the day the girl went missing, the same day Benton Hicks re-entered my life.

Without choosing to do so I was out of the truck and walking up the edge of the paved road. I stopped beside the SUV and looked in. The driver's seat was empty, the keys still hanging from the ignition. As I began to move again I paused and glanced back. The bracket that held the shotgun in place was open, the gun was gone.

I knew he wasn't here to talk. He was here to kill them. I didn't know how he'd answer to the state police about it. Maybe he'd say he misunderstood the message and went to talk to the residents and they attacked him. Maybe he just planned to be gone before they got here.

Moving past the SUV, I got to the edge of the gravel driveway and slowed my pace to keep from making noise on the loose stones. Even from a distance I heard raised voices through the thin walls, three of them from what I could tell. One was probably his cook, the man who makes the drugs that get sold all over this part of the state.

The voices grew louder, more heated, and I stopped. Looking down I was about to step off the gravel onto the soft dirt that made up the yard of the house, grass having given up trying to live there. I didn't want to leave my footprints in the dusty soil, one more thing for the investigators to find. I tried to pick out words and sentences, straining to hear in the still air, but it was all too muffled.

A man's voice raised louder, brassy even through the wall. "Don't! Please don't—"

The first blast made me stumble backward as the window flashed white, then three more shots, smaller, not as loud, rang out with their own flashes, then one more blast from what could only be the shotgun. The air was still again.

After what had to be a minute, maybe more, sounds came from the house. Something being pushed on the bare wood floors, an interior door slamming. I turned and meant to walk to keep my steps quiet but my body betrayed me and began to run. My boots made crunching noises and I wanted to slow but couldn't. Adrenaline pushed me forward. I heard another door slam then a voice yelling.

"Who's out there?"

I got to my truck and had the ignition on and the shifter in reverse, speeding quickly backward down the road with no lights. I felt the pavement give way to gravel beneath the tires and knew I was at the turn in the road, about to crash down the bank into the creek. I cranked my wheel left as I hit the brakes, threw the shifter into first, then sped forward. There was just enough moonlight that I kept from running off the next curve then turned my headlights on.

If he was dead, if Benton has been shot, there was nothing to worry about. Nobody was coming for me. Nobody was coming for Colleen.

I retraced my steps back to town then west to my house, the fastest route. I thought about going to Beasley's and sitting in a public place, somewhere he wouldn't try to kill me, but remembered it was closed, having belonged to Jared Walker. The funeral was today and people who went to it didn't know the true story yet, the proof of his guilt still living only with Benton and a few state police officers.

Back into my driveway I got inside and moved from room to room, not able to concentrate on anything. I needed to know what had happened, who had been shot. I needed to see it. My brother's pistol was now on the kitchen table, the box open in case I heard a car approach.

I had never tried to create a dream, to bring one up on my own. They had always just come. I didn't get to pick what I see. But I tried. I sat and closed my eyes and placed myself outside the house, walking up to the window. Without knowing what the inside looked like I couldn't put myself there. The curtains were thin and dirty, or at least I made them dirty in the dream I was trying to force.

The headache began, the pain growing from the inside as I pushed, fighting to connect to the moment that had passed. Sitting hurt more, so I stood and paced in the front room. My boots scuffed the freshly sanded wood and made a hollow sound in the emptiness, all the furniture relocated to the hallway and kitchen. Back and forth I walked, my hands held the side of my head, which felt like it would break in half, the pain growing stronger.

Shapes appeared. I could see the figures in the room, blurry. I walked faster in circles, my steps getting heavier and heavier. My head grew dizzy as it had when entering a dream before. I pushed harder. The shapes moved, now voices. What the fuck, Benton. I strained and tilted my head to hear, as if they were in the next room. You don't have to do this. Faster, circling, stepping louder, holding my head. Figures faded in and out of focus. I saw Benton, the shotgun held to his side. Faster. I saw another man, familiar. Greasy hair, dirty jeans. I saw him once, outside Jared's store, I think. A gun in his hand, large and black. Faster. The movement made things sharper, like adjusting rabbit ears on an old television.

Even faster, hands squeezed my temples, shadows moved in from the edges. A gun came up. Yelling. Warmth on my lips, dripping. My hand goes up and the dark red blood flowed down from me, over my fingers and onto the pale sanded wood floors. My feet stop moving but my head continued forward, balance gone. I had no control over my body, arms useless as they dropped to my sides.

I fell with nothing to block me, to break the impact. The side of my head crashed into the wood floor and I heard the crunch of bone cracking but felt no pain. I felt nothing, my body numb. My vision faded, darker and darker as it pulled in from the edges until only a pinpoint of light was left, then nothing.

When the light returned, it was brighter, colors oversaturated. I stood outside the old church, the stone walls were a deep, burnt orange. I reached out and touched them, the roughness on my fingertips familiar from my childhood, but I could tell it was only that, the memory of a sensation. I looked around at the landscape surrounding me, everything seemed too perfect but also misplaced, as if painted by an artist who had only seen photographs. The sky flashed, a shocking white, and the earth trembled beneath me, then all was still again. I walked around to the opening in the church and the tree was still there, so much larger now. The bark was aged and bulging, moving, as if something was working to get out. It scared me but I wanted to touch it, feel its life. As I placed my hand against it the flash of light and shaking ground came again, I stumbled forward into the tree and for a moment I felt it hold me up, invisible hands supporting me, then they were gone again.

I could see the tree better now and realized it had taken up the entire church, wall to wall. It pushed against the stones from the inside, forcing outward, threatening to knock the walls down if it grew only a little more. It had a life, a pulse. Something about it seemed familiar, a part of me, but frightening at the same time. I stretched my arms wide and leaned into the trunk and pressed my whole body against it and felt the beating, the constant drumbeat of life. The vibration of the tree matched my own.

A heat spread through my body, burning my arteries and veins, firing synapses in my brain faster than they should be, then the tree grabbed me. Branches reached down and held me against it, fighting to stay a part of me.

Another flash of light and the earthquake that followed, I felt the tree hold tighter, keeping me from falling, from running. The darkness came again, creeping in from the corners of my eyes until I could not see or feel.

Chapter 46

THERE WAS MOVEMENT, commotion, but my eyes were too heavy to open. Loud voices and electronic sounds sparked a memory I couldn't place. A hand on my arm then something sharp entering my skin. I fought the weight and opened my eyes. Everything was in shades of white. People moved around me as if I wasn't there. I couldn't be sure if it was a dream, it had the same feel. Then a voice.

"Dr. Duncan, he's awake."

A face I didn't know appeared in front of me, sterile eyes and no smile. "Mr. Hudson, you have nothing to worry about."

I tried to speak, ask questions, but nothing would come out. They weren't looking at me anymore, not talking to me, just to each other. Words moved in and out of conversations. Blood flow, pressure, mass. I struggled to turn my head and saw the flashing lights and numbers on the machines to my side, the flow of air through a tube that I realized was running to my face. Beeps got louder and faster along with my heartbeat, then the memory I hadn't been able to place came in, sharper and clearer than the room in front of me now. The hospital years ago when I'd held my father's hand as they took him off of these same machines, committing him to death. My eyes grew damp knowing now how he had felt in his final minutes. His memories and emotions had passed through me that day, that moment, the everything as I'd called it. I had nobody beside me to receive mine, to understand my life and see what I had gone through. There was only one person I'd want there, but she didn't know where I was, what was happening.

Never had I wondered what death felt like, even having experienced it so many times. The thought never entered my mind. It had always been from a distance, disembodied. I knew I was feeling it now. My life reduced to a body on a table. The energy inside me would be gone, the memories and emotions dead, too. There was no sadness for what I'd left behind, but no hope for what might still be ahead, because I've always felt that death was the ending, nothing came after. If a life had no meaning while blood still pumped through veins, then in death it would be forgotten, marked only by another dirt stained headstone in a church cemetery.

More pressure on my arm and I felt warmth enter my body as I had in my dream and my eyes grew heavy again but I strained to keep them open as long as I could. I wondered if it would even have worked, could she have felt my life as I died, or could only those with the dreams, with the growth inside their brains that caused the dreams, experience that?

"Wes," a soft voice from a woman I couldn't see. "Can you count backwards from a hundred for me, sweetie?"

It hit me, much slower than it should have, and I tried to fight. My arms wouldn't move and my entire body felt heavy like I was tied to the bed. I yelled but it came out only as sighs. Please don't. No one even looked my direction. Don't take it out. The dreams were a part of me and I was afraid for what my life would be without them. Without the growth, the tumor. The room dissolved to black.

Warm colors moved through and around me, swirling and swaying in the bright light as if being acted upon by a breeze I couldn't feel. I had no weight and walked easily through the colors, unaware of my feet touching anything solid to move me forward with each step. The swirls moved together as if organized, sentient, and my mother appeared in them, created in colors and light. She stood and smiled, and I felt the love she had for me travel through my body. I tried to reach her, move forward, but the distance between us remained the same. More motion, then she disappeared as another took her place. I watched and hoped and smiled when it took form.

Lawrence was ahead of me, just out of grasp as my mother had been. He wasn't in the uniform I'd last seen him wearing, but his faded jeans and a white tee shirt. Then swirling and he was gone.

The dream I'd had about my mother was my first, at least the first that mattered. Ones before that hadn't been fully formed, only fragments of people and events that had no meaning. I'd learned from Grandpa that they don't start until you are older, twelve years old, maybe thirteen. It wasn't until after Larry's death that I even gave more thought to the one of Mom pouring from that red box into her tea late at night when everyone else was sleeping.

The colors grew darker, slowly blending into each other in tones of grey, and I grew cold and heavy. Where moments earlier I felt airborne, now I could not lift an arm or move a leg to walk. Static built up, white noise so loud I needed to cover my ears but was unable to do so. Without having moved, I felt as if I were laying down with a great weight on top of me, not smashing me but forcing me into the ground. For a moment the pressure let off, then came down harder against me and I felt the surface give way and open up, accepting my body.

In the deepening darkness one more face emerged as fragments of shadows, almost imperceptible. Jake was there now, *Pyothopi* of the deer clan. Even in the absence of light I could see his thin lips and emotionless face. I wanted him to speak to me, to tell me why he had appeared, but he wouldn't. I had spent one afternoon with him at the church when we were boys, an event that seemed meaningless after the years that followed but for some reason he was here with me now. In the boy's eyes I saw his father all dressed in feathers and leather, dancing around the central fire, his face covered with tears of sadness and anger. I'd watched him dance and felt the emotion emanating from him. The vision of his father faded, and with it, Jake disappeared, too.

I was the last of my kind. No family left, nobody to inherit the so-called gift that had pushed me away from the world. But it was my own doing, my fault. I had thought it was better that way. I thought I was protecting others, but was just protecting myself from losing anyone else.

An edge came off of the cold and the grey lightened. The volume of the static eased lower.

I didn't want to be alone, I just thought I had to be.

Chapter 47

THE SOFT TOUCH on my arm moved through my skin, electric signals firing and spreading warmth. I could feel my body on a firm bed, rough sheets against my bare legs. There were no sounds, an eerie silence lacking echo or depth. The touch on my arm moved, stroking skin.

I could feel my body stirring, waking up after what felt like a year's sleep. Muscles began to respond, though slowly. Images still flashed through my mind at times, random memories I'd thought forgotten years ago. A dog we had on the farm for a summer until it died on the gravel road. Building a kite out of newspapers in the backyard with Larry. A girl's glance back at me down the rows of desks at school, Jennifer Smith's sweet smile.

There was motion around me though I couldn't hear it, still trapped in my isolation chamber. Vibrations of footsteps and bumps against the bed. Another brush against my arm, soft fingers touching lovingly.

Colleen. It had to be Colleen.

I wanted to see now, to open my eyes and answer the many questions growing inside of me. Though still heavy and tired, I forced my eyelids to move. The shades of white were still there from the last time I'd looked, the last time I'd been awake. Things were in focus now, though I was on my back facing the ceiling.

Still only silence.

The hand was on my arm and I wanted to let her know I was awake. I concentrated on my body, on muscles and bones, and sent signals to my right arm. I put so much energy to it I thought my hand would fly into the air.

A twitch.

That was it. A twitch. But it was enough. She came into view as she stood up and looked at me and I'd never seen anything more beautiful. I wanted to tell her that but the words were trapped behind the tube that ran down my throat. She was smiling at me. There was no makeup on her face and she looked tired but happy. So many things I wanted to say right then, how much I loved her and needed her in my life, how her touch on my face drove me crazy.

I tried to speak again, choking on the tube.

A man and a woman appeared on either side of me, pushing Colleen further away. I wanted her back. I needed to see her and only her. The man and woman moved with quick and efficient motions above me, wires and tubes being repositioned. The woman's face looked at mine and her lips moved, the words getting lost in the absence of sound. She took hold of the tube in my mouth then said something else. The memory of my father came again, my final moments with him that begun the same way. My hair on my arms stood up and my heart began to thud loudly inside my chest.

Is this it, my final seconds? Will I have only moments to say to Colleen everything I feel?

The nurse pulled and the tube was expelled from my throat with fluids dripping from it as I coughed, trying to lean forward to spit the dense liquid out, but they stopped me. Arms came to my shoulders and held me back as my throat became blocked and I gagged. A small hose was shoved into my mouth and I felt the vacuum, the air starting to enter once more. I gripped the blanket with both fists waiting for the end.

Still silence.

My face was wiped as wires were moved again then calm around me once more. She was back. Colleen leaned over me with that wonderful smile and sleepy eyes. She spoke and I did not hear but I watched her as if I did. My eyelids grew heavy and I couldn't fight them. The feeling was familiar from late nights drinking whisky in the leather recliner, a drugged and numbing type of tired you cannot fight. Still I feared I wouldn't wake up but there was nothing I could do to fight it, and the sleep came.

She had the same shirt on when I woke and again she was right there beside me, her hand on my arm. When she saw my eyes were open, her face came to mine and she kissed my cheek gently. The warmth flowed from her lips and I felt her emotions pass through to me. Muscles responded faster but still slow and my eyes were lighter. Progress. I was still alive.

Colleen sat on the edge of the bed, constantly checking all of the wires and tubes to make sure she wasn't blocking something. She stroked her hand across my forehead and spoke.

No sound.

I watched her talk, lips moving and her tongue touching the bottom of her top teeth between thoughts as she'd always done. I didn't want to stop her, just pretend I was listening. Her eyes narrowed as she held my hand. She was very serious. I tried to read her lips but couldn't catch all the words. My hand squeezed hers to try to tell her I couldn't hear her, to stop her but she just held tighter.

Tears formed in her eyes as the words kept coming and bouncing off of me unheard. I squeezed more and watched her lips. She was sobbing while speaking now, and I needed to hold her and tell her whatever it was would be fine. I'm here. I'm alive. Then one motion with her mouth caught me, a word formed, the shape of letters and syllables, and I knew everything she was telling me, everything she was feeling.

Benton.

And I knew so much that she didn't know.

My heart broke watching her tell me that the man she thought was my best friend was dead. I didn't know if she was telling me how but I already knew. In my silence I hadn't tried to speak, believing I had no voice if I could not hear. I didn't know what would come out and wouldn't know if anything had. But I tried.

My grip tightened on her hand. "I know."

I felt the vibration in my throat and knew sound had been formed. She stopped talking and looked at me as her confused smile widened through the tears.

Over the next two weeks in the hospital I watched conversations happen in front of me. Doctors wrote on white boards to explain what was happening. The pressure from the swelling in my brain was pushing on the area that controls hearing. The hope was that when the swelling went down, the sense would come back to me.

Colleen was never far away. She brought clothes from home and the nurses finally gave in and brought her a cot to sleep on each night. There were stacks of paper as she worked on cases, looking up at me every few seconds. When I was well enough to begin physical therapy, she would watch from the other end of the long room.

I woke in the middle of the night, my legs sore from the workout the day before. A hospital room is never really dark. There's a light always on that faces the ceiling and the machines to the side of the bed with glowing switches and screens. In a stream of light that spread above me I saw the dust floating, doing the same dance I had watched every morning from my bed back in Stroud as a boy. It was a perfect moment, a memory lost for years that returned with a smile and thoughts of my brother, my mother.

A sensation that seemed new and familiar at the same time made my skin bristle, goose bumps rising to provide more surface area to accept foreign input. I lay still and searched for it, to find what was happening, and it came to me with a drip of water in the bathroom sink. Then more came. My body had accepted them as normal, ambient noises that are filtered out to make you think you are in silence when you never truly are. A voice from the other side of my hospital room door as one night nurse spoke on the phone. The buzz of the light on the other wall.

"Colleen."

She didn't stir, tired from a drive to Jay and back the day before and hours of going over a case after I went to sleep. I'd awakened and seen her sitting there with papers all over the table and some even on the end of my bed. I didn't let her know, just watched her for a few moments before falling back to sleep.

"Colleen." A little louder.

Her body moved reluctantly, then gave in to the stimulus and her head came up. She looked at me.

"Come here."

In one motion she moved to me, a look of concern on her face. She looked at me and exaggerated her words as she spoke so I could read her lips. "Are you okay?"

I smiled. "Yeah. I'm okay."

Chapter 48

THE SAND WAS soft beneath my feet and the light jacket I wore did nothing to keep me warm against the cold air off the ocean. I'd been on the edge of Grand Lake more times than I could count, and had wondered how anything could be more amazing. Then I stood humbled before the swells and white caps of the Atlantic. I wanted to take off my shoes, to feel the wet sand between my toes, to be closer to the earth. I had done that the first day weeks earlier, nothing could have stopped me. If the water weren't so cold I'd have walked in up to my neck. Instead I let the salty brine splash against my legs.

The dreams stopped coming, for the most part. Occasionally a fragment would slip in during the night or a momentary flash while out walking. I would say I don't miss them, but when anything is part of you for so long, it leaves an emptiness behind. The tourniquet had tightened on my brain, blood flow slowed until any amount of stress would cause a seizure. It had happened the night I killed Jared Walker then again when I almost died a few nights later. Colleen found me and called for help. Before the ambulance could get me to Grove, a helicopter was en route from Tulsa and flew me away.

I didn't remember any of that. I wasn't awake for it and for a short time wasn't alive for it. The paramedics revived me somewhere over Chouteau with electric paddles to my chest. The tumor was killing me. After an MRI showed the mass, a brain surgeon was called in and he made the decision to remove it before it killed me, figuring I was dead anyway if he didn't.

The few things that survived were now glimpses of my past, not as many visions of the future. The red sea of maple leaves spread out on the ground outside my back door was perhaps the most common, one of the sights I ever felt was beautiful, perfect. None of the pain and death seeped in, unless I let it. Every so often I would, just to remember the people, a way of honoring the lives that no longer existed in mortal form. I wanted to remember some of the details. I felt it wasn't fair to let those fade away as I was the only one who knew them all, who could tell the complete story from beginning to end. I thought of writing them down, going back to my childhood love of putting stories together, and somehow on my deathbed release them to the world so loved ones of those lost would know the truth.

Ahead of me was a long black metal structure emerging from the beach, stained and scarred from years of abuse from the surf and wind. Children ran around it, coats too big for their bodies that looked to be moving independently of them as they turned and ran each and every way. I'd inspected the structure on my first walk down the beach, in the quiet morning hours before the tourists appeared and turned everything into a playground. It was refuse from what seemed an ancient time, left as a monument, a time capsule, to the brutality that had played out on this sand. Once, decades ago, it floated at sea just off the beach, an artificial harbor to aid in landing the Allied Forces.

Away from the water I entered the small town, shops and cafés lining each side of the narrow road. I was greeted in the bakery with a familiar wave as I pointed at the long loaves of bread.

"*Deux, s'il vous plait.*" I stuttered out a few of the words I could manage, though I knew the shopkeepers all spoke English. I fished through the change from my pocket and picked out two coins to pay. It was a daily stop, even if I didn't finish the bread. I needed it more for the normality and a sense of place. The cold, hard baguettes in baskets at Wal-Mart now seemed to mock the very nature of the ingredients compared to these.

The sidewalk wound through the small neighborhood, up and away from the beach. I climbed the few steps to the porch and entered the unlocked cottage. After putting the baguettes in the kitchen I sat down in the front room, the large picture window offering a view of the ocean down the hill. It had become my favorite spot.

I spent many hours with the old bible while recovering at Colleen's house. Along the bottom of one page was a row of numbers I'd never understood, along with a single name, Montandon. It was Colleen who figured it out. That's how we found ourselves walking into a small but very secured business in a Zurich office building. In a private room we were given access to a long silver box that held nothing but a notebook. Hesitantly, I opened it to find my grandfather's hand writing, so familiar to me from the bible.

I found it, Wesley. And if you are reading this then you have found it, too.

Live, Wesley. Explore. Love.

But most of all, have fun.

Jack
1971

It had been more than twenty years since he died but I could hear his voice in the words. The bank could offer no more information aside from the account balance and a card to access the money from anywhere. I didn't know how he had gotten it there, just another one of the secrets he took with him.

Several weeks were spent traveling country to country before landing in France. Between the money in Switzerland and what I'd made from selling the farm and

all of my tools and tractors I didn't have to work again if
I was cautious. I had nobody to leave the money to, so I
wasn't going to be frugal, either.

I'd walked through the trenches from World War I, now
preserved as a memorial. I couldn't say it brought me any
closer to Grandpa, but it was something I needed to do.
Omaha Beach was outside my window. I had feared that
the lives of thousands of young men would overtake my
dreams, each looking for an ending that made sense, far
more than the one they had received. But it was quiet.
Even a stroll through the American cemetery was peaceful.

I woke up in the chair, the sun setting over the Atlantic
out the window. The room had turned chilly so I reached
for a blanket on the floor and pulled it over my legs. It's
been six months since that night. State police found Benton
dead on the floor of the old house along with the man who
cooked his drugs. The third man was shot and a trail of
blood lead out of the house to Benton's SUV where he was
found unconscious but alive. He told them everything.

I've tried to miss Benton, to think of the years of
friendship before I knew who he truly was, but couldn't.
It's impossible to separate one man from the other and
all of those years are lost now. Memories of conversations
turn to new meanings with what I had learned. While the
world knows that Jared Walker killed Shawna Tate, I'll
still be the only one to know of Benton's involvement.

It's never truly quiet near an ocean. You can trick
yourself into thinking there's no sound, but the rumble
of the water moving in and out from the land is constant.

It becomes a heartbeat, something that is always there but you wouldn't notice unless it stopped. From my chair I almost thought I could feel the waves coming up on the beach half a mile a way. I closed my eyes to see if I could sense the vibration of the earth.

In searching for one sound, I didn't hear the steps behind me, a hand landing on my shoulder. It rested naturally and said so much with a simple touch. I smiled when she spoke.

"How was your day?"

About the Author

John H. Matthews has loved writing for most of his life. The walls of his childhood homes were lined with bookshelves instead of family photographs and he read his first Stephen King novel when he was way too young.

Born in New York City, he grew up in Arkansas and Oklahoma, and now resides in the Washington, D.C. suburbs of Northern Virginia with his wife and son.

A year living in the San Francisco bay area renewed his love of writing, spending all spare moments reading John Steinbeck novels near where many of them were written.

He spent several weeks at his grandfather's farm outside of Jay, Oklahoma, one summer when he was about twelve years old, riding in his grandpa's old GMC pickup around the farm. They spent hours driving up on top the hill looking for the bags of money.

Thank you to
Wyatt Akins
Tracy Brown
Mark Duncan
Edward Hutchison
Casey Jenkins
Mary Kauffman
Stephane Le Baud Roy
Jennifer Smith McCord
Shea Megale
Stephen Moriarty
Kim Saguinsin
Scott Smith

A special thank you to
Katie Thompson of the Sac and Fox Nation
in Stroud, Oklahoma, for her assistance
in proper translations from English to the
Sauk language.

Made in the USA
Middletown, DE
19 April 2019